EVERY TRICK IN THE ROOK

An absolutely gripping British cozy murder mystery

MARTY WINGATE

A Birds of a Feather Mystery Book 3

Revised edition 2024
Joffe Books, London
www.joffebooks.com

First published in Great Britain in 2017

This paperback edition was first published in Great Britain in 2024

Cover art by Imogen Buchanan

ISBN: 978-1-83526-471-3

To Leighton

CHAPTER 1

A distinctly steamy atmosphere filled the church hall at St. Swithun's on that early April Thursday evening, created by wet mackintoshes, dripping umbrellas, and leather boots that would not dry out until July, all combined with six oil-filled radiators plugged in along the walls. The aroma of damp wool hung heavily in the air. I had intended to take the chill off and accidentally created a sauna. Despite that, our organizational meeting of the Smeaton-under-Lyme Wednesday Farmers Market — its inaugural appearance in a fortnight's time — had gone well, if overly long. Farmers, cheese mongers, bakers, cider and perry makers, and a host of other food producers had attended so that we could talk through the last details. I glanced at my watch — just gone eleven. My God, don't these people have homes to go to?

A small woman in the front row raised her hand.

"Julia, have you heard from Health and Safety yet? Our equipment must pass inspection before I begin, and if I don't start soon, I won't have enough supply to hand out the free samples at the market, let alone for the grand opening of the shop."

"Right, Helen, I'll ring them tomorrow and secure an appointment." Helen Dunne, proprietor of the village's first sweets shop, Sugar for My Honey, looked as if she'd never popped a toffee in her entire life, but all of us at the Tourist Information Center had tasted her confections and given her top marks. I, for one, was particularly looking forward to her CocoJava fudge, although my co-workers, Vesta Widdersham and Willow Wynn-Finch, leaned toward the rose-and-lemon Turkish delights.

A clattering of metal folding chairs lifted my heart, as I thought everyone else had finally had enough, too, and had begun to pack it in. But instead of preparing to leave, the crowd had pulled back to watch two farmers go at each other like bulls.

"You'll never get away with it!" the short one shouted, as he threw a punch that made contact with a *crunch*.

"I'll not let you steal what I've worked my entire life for," the taller one responded, although thickly, as he covered his nose with one hand. He flew at the first man, they tumbled to the ground, and the pummeling continued.

"*Stop it!*" I shouted at them. "*Stop it this instant!*" I ran to them and took hold of the first one I could reach, grabbing the collar of his sweater and wrenching him back hard enough that I heard him gag. We both stumbled into the crowd, and I felt someone catch me before I landed on my bum. I let go of the one farmer and placed myself between them, pointing a finger at each to keep them still.

Bloody asparagus growers. The two of them had been bickering for the past month about who had the right to call himself King of Suffolk Asparagus. I'd tried arbitration, but it hadn't worked, and I'd had enough.

The little one jumped up as if to continue the scuffle, and the taller one flinched.

"Stop it, the pair of you," I warned, "or you'll both be banned from the market from day one."

"On whose say?" the taller one asked as he wiped a trickle of blood off his lip. "This is the Fotheringill estate, and you're only the tourist manager."

"On *my* say, with the full backing of Lord Fotheringill, as you well know. Shall I ring him now and we'll just verify that?" I whipped my phone out of my pocket and wiggled it in front of their faces. "Go on, try me — you know I'll do it."

The crowd held its breath. I could see Willow off to the side, her eyes wide. At last, the two farmers stuck their hands into the pockets of their grimy denims. Both shrugged.

"Right," I said, blowing my bangs out of my eyes and straightening my cardigan. "Now, we'll have no more of this. You two behave, or you'll find yourselves peddling your spears at the side of the road in Shimpling."

* * *

"Gosh, Julia, that was truly amazing. You're incredibly brave, and you have such a really, really bold spirit," Willow said as we stacked up chairs and cleared off the tea table. "Ooh, look — two fairy cakes left."

For just a moment we considered those little squares of sponge cake coated in pink-tinted fondant — the last survivors amid a platter of crumbs.

"Well, can't let those go to waste, now can we?" I asked. "What would Nuala say?" Nuala ran the tearoom in the village and supplied cakes, tarts, and scones for our every need. I counted myself as one of her most enthusiastic supporters.

The final fairy cakes dispatched, we washed out the tea urn and swept up.

"There now," Willow said, as we took a last look at the church hall, and she adjusted the knitted beret that sat atop her brown curls. "All put to rights. Well, Julia, as I won't see you before you get off, you have a lovely weekend."

I certainly intended to. "And you, Willow. Thanks for helping out this evening."

I walked down Church Lane, past the Stoat and Hare pub — not only a pub, but with ten lovely rooms available upstairs, a fact I always pointed out to visitors — and continued down the high street to my Pipit Cottage.

A warm glow emanated from the front window. I unlocked the door and stepped in, pausing for a moment to take a deep, cleansing breath. Home. I hung my coat on a peg, switched off the tiny lamp on the mantel, and climbed the steep stairs to the landing. I stopped in the bedroom doorway.

Michael, sound asleep on his stomach with arms flung out, had left the bedside lamp on for me. I watched him for a moment, listening to his heavy breathing. His black hair — always a bit shaggy — didn't quite cover that tiny white scar high on his cheek. Even in sleep, one side of his mouth tugged up into that lopsided smile. I smiled back.

As quiet as a mouse, I undressed and slipped into bed beside him. When I turned to switch off the light, I saw he'd left the printed confirmation from The Ship pub in Dunwich: Marsh View Room for two booked for Michael Sedgwick starting tomorrow evening, Friday. I sighed. This had been our goal for weeks now — a weekend away on the coast, apart from our hectic work schedules. Time together. No wonder he was already asleep — he'd be up at four in the morning tomorrow, as he had been every morning that week.

Michael held my former post of personal assistant to celebrity ornithologist Rupert Lanchester who was also my father. This meant Michael not only organized Dad's appearance schedule, but also produced his BBC Two television program *A Bird in the Hand*. In case he didn't have enough to do, Michael had created the Rupert Lanchester Foundation, which would award grants to worthy groups, institutes, and schools to further nature studies. The first grant was to be awarded soon. To say he was busy didn't cover it by half.

And just as Michael had been up before dawn every morning, I'd been in late every evening with meetings about the market, the Walking Festival and Smeaton's Summer Supper. But when I locked the door of the Tourist Information Center tomorrow, Friday at five o'clock, there would be no more of that. I'd get in my little Fiat and head for the coast. We'd meet up and not look back. At least until Monday.

* * *

A heavy mist threatened to soak me through the minute I closed the door of my cottage the next morning, but I set my mind to better thoughts — get through this last workday before the weekend. I clamped half a slice of toast in my mouth as I zipped my mackintosh, pulled the hood up, and hitched my weekend bag higher on my shoulder. A blob of marmalade slid off the corner of the toast and plopped onto my chest, but before I had a chance to nab it, the rain had washed it off and the marmalade landed on the toe of one of my shoes. *Welcome to Friday.*

A loud *caw-caw* from across the deserted high street made me look up to see a rook perched atop a chimney pot. The bird spread his wings, glided to the roof's edge, and turned his head to peer down at me, in the process showing off his white chin and long, pale gray beak. A sage look that was contradicted by his pantaloon-like leg feathers, which gave him the appearance of a court jester.

"'Morning," I called to the bird, biting off the end of my toast as I clattered down the pavement in my spike heels. "The rook is a sociable bird," I murmured with my mouth full. I paraphrased *The Observer's Book of British Birds*, a copy of which I had kept close at hand for nearly thirty years, since buying it for a pound at a church jumble sale when I was twelve. With a couple of flaps, the rook arose and flew off in the same direction I headed — down the high street toward the TIC.

Perhaps he'd like a leaflet on available nesting sights on the Fotheringill estate. More likely he already knew and had come from the rookery just at the edge of the village, near the bridge that spanned the brook. I'd mentioned the rookery in a recent and already quite popular leaflet, *Birds of Hoggin Hall.* As manager of the TIC, I had written a leaflet on just about every imaginable topic with a connection to our village, the estate, and the Fotheringills, including *What the Vikings Left Behind — Do You Have Danish Blood?* and *Henry VIII and Fotheringill Abbey: A Tale of Jealousy and Intrigue.*

The rook waited for me across the road at the TIC — at least, I decided he was the same one. He strutted along the gutter of the slate roof, and I could hear the *scritching* of his toes when he stopped to shake the rain off. He sailed toward me, landed on the black iron bollard next to the curb, and gave the last bite of toast in my hand a significant look.

"Oh, well, go on then," I said, and tossed it onto the pavement.

He dropped and spread his wings, giving me a bow before seizing it. I heard a chortling sound as he flew off.

"You're very welcome," I called after.

Breakfast on the wing — well and good for the rook, although not my favorite way of eating. But I had left it too late for a proper meal, because I had needed to pack for the weekend, and I'd also taken time to refill the feeders in the back garden. I wouldn't want to leave the garden birds without for three days — not in April, when they were so busy nesting and needed all the food they could get.

I went through the activities that started each workday — unlock the door, switch on the lights, turn the sign in the window to Open. I paused for a moment to take in the first impression our tiny shop-sized tourist office would present to a visitor. A short counter very nearly split the place in two. In front, racks of leaflets covered the wall, as well as maps, booklets, and posters touting the Fotheringill estate as a wonderful place to spend time. On the counter, an introductory leaflet — *Who Are the Fotheringills?* — along with our business cards (Julia Lanchester, manager; Vesta Widdersham, associate) and an assortment of pencils and erasers. A tray held key chains in two styles — one with a miniature Hoggin Hall and its distinctive turrets, the other the Fotheringill family coat of arms. These were the only items for sale, as we had no desire to compete with shops in the village. Behind the counter lay our workspace comprised of a small table and four chairs, two of which were usually stacked up in the corner, plus all the work necessities from computer to tiny fridge. Behind a concertina door, in what looked like a cupboard, was the loo.

We had increased traffic into the TIC these days, in part, because of our website. It had a smart and appealing look.

The home page displayed a warm welcome from Linus — the Earl Fotheringill — and a separate page that told the family history through the centuries. We had sprinkled in loads of photos and drawings, added an interactive map of the estate, and uploaded all our leaflets, which could be printed out at home. The project had consumed my January but had been up and running for two months now.

I dropped my bags, switched on the electric kettle, and breathed a sigh of relief. There — tea on its way. I rinsed marmalade off my fingers, nudged my weekend bag under the counter, and rummaged in my enormous day bag, pulling out a large slice of Madeira cake from Nuala's, nabbed from the tea table at last evening's meeting just before the farmers began to arrive. Good for my morning tea, but my favorite of Nuala's cakes would always be the chocolate with chocolate fudge frosting, which I indulged in on a regular basis — blessed, as I had been, with my mother's ability to eat almost continually and still keep a reasonable figure.

As I waited for our cranky kettle to rattle and wheeze its way to boil, my mind drifted off to pleasant thoughts. Michael and I had been a couple — mostly — for nearly a year, which astonished me just as much as it did everyone else. Not only that, we'd been living together in my little Pipit Cottage for almost five months. I felt like a grown-up and, as my sister, Bianca, would say and has said, "About time, too, as you'll be forty before you can take another breath."

At her words, my hand had flown up to my hair — dark blond cut in a bob. Rosy at The Hair Strand had been pushing me to get highlights, and I'd spotted two gray hairs not long ago. Still, not enough to worry about.

But living together, it turns out, doesn't necessarily mean seeing a lot of each other. In fact, for Michael and me, lately, it had been quite the opposite.

And so, we'd needed to go away to be together, although work and life did seem to have a way of following along. We had promised Dad we'd scout a few film sites while we strolled Minsmere, a Royal Society for the Protection of

Birds reserve quite near our pub. Also, I had a bit of business to bring up. I wanted to tell Michael about an email I'd received. Really, it was only to clear the air. I'd give it five minutes, and then we could forget it.

* * *

I spent a pleasant morning with a steady stream of visitors, mostly walkers who were more than happy to learn that most of our footpaths came within shouting distance of both of the two pubs on the estate — the Royal Oak and the Stoat and Hare. Over lunch, I texted Michael for no other reason than to act as a bit of foreplay, after which I jotted down a few notes about summer activities. I yawned.

No, mustn't be snoring on the worktable when a visitor appeared. I stood, stretched, and glanced round the front of the TIC. Time to put the wall of leaflets to rights.

We took on this task three times a week and daily in the high season, refilling, re-sorting — it seemed many visitors had a difficult time remembering in just which slot they'd found *The Royal Welcome Mat: Queen Charlotte's 1802 Visit* and thought that it might quite easily fit with the leaflet about native butterflies in the meadows. Also, tidying gave me the opportunity to pull out leaflets that needed updating — this one, for example: *The Fotheringill Family Tree.*

Past four o'clock, the bell above the door jingled. I was on my hands and knees, having knocked the tray of key rings off the counter as I'd grabbed for a handful of fresh foldout maps. I straightened, still on my knees, and looked up at my visitor — a slight girl with wide brown eyes and long, sleek chestnut hair that hung in a single sausage curl over her shoulder. She looked about the age of my niece Emmy, who had turned eleven not long ago.

"Good afternoon," I said, flinging my handful of key rings back into the tray. One of them tumbled out onto the counter and I reached for it, only to be beaten to the prize when, from behind the girl, hopped a rook.

CHAPTER 2

I opened my mouth in surprise and watched as the bird picked up the stray key ring and deposited it with the rest, shook his feathers, and sidled down to the corner of the countertop, his toes clicking on the glass.

"Hello, good afternoon," the girl said quickly. "My name is Tennyson. And this is Alfie. Is it all right if he comes in?"

A moot point as Alfie, who looked as big as a chicken at close range, seemed to be making himself at home.

"Yes, of course — you're both very welcome." Alfie may have been the first rook inside the TIC, but birds, up close and personal, had been a part of my entire life. People were continually telling Dad personal bird tales — tame robins that would eat out of your hand, a pink-footed goose that became best friends with the dog. Perhaps Rupert hadn't seen it all, but he'd seen a great deal, and his family had been witness to most of it.

I stood and brushed off my knees, remembering this wasn't my first encounter with a rook that day. "Do I know your Alfie?"

Alfie turned his head to give me his strong profile as if I needed to identify him in a police lineup.

"He may have paid you a visit this morning after I was in school," Tennyson said, dropping her schoolbag on the floor.

"We've walked by several times this week, and we wanted to come in, but you all looked quite busy and we didn't want to be a bother."

"It's never a bother, you're welcome anytime," I said, getting a vague notion of what this was about, but becoming distracted by Alfie, who had started to rummage round in the tray of key rings. "How can I help you today?"

A cluster of children passed the window, the boys with white shirts half pulled out of trousers, girls with skirts hitched up an extra inch and all dragging their school bags behind them as they laughed and called to another group across the road. They wore the same uniform as Tennyson — green plaid skirts and trousers and green pullovers from the village school — and looked about her age. They glanced in the window and Tennyson looked back, but neither side waved.

"My mum and I moved here last month, you see," Tennyson said, explaining, perhaps unintentionally, the non-exchange with her schoolmates. "She works for Dot in her dress shop and Dot told my mum who you are. That is, who your father is."

Just as I thought — a Rupert fan. "Do you watch *A Bird in the Hand*?" I asked.

Tennyson grinned, the first one she'd offered, full of girlish charm and teeth. "I mostly catch up with the programs when I can stay after school in the computer room. Or I go to the library. The program is quite good. I've learned loads."

"That's just what Rupert likes to hear. Look, I'll be seeing him soon, and I know he'll be interested to hear about you and Alfie. I could bring you a copy of the booklet that talks about the program — an autographed copy."

"Oh yes, thank you, that would be lovely," Tennyson said politely, but hurried on. "Actually, I'd like Rupert's advice. You see, I want to study to become an ornithologist. I've always wanted to. At least, since I've known Alfie. I'm quite interested in the interaction between birds and people — how it changes each of us, you know, and alters our perception of nature. I'm hoping to get as much field experience as possible, and if I work hard, I may qualify for a bursary to uni. That would be the only way I could do it, you see."

Field experience? University? "Aren't you a bit young to worry about that?" I asked.

"I'm almost eleven. There's no time to waste."

Alfie chortled in a self-satisfied sort of way and returned to the end of the counter. I glanced in the tray, which had been one heap of key rings and was now sorted into two smaller heaps according to type — miniature Hoggin Halls here, Fotheringill coats of arms there. I looked at Alfie and then at Tennyson.

"He likes to keep busy," she explained.

At that, Alfie ruffled his feathers, flapped his wings, and did what birds do — and right on the glass counter. *Splat.*

"I'll get that," Tennyson said in a matter-of-fact tone. She unbuckled her schoolbag and took out a roll of kitchen towels and a spray bottle of Dettol, the all-purpose cleaner. In no time, she had taken care of the situation. Alfie hopped to the back of a chair in our work area and eyed the kettle.

"Is your mum expecting you home?" I asked.

"Mum's working at the Stoat and Hare, but I told her where I'd be. She said it would be all right for me to visit you, because you've been vouched for on account of Dot knowing you. And Peg and Fred at the pub. In fact, everyone knows you."

"Well, in that case, fancy a cup of tea?"

* * *

Given a choice, Alfie preferred ginger biscuits to Bourbon creams, dropping half into his mug of tea and occupying himself the rest of the time by finding a proper hiding place for the other half. First, he stashed it behind the rubbish bin and returned to his seat, but a moment later he retrieved the hidden morsel and, after some consideration, chose instead the pocket of my mackintosh.

As Tennyson and I drank our tea, I felt the minute hand of the clock edging its way toward five. She didn't seem to be in a hurry, and I couldn't show the girl out just so I could be on my way to a weekend break. And, also, I couldn't help but be concerned, thinking that my sister, Bianca, wouldn't let Emmy wander the streets of St. Ives with only a bird for a companion and no one waiting for her at home.

"I haven't met your mum yet, have I? She works at the pub?" I asked.

"Well, she works on the hotel side in the mornings, but helps out in the kitchen three times a week in the early evening," Tennyson said, looking into the biscuit tin and pulling out the tail end of a wrapper. "There are two chocolate digestives left."

"Why don't we each take one?" Hotel side. Peg and her husband, Fred, were proprietors of the Stoat and Hare, and I now recalled Peg saying they'd hired a new cleaner. "Did you say your mum works for Dot as well?"

"A couple of afternoons a week and early on Saturday. But she's home the other evenings, because she's busy with ironing."

This was beginning to sound quite Dickensian.

"Is Smeaton very different from where you lived before?" I tried to make it sound like a casual question, but it didn't come off well. Tennyson's face darkened and she paused for a moment.

"We lived with my gran before, but she died."

Great work, Julia, make the little girl cry. Alfie, on the back of Tennyson's chair, stuck his beak in her hair and murmured.

Tennyson smiled. "I found Alfie two years ago. He was just a fledgling, and he'd fallen from his nest. Although" — she leaned forward, her voice dropping — "we realize that it might have been deliberate. Sibling rivalry, you know. I took him home, and Gran told Mum that I should take care of him. Well, we say 'him,' but of course, Alfie could be a 'her.' We're not sure about that either."

True — male and female rooks looked the same — no colorful plumage for the boys and drab feathers for the girls.

Good humor restored, Tennyson popped the last of the biscuit in her mouth and said, "We've been friends ever since."

* * *

Girl and bird left just after five o'clock. We should all have a friend like Alfie, I thought as I fished the ginger biscuit out of my mackintosh pocket. I had enjoyed Tennyson's company, but it made me miss my eldest niece as well as the younger ones, Enid and Estella. And nephew Emmet, too, poor sausage, only boy stuck in the middle of a load of female siblings. All lived far away in Cornwall.

My departure was delayed a further half hour while I wrote up notes for Vesta and Willow, who would fill in for me on Saturday and Sunday — we were closed on Monday, our only true day of rest. My last task put to bed and the TIC tidied, I switched off the lights, turned the sign to Closed and locked up. At last, the weekend had arrived.

* * *

The evening before, I had stashed my little Fiat just round the corner from the TIC. It usually lives in a lockup beyond my cottage, in a lane behind Nuala's Tea Room, but I hadn't wanted to delay the start of my journey even the ten minutes it took to walk up there. I tossed my bag in the boot, but hesitated. I was a bit peckish. It occurred to me that it would be ages before I arrived at our weekend digs, and so I took a brief detour into the corner shop for a packet of crisps and a coffee for the journey.

As I headed out the north end of the village, past my cottage, past Nuala's, I inched along with the other cars creeping up the London road and tried to enjoy the cowslips that had started to bloom in the verge. Just past the long gravel drive on my right that led to Hoggin Hall, I glanced left to the Stoat and Hare. The lane that ran from the church to the pub and hotel was clogged with parked cars. The rain had let up, and a crowd congregated on the pavement, while at least a dozen small children dashed about, chasing one another round the clusters of adults. Everyone well dressed, laughing and talking. Had there been a wedding? I preferred to know when there was any sort of celebration in the village, not because I was a nosy parker, but because it was important for the manager of the TIC to keep her finger on the pulse of the estate. I made a mental note to ask Peg.

* * *

I arrived in Dunwich ahead of Michael and lugged my bag up the stairs. He'd booked us a lovely room that had a view to the east, out across the marsh to the sea beyond. Sunrise would be gorgeous — not that I intended either of us to be up and about for it. I filled the kettle, switched it on, and opened a packet of Hobnobs from the tea tray. I drank my tea as I watched the sky over the water dim. I had stretched out on the bed for only a moment when the next thing I knew, I awoke to a darkened room and a man beside me.

I giggled and leaned over, bumping my nose on his cheek before nipping at his earlobe. "Took you long enough."

"Yeah," Michael said slipping his arms round my waist and pulling me close. He sighed deeply. "Late — that was my day. Late for everything. Couldn't get the crew scheduled at Marshy End until Basil Blandy arrived and spent two hours in a foundation meeting in Cambridge during which we should've been going over grant applications, but turned out they hadn't been copied yet. I was harassed by one of the applicants in the pub, got all the way to the village before I remembered we weren't driving here together, and pulled up in front of the visitors' center at Lackford Lakes outside of Bury to find Rupert blaming me that he'd missed a short-eared owl."

"It isn't wise to stand between Dad and a short-eared owl," I commiserated. Michael sighed, reached over, and switched on the lamp. We both blinked.

"Look, Julia, I want to tell you something else. I got an email."

"Wait." I pressed my fingers to his lips. "For the next three days, no more talk of work or schedules or emails. We need this weekend to ourselves, no outside interruptions." There, I'd said it. This proposal had been simmering at the back of my mind, and I sighed with relief at letting it out. If both of us had something to explain, this was a good idea all round. Although, I'd say my email would be the bigger surprise — it had certainly stunned me. But this wasn't the time.

I gasped as inspiration struck. "Let's switch off our phones, so no one can bother us. What do you say?"

The corner of Michael's mouth pulled up and his blue eyes were like midnight. "I say yes to that."

* * *

We lazed our way through the weekend, spending most of Saturday strolling the promenade at Southwold and snapping photos of the long line of colorful beach huts.

"Look now," Michael said, pointing to one painted with red-and-white stripes. "For sale — only a hundred thousand."

We peered in the windows. "I could barely turn round in there," I said, but then realized it looked about the size of my cottage's sitting room.

We ate ice cream on the pier — a bit on the chilly side for it, but it seemed the thing to do — had a lovely lunch at Two Magpies Bakery on the high street, and when we returned to Dunwich and our room in the late afternoon, we didn't come out again until time for dinner. Cod-and-salmon fish cake with fresh spinach for me, and pork belly for Michael. What a perfect day.

On Sunday morning we spent hours wandering the paths at Minsmere. I wanted Michael to see a firecrest. It's such a lovely, tiny bird with that band of orange right on the top of its head, and one had been spotted in the wood not far from the visitors' center. We didn't find him, but we were not short of bird sightings. At the feeders we saw goldfinch, chaffinch, chiffchaff, robin, dunnock, blue tit, long-tailed tit, coal tit. In the sky were marsh harriers with eyes on the ground, hunting. And on the water, avocets, widgeons, teals, all manner of gulls, and greylag geese.

We were in the south hide, sitting on stools with elbows on the wooden bar, propping up our binoculars. Down the other end, two couples chatted about sand martins.

"Too bad we won't see a bean goose," I said. "I'd say they've all gone back to Russia by now."

"Does a bean goose eat beans?" Michael asked.

I snorted. "Yes, beans on toast, every morning. Really, you know — apart from the bean goose — you've learned a great deal about birds in only a year."

"Rupert's a good teacher." He nudged my shoulder with his. "I have two good teachers."

"Who's the other one?" I asked. "Basil Blandy?" Michael grinned and gave me a quick kiss. "This is lovely," I whispered.

He watched me for a moment. His eyes were that iridescent turquoise of a kingfisher. "Come away with me," he said.

If we'd been alone, I would've thrown myself in his arms at this invitation.

"A holiday," he continued. "A real one." His eyes sparked. "Where would you like to go?"

"Far away," I said. Having been off this island home only once in my life for a weekend in Paris, my vision was limited, and I took a stab at a remote and secluded spot. "John o' Groats?"

Michael laughed. "We'll have to do better than that to escape work. Rupert wants to do an entire program up there on puffins."

I looped my arm through his. "We'll have to think on it then." We returned to scanning the scrape, as a dozen lapwings came in to land. "They saw a Slavonian grebe here not long ago," I said. "Rare and a real surprise. But of course, it's spring migration. At this time of year, anything can happen."

* * *

Outside the pub, we stamped our feet to get the sand off before going in and tramping up the stairs.

"I could just do with a bath," I said over my shoulder.

"Ms. Lanchester?" The fellow from the bar popped his head round the corner. "You had a phone call earlier from your father." Dad was no stranger to these parts or this pub, and so no one needed to get all aflutter when Rupert Lanchester was on the other end of the line.

I rolled my eyes at Michael. "Busted."

"He asked that you ring him as soon as possible."

"Right, thanks," I said cheerfully to the fellow, but grumbled out of the corner of my mouth to Michael, "We shouldn't be made to work on our holiday."

"Our working holiday," he reminded me.

"And you, Mr. Sedgwick," the fellow continued, "you had a phone call as well."

"Rupert?" Michael asked.

"No sir, Sudbury Constabulary. A Detective Inspector Callow."

CHAPTER 3

Detective Inspector Tess Callow — that name stunned my senses and froze me to the spot. Sudbury, the nearest town to Smeaton, was only ten minutes down the road, and home of our local constabulary. Michael and I had met her in the autumn when she investigated a "suspicious" death at Hoggin Hall. I had been in temporary residence at the time as my cottage was undergoing a repair, and had found the body. I'd mostly put all that behind me until this moment.

Michael called out "Thanks" to the fellow from the pub, grabbed my hand, and pulled me up the stairs to our room. Inside, we both dived for our phones, and as we waited for them to fire up, he said, "It might be nothing. Your dad, Callow — it might not be related at all." But we both knew better. My heart thumped in my chest.

The moment the phones were live, beeps, chirps, and dings chastised us. Seven texts on mine, nine missed calls, and four voice messages. Listen or read? I couldn't seem to make up my mind. I saw Michael, too, staring at his screen. When my phone rang with a real call, I jumped as if I'd been slapped.

"Dad?" I asked. "What is it?"

He said something I couldn't understand, because the sound was muffled as if he'd turned away. In the background

I heard another voice. Beryl, I think — Dad's wife and my stepmum. He came back on the line, his voice strained and tired. "Julia? Where are you? Are you still in Dunwich? Why haven't you been answering?"

"We were having a bit of a break, that's all."

Michael's phone rang. He looked at the screen and up at me, nodding once. Callow. He walked into the bathroom to answer.

A pricking sensation like little needles crept up my arm. "Dad, is something wrong?"

I tried to listen to Michael's side of his conversation, hoping to understand why the police would need him. "Friday," I heard him tell Callow.

"There's a bit of bad news," Rupert said to me, "but I—"

"Is it Bee?" I asked, jumping in feet first, assuming the worst. Something must've happened to my sister. "One of the children? Paul?"

"No, it isn't Bianca or any of them—"

"Are you ill? Is Beryl?"

"No, we are both fine, but I need to—"

"Stephen?" I asked. If it wasn't my sister or Dad or his wife, Beryl, it must be my best friend from childhood, who was also Beryl's son.

"Jools, listen to me." I could hear the frustration in his voice. "We are all well, but there's been an unfortunate event on the estate."

Another one? My heart leapt into my throat. The police. "Oh God, not Linus."

In the bathroom, I heard Michael say, "No, I don't know him."

"Not Linus," Dad said. "Or Cecil. Julia, you must let me say this. The police found Nick near the Hall. He's dead."

In some creepy time warp, I was transported to four years ago — no five, now — and saw a slight figure with mousy brown hair that he kept cut short and that odd bend to his nose where he'd broken it in a fall. And I heard him saying, "Well, see ya," before he left for St. Kilda in the Outer

Hebrides. The image was dull and colorless. The last time I saw my ex-husband, Nick Hawkins.

I felt nothing. It was as if my mind had been shot with novocaine — my entire body, too.

"Yes, I can come in," Michael said, his eyes on me. "Does it need to be today?"

"Julia?" Dad called to me from his end of the phone. "Are you all right?"

"What happened?" I croaked.

"Listen, come back now — you and Michael. It shouldn't take you more than an hour and a half. Beryl and I will meet you both."

"At my cottage?" I asked, trying to grasp some mundane detail that would make sense. "At the Hall? Cambridge — should we go to your house?"

Michael turned away from me, but I heard him say, "Right, we're on our way."

"No, Jools," Dad said, "not the village — at the police station in Sudbury."

"Dad—"

"It's a suspicious death — that's what DI Callow says. Let's not do this now. Can you leave soon? Will you be all right to drive? You could leave your car and come back with Michael."

"I'm not leaving my car in the middle of nowhere," I said hotly. "That's ridiculous — how would I ever get it back again?" Anger boiled up in me, and I had no idea where to direct it, so Rupert took the brunt.

"All right, drive back," Dad said in that soothing tone meant to pacify a screaming child. "You'll be careful?"

"Yes, of course," I acquiesced, all the fight gone out of me. I rang off.

Michael had already finished his conversation, and dropped his phone on the bed as he came out of the bathroom. He hesitated, but I pulled him to me, clasping my arms round his neck and holding tight. He responded in kind, and the strength of his embrace brought feeling back into my limbs and my mind.

"We've got to go," I said. "Did Callow tell you?"

"Yes. I'm sorry, Julia."

My grip on Michael's neck loosened. "Sus . . . suspicious death," I sputtered. "The police will explain what happened, they have to."

I began to stuff clothes into my bag as Michael gathered his things. In only a moment, we stood at the door of the room, bags in hand. Out the window, I could see the midday sun sparkling on the sea and a gull of some sort gliding by in the distance. I grabbed Michael's hand.

"It was such a lovely weekend." My voice caught in my throat.

"We'll come back," Michael said.

I dropped my bag to reach over with my other hand and touch his cheek. "I'm very glad you're with me."

He kissed the palm of my hand. "We'd best be off."

It had been all of ten minutes since we'd returned to the pub, and now here we were heading back down the stairs and outdoors. We stowed our bags in our cars and stood with keys in our hands as a salty breeze circled us. I, for one, was afraid to break this last contact.

"Julia—" Michael began.

"Michael, I had an email from Nick." There, I'd said it — my confession blurted out, because I couldn't think of a way to introduce it. I had been keeping the news until after our weekend, when the real world would insinuate itself into our lives again. But that wasn't to be. "Thursday. Five years with no contact apart from when we signed the divorce papers, and then Thursday, an email."

Michael looked out across the road for a moment, and then back at me. His eyes were a sharp, flinty blue.

"I had an email from Nick, too."

* * *

One of the voice messages had been from Vesta. And so before I pulled out of the car park, I rang her, switched to "speaker," and set my phone in the cup holder so that I could talk as I drove.

"Julia!" she answered, her voice full of relief. "Are you all right?"

"You've heard?" I asked.

"I've heard nothing, but yesterday afternoon, that Detective Inspector Callow from Sudbury rang looking for you."

And so I explained the few details I knew.

"What an awful thing to happen," Vesta said. "And how difficult for you."

Vesta, who always seemed to understand more than was said, knew of my ambivalence toward Nick. She had heard more about it than Michael had. I couldn't tell the man in my life now that I had never loved my husband — before or during our marriage. I hadn't hated Nick, but I certainly hadn't loved him, either. What sort of person has no feelings whatsoever?

Vesta asked nothing else, and I told her I'd see her on Tuesday, when I was sure I could explain further.

I've no idea how long the journey to Sudbury took. I kept myself well occupied by sorting through the incongruous jumble of facts I'd been presented and trying to build them into a story that made sense.

The last thing Michael had said to me was, "Are you all right?"

I'd nodded, but couldn't look at him. I wasn't all right, but neither had I collapsed in a puddle of anguish and despair. My ex-husband was dead, and so shouldn't those be the normal emotions, at least to some degree? At the very least I should feel sad. But instead, I felt an old dullness creep over me, at once familiar and unpleasant. A small, but heavy, stone of guilt dropped into the pit of my stomach — and running through the stone, a blood-red vein of angry resentment.

Questions flooded my mind. How had Nick died? In a "suspicious" manner. The police couldn't fool me — I knew that to be a thinly veiled euphemism for murder.

Merely thinking the word caused me to take a sharp breath. Someone had killed Nick. Did his death have something to do with the Fotheringills? Where had he been found? I had a sudden picture in my mind of the butler, Thorne, pulling open the enormous oak front door of Hoggin Hall to find Nick's body flung across the flagstone step. The image made me giggle, after which I felt even more wretched than before.

Nick had left St. Kilda — his home these past five years — and come to Smeaton. Why? He had contacted both Michael and me and asked to meet. For the same reason or did he have a separate agenda with each of us?

"He wanted to see me, but he didn't say why." It was all Michael had said before we had left the coast. I had said the same.

Nick had revealed nothing in his email. "Julia, I'm back on land and I'd like to see you. What do you say?" Never one for flowery words, not even a "Hasn't it been a long time," or "I hope you are well" or "I was sorry to hear about your mum." That's right — nearly two years ago, when my mum was run over and killed while out for a walk, we'd had an outpouring of sympathy from well-wishers everywhere. Nick's sister, Kathleen, seventeen years his senior, had even sent a card, although she'd added nothing but her signature to the printed message "Our condolences at your loss." Perhaps that "our" was meant to cover Nick, too. How convenient.

Nick's email had caught me by surprise, a reaction I immediately had squashed, moving on to other things. But I had meant to ignore it for three days only and had every intention of answering him after the weekend. So much for that.

* * *

A dull pain in my right temple had blossomed into a full-blown headache by the time we arrived at the Sudbury police station. I pulled my sky-blue Fiat into a space in the car park and Michael, driving his sea-foam-green model, parked just next to me.

At the door of the building, I reached for his hand. Once inside, I took in the scene a moment before they noticed us. Rupert and Linus — who had become quite good friends over the past few months — were standing in the corner, speaking quietly. Dad wore his safari jacket and khaki trousers, but not his wide-brimmed leather hat. Linus, well dressed as always, wore a lightweight checked wool suit, although I could see the shape of his bicycle trouser clip in the pocket of his jacket. Beryl, in an uncharacteristically mismatched pink-and-green sweater set, sat nearby, tapping her fingers on an unopened magazine.

The tableau crumbled the moment they spotted us. Beryl jumped up and gave me a hug, and Dad and Linus hurried over. They all began to speak at once, and then all stopped, leaving a chasm of silence in the room.

The desk sergeant picked up his phone.

"Will someone please tell me how it happened?" I asked. "What was Nick doing at the Hall? Did you see him, Linus?"

Linus shook his head. "No, I'm so sorry, Julia. I have no idea of the circumstances. He was found" — he shook his head at his own words — "in the summerhouse."

"The summerhouse?"

My sluggish brain lurched forward, searching the map of the estate I had memorized. I could see it — the small, derelict, octagonal building on the other side of the drive from Hoggin Hall. It sat on a knoll and had overlooked the fields and wood to both the east and west, until a new beech wood had grown up around it, obscuring the view. Linus said it had been his grandmother's favorite spot for dinners during long summer evenings, and so on the website, we had used a lovely old photo of him in short trousers standing on its steps next to her. I thought she looked rather severe, a bit like a peregrine staring at you head-on, but Linus spoke fondly of her.

The summerhouse had fallen out of favor after she died, and then thirty years ago, when Linus inherited, he began his austerity program, which had meant some parts of the estate had been neglected. The summerhouse, unused for decades, was abandoned completely. Now, the beech grove hid it from even the most discerning gaze, and a person had to go searching for it to find it. Out of sight, out of mind. Although Linus had brought the estate back into solvency, the summerhouse had yet to appear on a list for refurbishment.

"The summerhouse," I repeated. "What possible reason could he have for being there?"

"That's just what we hope to learn, Ms. Lanchester," a voice behind me said.

I whirled round to find Detective Inspector Callow. I hadn't seen her in a few months, but found her cool gaze, steel-rod posture, and tailored dark trouser suit just as intimidating as before. She kept her silver-gray hair quite short on top and a bit longer on the sides, where it was swept back. No doubt her smooth skin was the result of showing no emotion — although a few worry lines seemed to have sprouted between her brows.

"Inspector Callow," I said, raising my chin. "Good. Will you tell us why we're all here? How did Nick die? Why was he on the estate?"

"Ms. Lanchester, would you and Mr. Sedgwick come with me?" she asked, gesturing toward the door that led to the bowels of the building.

I cast a brief glance back to Rupert, Beryl, and Linus as Michael and I were led off.

"We'll wait for you," Dad said.

CHAPTER 4

We sat at a table in interview room one — according to the sign by the door — with DI Callow across from us, and a thin file folder in front of her. Michael caught my eye and I gave him a small "I'm all right" smile. He took my hand.

Callow had started the recorder just as the door bumped open and in came Detective Sergeant Glossop carrying two takeaway cups of tea, steam rising from them.

"I thought you could use these," he said, setting them gently on the table. "There's a wee bit of sugar in it."

I was desperate for a cup, but when I took a sip, I coughed. This was a cup my dad — a three-sugars-please tea drinker — would love. "Thank you, Sergeant," I said.

Natty Glossop flashed a smile, looked at his boss, and the smile disappeared. He nodded and straightened his jacket before sitting.

I set my tea on the table. "I appreciate you wanting to tell me about Nick's death, but I'm not his next-of-kin. We've been divorced for three years. You should be in touch with his sister. I may have her contact details."

"Thank you," Glossop said, "but your father has provided us with those. The deceased's sister, Kathleen Hawkins, will be here day after tomorrow. She's traveling from Nova Scotia."

"Well, then, did you want to explain to me how he died?"

"When were you last on the grounds of Hoggin Hall, Ms. Lanchester?" Callow asked.

I sensed the dance had begun — I asked a question, Callow sidestepped. What I didn't understand was why.

"I was there Thursday late afternoon," I said. "Akash Kumar runs the docent program for our open days, and we had a retraining scheduled to get ready for the increase in visitors during the late spring and summer. When did Nick die? When was he found?"

"Mr. Sedgwick?"

"Julia and I were there for dinner on Sunday," Michael said, cool as a cucumber, a facade he had perfected when he worked in public relations. "Rupert and Beryl, too."

"Cecil and Willow," I added. "And Nuala." It had been a jolly evening. "Inspector, how did Nick die?"

She shot me a brief look. "Have you not been on the grounds since then, Mr. Sedgwick? Not Friday afternoon?"

Michael cocked his head. "I—"

"Because we have a witness who saw you turning down the drive to Hoggin Hall Friday at about three o'clock."

"Is that when he died — Friday?" I asked.

"Body was found by police at four-seventeen Saturday afternoon, Ms. Lanchester," Glossop said. "The pathologist says that rigor mortis was on its way out at that point. It allows us to estimate time of death as sometime Friday afternoon."

"Hang on," I said, too loudly, my voice echoing off the hard surfaces of the room. "Are you accusing Michael of . . . of . . ."

"We're making no accusations, Ms. Lanchester," Callow shot back. DS Glossop shifted in his chair. "I'm gathering information in a murder enquiry. You remember how that goes, I presume?"

"What could we possibly have to tell you that would help — we were both away for the weekend." We both of us did have something to tell her, it was true, but she hadn't actually provided the opportunity yet, had she? I took a slug of my tea, forgetting how sugary it was, and almost gagged.

"It's all right," Michael said. "Yes, I was on the grounds Friday afternoon, if you could call it that. For all of two minutes. I pulled into the drive, turned round, and headed out. I had forgotten that Julia and I arranged to meet at the coast, not drive together. Did your witness tell you that?"

"Who found Nick's body?" I persisted. I would play the role of midge and buzz in front of Callow's face as long as it took to get a detail of any sort out of her. Surely she remembered that. "No one goes out to the summerhouse. How did anyone come across him?"

"We received an anonymous phone call on Saturday afternoon," Glossop said.

"Sergeant," the DI warned, sending her DS an icy glare.

"They deserve to know that much, don't they?" he asked.

Six months had gone by since the last time I saw DS Glossop. He had been new to the job then — a bit brash, a bit unsure of himself, but full of humanity. I could see he'd gained both poise and confidence, but without any of Callow's cold demeanor rubbing off on him.

The DI nodded once. "Yes, fine. Go ahead."

He continued. "The desk sergeant took it. The person identified himself or possibly herself — it was difficult to tell — as a rambler and reported seeing a man's body in a derelict building on the estate quite near the Hall."

"It isn't derelict," I said, unable to think of anything else to say at the thought of Nick's body in the summerhouse. "It only needs a bit of refurbishment." I straightened up in my chair. "Are you going to tell us how Nick died?"

"He died from a stab wound to the back," Callow said, her eyes darting from my face to Michael's and back again. "A long, thin, sharp blade, possibly a filleting knife. We haven't found it. The blade entered the upper body, narrowly missing the spinal cord. A clean entry, but it ran straight through a major artery."

Blood. I saw blood everywhere — my mind was covered in a curtain of red. I grabbed for my tea, but my hand shook so much that a tsunami of lukewarm liquid sloshed over the side, across my hand and onto my trousers. I looked down at the dark stain and shuddered. Michael gently took the cup from me, and the DS retrieved a box of tissues from the windowsill.

As I mopped myself up, I said, "Inspector, Nick emailed me on Thursday."

"He emailed me, too," Michael said. "Thursday."

There, our cards were on the table. Callow didn't react, of course, but answered smoothly. "And what were the contents of those emails?"

I shrugged. "He wanted to meet. He lives on St. Kilda year-round tracking vagrant birds. Research. But he said he was back. I don't know why."

"And did you meet?"

"No. I didn't even reply. Michael and I were going to the coast for the weekend, and I thought I'd answer on Monday. Tomorrow."

"Mr. Sedgwick?"

Michael already had the email pulled up on his phone, which he set on the table and pushed over to the officers. They leaned over and the DS read aloud: "Nick Hawkins here. You know who I am? I'd like to meet. Tomorrow afternoon — someplace we can talk. I'll come to Julia's village."

My village. The drive to Hoggin Hall. The summerhouse, although mostly hidden from view, was not far off the drive. I logged these facts as I'm sure Callow did, but I doubt if we came to the same conclusion.

"And did you, Mr. Sedgwick? Did you meet him?"

"No," Michael said. "I've already told you that. I sent no reply. I wanted to talk with Julia about it first."

"Had you ever met Mr. Hawkins? Ever seen him?"

"I—" Michael's expression shifted slightly, and he glanced away and back again before saying, "I don't know what he looks like."

Don't think I didn't see Callow cut her eyes at me.

"It isn't as if I keep old wedding photos on the mantel," I told her.

She reached inside the file folder and took something out. Before I could think, I gasped and recoiled, covering my mouth with my hand.

Callow leaned forward and said, "It's only the photo from the identification he had with him." But I knew there were more photos in that folder — there had to be. Photos of Nick from every angle, dead and lying in a pool of his own blood. That's what police do; they collect photos of bodies.

"AIL," Michael said, looking at Nick's ID.

AIL. I knew those letters. "Avian Institute of Learning," I said. "The place he worked." I leaned over to look and frowned at the identification photo. Nick had let his hair grow — it came down to his shoulders, scraggly and thin. He wasn't smiling. Typical.

Michael exhaled deeply and shook his head. "No, I've never seen him."

Callow nodded toward the DS who pulled a flat plastic bag out from beneath the file folder.

"We found this clutched in Mr. Hawkins's hand," she said. "Can either of you tell me why he might have had it?"

The bag held a piece of paper about the size of an index card with a black-and-white photo. The paper looked as if it had been torn off a larger sheet and wrinkled, but flattened out again, with reddish-brown stains around the edges. The photo on it may have been a black-and-white copy, but the colors came to life in my mind. Michael and I smiling at the camera. I wore my flirty pink dress — long sleeves, short hem, plunging back — and Michael, a tux. I remembered the night. It had been two months ago, and we were all dressed up for a fundraising dinner for the Rupert Lanchester Foundation. It had been a lovely evening and had raised buckets of money. The photo looked as if it had been printed off an online news site — one of those social events pages. Part of the caption was missing, but our names were legible, as well as the phrase "busy couple who still find time to . . ." *Find time to what,* I wondered.

"Why would Mr. Hawkins have this?" Callow asked. "And if he'd been away for three years—"

"Five," I corrected her. "He left for St. Kilda five years ago. We were divorced three years ago." I waited for her to ask why it took us so long, but she followed her own train of thought.

"If he'd been away for that long, it might make sense he would want to see you, Ms. Lanchester." — It made no sense to me, but I kept my mouth shut and let her continue. "But why would he want to talk with you, Mr. Sedgwick?"

"I've no idea."

"Are you asking them" — I nodded toward Nick's ID — "the rest of the people in AIL? Are you asking them about Nick?"

"We would if we could find them," Glossop said.

"You mean they're in hiding?"

"Do you know how many people live on Hirta?" Callow asked. "It's the only inhabited island of St. Kilda."

I shrugged. "Not too many, I would think."

"Ten year-round," Callow said. "For two months in the summer, the researchers move in and the tour boats arrive. The population swells to about thirty-five. Mr. Hawkins was one of the few who lived there throughout the year. Sounds like a lonely life for a young man."

"Sounds like it would suit Nick." My face reddened as I heard my words as they would hear them — callous, cold.

The DI stood, signaling an imminent dismissal. She rested her fingertips on the table and stood straight and tall.

"We are at the beginning of this investigation, and I may need to reach you with further questions. I know you both realize" — *right, here it is* — "how important it is that you do nothing on your own. If you accidentally come across even the smallest piece of information that may have to do with Mr. Hawkins's death, you will turn it over to me or to DS Glossop and not pursue it yourselves. Am I understood?"

It was as if I was in school again. I almost replied, "Yes, miss," but stopped myself in time and nodded.

"And Mr. Sedgwick — we'll need you to give us your schedule for Friday and anyone who can verify your whereabouts."

I shot out of my chair. "You can't be seriously keeping that up. Why in God's name would Michael want to kill Nick?"

Before Callow could answer, Michael put a hand on my arm and said, "I don't mind. You know how it is, Julia."

Only too well.

* * *

"Come back to the house with us," Dad said as he, Beryl, and Linus clustered round Michael and me when we emerged.

"Yes," Beryl said. "We'll cook a meal together — just have a quiet evening."

I shook my head. "I want to go home. Come by the cottage, why don't you? Linus, you too."

"Thank you, Julia," Linus replied, pulling his trouser clip from his pocket. "I'll go back to the Hall. I know the others will be waiting to hear you're all right."

"You didn't cycle over, did you?" Linus rode his bike all over the estate and the journey to the police station wasn't that far, but still, it seemed a bit extreme. The road between Sudbury and Smeaton could be quite busy.

He looked down at the clip in his hand and smiled. "No, sorry. Automatic response, I suppose." Back went the clip. "Please let me know if you need anything. The TIC is closed tomorrow, but why don't you take Tuesday off as well. Surely Vesta could fill in?"

"No, tomorrow will be enough." I didn't know what everyone expected me to do — wear black? Plan the funeral? In my stomach, the lump of guilt began to swell.

We walked out and down the steps to the car park, and I heard someone call my name.

"Julia?"

I turned toward the voice and heard the *click* of a camera. Five or six people, strung out along the edge of the pavement, all began talking at once, their volume increasing into a Tower of Babel.

"Rupert! Is it true your son-in-law was murdered?"

"Michael! How will this affect your relationship with Julia?"

"Julia! Did you find the body? What went through your mind? Are you sorry for the divorce now?"

For a moment, we stood frozen as the questions pelted us. A woman in a brown duffel coat — her head close-cropped on one side, with a severe wedge of frizzy auburn hair on the other — thrust something furry at me. I could see scratches on her hand and arm, and for a second I thought she held a kitten, but then realized it was a windscreen, like a tiny muff, that fit on a hand-held recorder. Recorder? I jumped away from the thing.

"Michael!" A tall, wide fellow pushed his way forward. "Were you arguing with him and it turned violent? Tell us your side of the story."

Dad spread his arms and hurried us away.

"Rupert! You didn't see any carrion crows, did you? Not like in the film, eh? Pecking his eyes out?"

We all stopped at that last one. I whirled round, scanned the group, and saw a man at the back standing up on the curb. He was short and balding with wispy blond hair. He had two cameras round his neck and an iPhone in his hand, and he wore one of those canvas waistcoats with a million tiny Velcro pockets. His face was flushed, and I knew he had been the one.

Rupert took a sharp breath. "Now then, this is a private matter," he called in a friendly manner — I doubted that any in that group could hear the underlying fury. "I'm sure you'll respect that."

"Lord Fotheringill?" One of the other men asked this with a note of delighted incredulity in his voice. They all turned on Linus, who held his head high and gave us a nod. Rupert herded us away.

"Your Lordship," we heard one say, "bad luck for the estate. Or will you start conducting murder tours round the Hall?"

CHAPTER 5

When we'd arrived at my Pipit Cottage, Beryl had nipped into Akash's shop for sandwiches and now had them arranged on a plate, which she set on the coffee table.

I brought the tea in. Dad sat in the one armchair and the rest of us crowded onto the sofa. I spotted the roast chicken-and-stuffing sandwich and nabbed a half. It had been hours and hours since breakfast.

The first topic of discussion was "How did they know?" 'They' meaning the press, the media, whoever that lot was outside the station.

"Police reports go online quickly, don't they?" Dad asked. "Incident reports and the like."

"Sounded as if they knew more than would be in an incident report," I said.

"Journos are free with their suppositions — at least some types are," Michael said. He knew a thing or two about the press, because he'd worked in his family's PR business, HMS, Ltd., before getting a job with Rupert. "They'll say anything and look for a reaction. If they get one, that's what they'll pursue."

"It'll die down, this attention," Beryl said. "Just don't engage. Don't react or lash out."

I saw the three of them exchange looks. That advice was meant for me, of course. But I could behave when I had to, although I hoped it wouldn't come to me needing to monitor every word that came out of my mouth. Perhaps they would just leave us alone.

* * *

Michael and I went over everything Callow and Glossop had asked and what we had told them, and Beryl and Rupert began to fill in their side of the story. Late Saturday afternoon — only the day before — the police appeared at Hoggin Hall to inform Linus a man's body had been found on the grounds. As they scoured the scene and, no doubt, rummaged through Nick's pockets, police discovered his identity, and made the connection with us when they found the crumpled paper in Nick's hand. Michael and I were out of touch at the coast, and so when they couldn't find us, they found Rupert instead. He and Beryl were in Bristol, where Dad had given a talk at the university on Friday.

"I explained who Nick was," Dad said.

"And we came straight back," Beryl added.

"Did you have to" — I swallowed hard — "identify him?"

Dad nodded once. "Yes. But I told them I had no idea how Nick came to be there."

"Nick called Smeaton 'my village' in the email to Michael. How did he even know where I was?"

"How does anyone know anything these days?" Michael asked. "He probably found you online."

"Oh, right." Our website for the estate included a staff page with a photo of Vesta, Willow, and me — all smiling, wearing our uniforms of navy pencil skirt, cardigan, and white blouse. Well, not Willow, of course. Instead, she sported one of her usual hodgepodge outfits of batik-print skirt, crocheted waistcoat, and beret.

"And you've had no word from him all this time?" Dad asked.

"Nothing for five years."

"And you, Michael? Nick has never tried to get in touch with you before this? What about your family business?"

I couldn't imagine what Nick would need with HMS, Ltd., now run by Miles, Michael's older brother. Send out press releases for the latest vagrant-bird sightings? *Red-crested pochard drops in for a visit!*

"No, sir." Michael picked up his mug of tea and stared into it.

"Dad, do you know the people Nick worked with — AIL, the Avian Institute of Learning?"

"I've no idea who they are," Rupert said.

"Would they be from Cambridge, do you think?"

"Entirely possible, but it's not for us to find out. We'll have to leave it to the police." Dad apparently didn't like the silence that followed his statement. "Won't we, Jools?"

"Yes, of course. But I do hope they'll tell us what happened." The sandwiches had been reduced to crumbs, and the teapot held only sodden lumps. "Shall I do us another pot?"

"I'd say we'd best be off," Beryl said, gathering dishes and setting them on the tray. I followed her into the kitchen, where she turned to me and said, "You'll ring Bianca, won't you? Your father sent her a text to say we'd found you, so she knows you're safe, but she'll want to hear from you."

"Of course I will. Did you tell Stephen?"

Beryl shook her head and frowned. "Have you spoken to him lately?"

"It's been two or three weeks," I said. Bee and I had grown up with Beryl's son, Stephen. We had been, as my mum used to say, thick as thieves — our parents had called us the gang of three. Bee and I still kept in touch with Stephen, although we were geographically scattered, Stephen in London, Bee in Cornwall, and I in Suffolk.

"I understand you want to stay here, Julia, but won't you come over to Cambridge tomorrow?"

"Michael and I have the next month's schedule to sort," Dad said as he took his jacket and helped Beryl into hers. "It's your day off, come along."

"Yes, all right," I said.

We walked out onto the pavement with them. One moment the street was quiet, and the next, pandemonium.

"Julia! Can you bear to have him touch you knowing what he did?"

"Rupert! Do you regret hiring Michael?"

There they were, rushing at us from across the road. It looked like the same ones, all snapping photos and waving phones in the air — the large one, two men wearing identical jackets, that woman in the brown duffel coat with her kitten microphone, the short one with the pockets — all hoping for a juicy sound bite. But above it all, and almost drowning out the hateful questions, was a raucous cawing from above. Out of the corner of my eye I saw a dark figure drop from the sky and looked up in time to see a rook divebomb the group of journos. They scattered, but the big one tripped and fell flat. The others laughed.

Dad seized this moment of distraction and said to us, "Go back inside," as he and Beryl made for their car. Michael and I retreated indoors and moved to the window, peering through a slit in the curtains. Three of them — the large one and the twin jackets — followed the famous Rupert Lanchester to his car, but kitten woman stayed across the road. She stood next to the balding fellow with the cameras — the little weasel — but when she said something to him, he stepped away.

"Talk about carrion crows," I said. "I should ring Callow. Couldn't she send someone to drive them off?"

"They'll get tired of it," Michael said. "Was that a crow out there?"

"No, a rook," I said. "He had a long, pale beak, you know. And his leg feathers." I peeked out the slit, scanning the rooftops across the road. "I met a rook the other day."

"Did you now?" I noted the relief in Michael's voice as the subject shifted. I looked over to see one corner of his mouth tug into a grin. "And what's he called?"

"He's called Alfie," I said and smiled back. "He was with his friend, a little girl named Tennyson. They stopped in at the TIC Friday afternoon." That reminder brought the light moment to an abrupt end. Friday afternoon, when Nick was murdered.

"We might as well stay indoors this evening," Michael suggested. "What do you say?"

"Yes, perfect," I said with false cheer. "We'll watch a movie. I'll do us a pasta." We looked out at the empty street. "What did Nick want with us, Michael?"

* * *

I came down the next morning to find Michael at the same spot near the window, peering through the curtains.

"Are they still there?" I asked.

"They're reassembling, I'd say."

"The absolute nerve of them." I took two decisive steps toward the door, but Michael caught my hand. "Yes, all right," I huffed. "Don't engage."

"Tea's ready," Michael said as I heard the toast pop.

We sat in the kitchen. "Why don't I follow you over to Cambridge in a bit?" I asked as I reached for the butter. "I think I'll ring Bee again. She'll have a bit more free time this morning."

My sister, Bianca, deftly juggled a husband and four children. Evenings could be chaotic, which had been the case when we'd tried to talk the evening before, but now, with husband Paul at his gallery, and Emelia, Enid, and Emmet in their various schools, she'd have only baby Estella to deal with. And me.

"Yeah," Michael said, "that's fine. And listen, don't go online this morning, all right?" I grabbed for my phone and Michael put his hand over mine. "I mean it, Julia. What good will it do except to get you angry?"

"I can't not look. I can't avoid the whole matter. I'll be fine."

"Will you? Reacting will only make it worse. They'd seize on it and use it against you."

I nodded vigorously. "Yes, all right."

A few minutes later when Michael stepped out, a cacophony of rapid-fire questions hit us like pellets, accompanied, once again, by a rook's harsh descant from above.

"Michael! Did Nick attack you? Were you defending yourself? Tell us how it happened!"

"Were you in it together, Julia? Was Michael saving you?"

I swallowed a retort as Michael yanked the door out of my hand and closed it with a shudder. I watched from our lookout as he walked to his car, acting as if he was entirely alone on the street instead of being trailed by a gaggle of angry geese, nipping at his heels. As yesterday, the rook flew at the group, scattering them as they ducked his attack. Rooks, as well as crows, magpies, and jackdaws, took offense easily and didn't forget a slight soon. Had one of these journos — or perhaps the lot of them — done the bird some wrong? Steal a rock bun he had saved? Wouldn't give up a bit of ham sandwich? I squinted at the bird. Was that Alfie?

Michael drove off and the reporters slunk back, keeping to under the eaves and darting in doorways. *You can't hide — I see you.* I clamped my eyes on the little weasel, who brought up the rear. *Especially you.* He might look innocent hanging back like that, but I knew better and was happy to make him the figurehead. It felt good to have a target.

Love Nest Torn Apart by Murder!
Rupert's Shock Over Daughter's Tryst with Ex
The Birds Told Him to Do It!
The Rival for Her Affections — Did Boyfriend Go Too Far?

The headlines went from bad to worse. I had the windows tiled on my laptop, so that the impact quadrupled. *The People's News, Sightings, Suffolk Echo, Cambridge Mercury and Reformer.* I'd never heard of those sites. The photos of us showed mostly Michael and me and Dad, but with Beryl in the background. One showed Linus holding his hand up. Awful catch-you-off-guard sorts of photos with mouths open, arms waving as if we were trying to get away from it all. And so we were.

I kept the images on the screen as I rang Bee, anger fueling the fiery pain in my chest. I desperately needed a load of good sense.

"They're toerags, every last one of them," Bianca spat into the phone. "They don't care how this rubbish affects people's lives; they only care about selling their gossip. And will they retract any of these allegations when they find out what really happened? Bloody unlikely, I'd say."

I felt better immediately. "It's as if they're an entirely different breed from the press that write about Dad and his teaching and the program," I said as I switched on the kettle. "Where do these people come from?"

"Crawled out from under a rock."

"And so where are all the good ones, and why don't they write something to counteract this trash? Everyone loved the piece written about Dad and the oystercatchers in Morecambe Bay."

"Well, that's Michael's remit, isn't it? He'll put out a load of lovely articles and drown these hacks out."

"I'd say he's already on it, but he's got the television schedule and the foundation as well. It's such a terrible time for this to . . ." I caught myself. "It's terrible for it to happen at all."

"God, Nick," Bee said. "This is bizarre."

We settled into a moment of silence. The kettle switched off, and I poured out my mug of tea. A thought had formed during the night, and I needed for it to see the light of day to know if it had any weight or if it arose from the guilt of the living.

"If I had answered his email," I said, "if I had gone to meet him, perhaps he wouldn't've been killed."

"No, Jools, don't say that. What if you *had* gone to meet him — what then? You could've been there when this person killed him. And you could be dead now, too." Bianca's voice shook, and I heard her sniff.

"All these journos" — I nodded at the screaming headlines on my laptop screen — "they're trying to make out Michael had something to do with it."

"What do they think — that Nick came to win you back and Michael tried to stop him? Ha! That's a load of bollocks, and if they had known Nick, they would know that."

* * *

I checked the street from the cottage lookout window, saw no one loitering, and so slipped out and dashed down the pavement toward my car.

"Ms. Lanchester?"

Only one voice, and it sounded respectful, and so I made the mistake of turning. The little weasel with the cameras and the waistcoat made up of pockets had ducked out from between the wool shop and Dresses by Dot.

"Ms. Lanchester, may I have a word?"

Don't react, Julia. Don't engage.

I bit back my reply and hurried off, getting to my car and pulling away before I checked the wing mirror. He hadn't followed — perhaps he had been assigned to that spot of pavement. Good, stand right there. Don't move. A sharp shower began, and with grim delight I saw he had no hat. I switched on the wipers.

CHAPTER 6

The journey to Cambridge didn't take long, only forty minutes, but I added another half hour when I dropped in at the marquee hire business to confirm details for the farmers market. When we'd confirmed the number of stalls and size of the tents needed, I ticked that box on my mental list — one of a myriad of tasks that would keep me busy throughout the week. I felt grateful for the work, because it would be a good distraction. Many details remained to be sorted for the market, including final stall assignments and rubbish removal.

Beyond the market business, I had the Saturday mini-coach tours that came out from Colchester and stopped at the TIC for a brief introduction to the estate and to collect their lunches from Akash. Plus, the guided walk — we had joined the official Suffolk Walking Festival by organizing a birding event on the grounds of Hoggin Hall. It wasn't until Friday, so five days away. Would the police make us change the venue? Perhaps I could let Vesta deal with that one.

Michael had recommended that I avoid parking in front of Dad's house, and so I did as he suggested, finding a place two streets over and setting out on foot. But when I turned the corner, I saw them — the reporters — strung along the pavement in front of the house. Even the little weasel had made it in time for my arrival. I hesitated for a moment and then marched on with purpose, my head held high.

"Julia! Did you know Michael was going to meet your ex?"

"Don't you want everyone to know the truth? Give us your side!"

"Michael was jealous and lashed out — is that what happened?"

"Did Nick have your picture on him, Julia? Did he still love you?"

With every step and every question, my muscles tightened. The rabble followed me up the front walk and by the time I reached the door, I vibrated with fury.

"Was it a sex game gone wrong, Julia?"

It was the woman, that last one, and like Vesuvius, I erupted.

"*You stupid cow!*" I shrieked, swinging wildly, trying to knock the muffed recorder out of her hand. "*What do you know about anything?*"

The others — cowards — leapt away. I would've gone for her but behind me, the door opened. Michael grabbed me by the arms and pulled me in. He slammed the door shut, but not before I saw the smirk on her face.

Dad threw the latch, and Beryl pulled the blinds. Michael lessened his tight grip as I tried to catch my breath.

"They're evil," I whispered. "All of them."

"I don't know how they can live with themselves," Beryl said. She helped me out of my coat as if I were a child. "Listen now, I've pea-and-ham soup. When you're ready."

"Are you all right?" Michael asked, kissing my cheek. I nodded. I noticed the three of them exchanging glances. We were crowded in the small entry, but no one moved.

"I tell you what," Dad said, a bit too heartily, "why don't we have our lunch and then we can sit down for a chat." I cut my eyes at him. He smiled but didn't look directly at me. He'd always been terrible at deception — Mum had always known she couldn't tell him where she'd hidden our

Christmas gifts for fear we would read it on his face. And so I knew that something was up.

"Why don't we have a chat first," I replied. "It's a bit early for lunch, isn't it?"

Beryl's gaze darted among us. Rupert looked at Michael.

"Yes," Michael said. "Now's a good time."

He led me to the floral sofa, and we sat. Dad and Beryl each took an armchair. No one spoke.

When I couldn't take it any longer, the questions burst forth. "Right, out with it. Have you heard something else from the police? Have they caught the person? Did Linus ring. Am I fired? Is he closing the TIC?"

"No, no, of course not," Dad said.

"Well, then, what? Just say it."

"Julia," Dad began, "this is a dreadful thing that's happened, and I'm so sorry that you've been caught up in it." I noted two things here. First, he sounded as if he were introducing a lecture on the decline in the sparrow population, and second, he used my real name. "We don't know how long it will take the police to discover who did this. We hope it's only a day or two, but it could be longer. The longer it takes, the more difficult it will be for us to get on with things, the way those people are hanging on." He nodded out toward the front gate. "And," he added, "they seem to be focusing a great deal of their attention on Michael."

"Yes," I said, seizing on this, "and why is that? An anonymous caller who saw Michael turn into the drive and just happened upon Nick's body on Saturday? You can't tell me this was a rambler." I snapped my fingers. "Friday was an open afternoon. We'll check with Akash — no, not Akash, he and Vesta were away on Friday. Willow! She ran the opening on Friday afternoon. She might've seen something. I'll have a word with her."

"You will do no such thing," Rupert said. "That's for the police to see to."

I opened my mouth to tell my father that I bloody well would do such a thing, but Michael cut in. "What we need at this moment is to take the spotlight off Rupert," he said, raising his eyebrows at me. "And you."

"And *you*," I said.

"If we divert their attention long enough and give them nothing," Michael said, "they'll lose interest. These aren't the mainstream press; these are low-class scandal sheets looking to make up the news if the truth doesn't suit their purposes."

"Horrible people," Beryl contributed.

"As Michael says," Dad continued, "we need to shift the attention away from you, the program, and all our events. Remember, the foundation is looking to award its first grant to a worthy project — we can't taint that. Michael has come up with an idea."

I looked at Michael hopefully. He's quite good at ideas. He sees the big picture and can come up with really fabulous concepts. The Rupert Lanchester Foundation was his idea — a way to reward companies that support good causes and give money to individuals and groups that need it. I don't mind saying that I excel at the day-to-day problems. It's as we tell people — Michael's the what and who, and I'm the when and how.

Michael hesitated for a moment, as if bracing himself. "I'm stepping away until this is all settled," he said.

"Stepping away from what?"

"I won't be Rupert's personal assistant. I won't work on the television program, set his schedule, arrange lectures and appearances. We'll put a hold on the foundation grant — postpone the decision. I'll post an official statement on the website that I no longer have anything to do with Rupert Lanchester, the foundation, or *A Bird in the Hand*. This way, if the media want to speculate on my involvement in a murder, it'll be me they focus on, and they'll leave the rest of you alone."

All eyes were on me as I tried to sort this out. "You mean that you'll work behind the scenes?"

"I mean that it's for the best that we carry through on what we say. I will leave my post." A second's pause. "And I'll move out of the cottage."

He took my hand, and I took it back as a pricking sensation danced up my arm.

"You're breaking up with me?"

Dad's voice was quiet. "That isn't what he said, Jools."

My voice was not quiet. "It *is* what he said. You're breaking up with me *and* quitting your post all because of" — I waved my hand toward the front window — "because of them?"

"Because Nick is dead, and someone unknown person has dropped enough of a hint to hope these journos will stitch me up for it," Michael said, his eyes sharp like sapphires. "And while they're at it, they'll try to find a way to make their allegations stick to you, too, and I will not allow that to happen."

"He's drawing them away, Jools. It's a good idea. We've got to at least try to see if it will work."

I sniffed but didn't speak. It was a terrible idea, and I would not capitulate. It's only that I needed time to figure out how it wouldn't work and come up with a better plan.

Beryl stood up and brushed off her apron. "Let's go eat our lunch."

Dad followed Beryl, and they began to make noise in the kitchen with dishes and cutlery. I got as far as the foot of the stairs before Michael caught me. He ran a finger down my hand and caressed my palm.

"Let me do this for you. Please."

His words brought tears to my eyes. He wouldn't offer to sacrifice himself if he knew what a coldhearted person I was — unable to even grieve for Nick. Alive, I never thought about my ex-husband, and now dead, I resented his intrusion into my life.

"But we can still be in touch. Email, phone."

"They're devious, Julia. They can hack email accounts and phone records. You've only to look at the headlines every day to see that. The point is for you to distance yourself from me."

"But doesn't that just serve their purpose. It makes you look guilty?"

"Let them turn all their attention on me, I don't care. It can't last forever."

Of course, it was just possible that Michael *could* see what a shallow person I was. Perhaps this was at least partly why he was stepping back — one step, two steps, until eventually we were apart all the time. And it *would* last forever.

I looked at the floor. "Yeah, all right."

* * *

We ate lunch at the kitchen table in silence. Beryl's pea-and-ham soup was quite good, as always, but I couldn't give it my full attention as I'd had an idea and needed to work it through before I presented it. I felt their eyes on me — one at a time, and briefly, as if they needed to keep track of my whereabouts, because I just might fly into a sudden rage and run out the door screaming like a madwoman. I kept my counsel until, as I chased a last bit of carrot round my bowl, I made what I hoped sounded like a casual observation.

"You'll have a terrible time finding a replacement for Michael," I said to Dad. "You bring someone on board now, you'll spend all your time training him. You've far too many things going on."

"I won't look for anyone," Dad said. "We'll take a short break from filming, and I'll cancel all appearances until this is finished." I could tell he was feeling his way through this, and I also knew he hated to pull back from the work he loved. He'd paused in his work when Mum had died, but when he had resumed, it had made everyone feel better. Of course, six months later when he'd married Beryl, there'd been a longer pause, because I had reacted badly and quit as his assistant, departing in short order for new territory on the Fotheringill estate. That's when he'd hired Michael — the best thing that had happened in a long time to Rupert. And to me, too.

"At least I'll have time to write those books Michael has promised the publisher," Dad continued with an encouraging smile. "There now, that's my time sorted."

"That's ridiculous," I said. "How will this help? Michael Sedgwick disappears, and Rupert Lanchester closes up shop? That'll look worse."

Dad frowned. I held my breath.

"I'll make Basil my PA." He offered this with a lack of conviction.

"Basil Blandy?" I exclaimed. "You must be joking. I can see it now. You'll be scheduled for a lecture in Cumbria, and he'll send you off to Cornwall by mistake." I'd worked with Basil when I was Dad's assistant. He was a young fellow — at least, younger than I, probably in his late twenties — and was only a techie on the set. He was not known for his quickness or his efficiency, but he possessed a pleasant, unruffled demeanor, and Dad liked him. I considered him fairly useless.

"He's already produced segments for the program," Michael said. "He's more capable than you think. With me out of the way, he'll shine."

When pigs flew, I thought, but Michael out of the way reminded me of my more immediate loss. "Where will you go?"

"My old flat in Haverhill is vacant — I rang earlier. I'll go back there."

I was sure that Nick had not arranged to have himself murdered on the Fotheringill estate, but I couldn't help blaming him. My life was falling apart, and its downfall had been orchestrated by a man I hadn't laid eyes on in five years. A jolt of anger shot through me, followed quickly by a wave of guilt.

* * *

The blinds on the front window were drawn, but we each peered through a tiny opening as we passed by, taking our mugs of tea into the sitting room. They were still there — minus the big one, I thought. Now, the twin jackets stood to one side, smoking. kitten woman with her half-cropped and half-wedged auburn hair lingered nearby, and several feet away from her, the little weasel. They were all one to me — one miserable, monstrous entity.

I set my tea on the table, inhaled deeply, and said, "Right, Dad, well, you cannot cancel any of your engagements, articles, or the filming for the program — it just won't do. I'll step in and take over my old post as your assistant. As a *temporary* replacement, until Michael returns."

Dad sputtered.

"You already work full-time," Michael reminded me. "More than full-time."

"*Pfft*," I said. "It was only last week that was truly too much, because I had all those organizational meetings — everything's ticking along fine now. Every day at the TIC I have buckets of free time when no one comes in, and Vesta will be more than willing to add a few hours to her schedule when I need to nip out for anything. Willow — we've got Willow, remember." Did we? There was something about Willow I should remember, but at that moment, couldn't quite chase it down.

"No," Dad said, shaking his head. "No." He exhaled in a huff, but I could see a sense of relief on his face. "Well, at least we couldn't keep up the filming."

I was nearly in. "Nonsense. It's spring, we've more and more daylight, and so I'm well able to attend early-morning or evening shoots and still work at the TIC between. Just no filming too far away — we'll make sure we stay at Marshy End or Lackford or at the most, Minsmere, not John o' Groats."

I meant it as a joke, but my chin trembled thinking of the weekend Michael and I weren't allowed to finish and our talk of a holiday far away. I pressed my lips together.

"It would take up so much of your time," Dad complained, but in a weak sort of way. I knew I had won. He probably thought it would be a good excuse to keep an eye on me. I, on the other hand, thought it might be a good excuse to stay in touch with Michael, regardless of his intent to stay away.

* * *

We started to work. Dad drafted a brief statement about Michael's stepping away because of his concern for Rupert and the Lanchester family during this difficult time. This would be posted on the website, but not sent out as a news release — no need to call attention to the move. Michael had been a hard sell for my idea of filling in and had relented only when I'd begged. "I have to do my part," I had said. "I have to."

Michael insisted we sort through Rupert's entire schedule for the upcoming fortnight. "Not that long, surely?" I asked, but Michael said, "To be on the safe side."

"What about Dad's website?"

"I can keep that up," Michael replied. "Remote work — they won't know I have my hands on it."

At least he'd still have his hands on something — just not me.

Michael emailed me everything, but I also wanted it on paper, and so we stood quietly while the printer whirred and hummed and chugged. I noticed that I'd have an early filming at Marshy End on Wednesday. That meant I would need to leave the village by four o'clock that morning to get up there and back to the TIC. But Vesta could open, so I wouldn't be under too strict a time constraint.

"Will you see Nick's sister when she arrives?"

Lost in arranging my new single life, Michael's question startled me. "I certainly hope not," I said, and then heard my own words. "It's just that, I only ever met her once — they weren't close. Nick wasn't terribly close to anyone." I lifted my eyes and saw Michael shift his gaze away from me. I drew in a ragged breath. "What about the foundation?" I asked, turning away to wipe my nose on my sleeve.

"Let's not worry about that now," he said, "we'll postpone the decision on the grant. I believe there are five applications, but I'm not entirely sure. I didn't want to take a look until they were all ready to be reviewed."

"Michael, I'm so sorry about this. And I really don't see why you have to go away. Apart from distracting those journos, I mean."

He studied the pieces of paper as they were pulled in and pushed out of the printer. Without looking at me, he said, "I want to give you the space you need."

Space for what? But I didn't say it aloud. He reached for me, and I threw my arms round his neck and clung to him.

"Look now," he said, his lips against my temple, "I'll head out first, go to the cottage, and collect my things. You wait here a bit — with any luck they'll follow me to the village and away again. And remember" — he leaned back and gazed at me, his eyes a midnight blue — "the police will find out who killed Nick."

* * *

The police — I had a thing or two to say to them.

Michael had given me a quick kiss before he left. We watched him walk out and speak to the group of leeches, after which they trailed after him. I stayed in Cambridge for thirty minutes more, helping to wash up.

"You should wait a bit longer," Dad said. "Stay the night, why don't you?"

"No, I'm fine. I need to do a bit of shopping before I go home. Don't worry — it looks as if Michael's taken care of them. Right, well. I'll let you know how filming goes on Wednesday morning."

At their front gate I turned, waved the all-clear and hurried to my car. I drove straight to the police station in Sudbury — well, not straight, as the two main routes would take me through either the village or near Haverhill, and I certainly didn't want to see Michael, his Fiat packed with his belongings, as he left me.

* * *

It had gone six o'clock, as I approached the Sudbury station. It had been a mucky drive, rain keeping me company the entire way. I hesitated before I entered the car park, but I saw no one waiting on the pavement. They wouldn't dare harass a citizen on police property, would they? And no one would shout insults and insinuations with an officer nearby who could toss them in the nick. I sat in my car for a moment, gathering my nerve to go in.

Then, through the rain cascading down the windshield, I saw a familiar figure walk out the door of the station. Yes! Detective Sergeant Natty Glossop — the soft touch of the Callow-Glossop investigative team. Buoyed by my good luck, I popped out and called out to him.

"Ms. Lanchester?" he asked, glancing past me.

"I'm alone, Sergeant. I stopped by to have a word with you."

"You've no coat — you'd better come in," Glossop said, reaching for the door.

"No, really this is fine," I said, huddling under the narrow overhang. I'd take the rain over going inside the station and running into DI Callow, she who played her cards close to her chest. I wanted information and, in the past, DS Glossop had very kindly provided it. "Sergeant, the press — reporters and photographers from those awful online websites — are harassing us. Harassing Michael. They seem to know details about what happened to Nick. Did you tell them?"

Glossop took a step back and straightened his shoulders. "Our team would never leak information on an investigation."

"But then, how do those people know so much?"

The DS took a deep breath. His eyes darted to his wristwatch, reminding me of the time of day and how many people actually wanted to go home.

"This is a bad time," I said.

"Not a problem, Ms. Lanchester." Glossop shook his head. "It's only that, well, my mum, you see. On her own now, and I usually stop there for my tea in the evening."

"I'm sorry, Sergeant," I said "Please, you go on." How lovely he had someone waiting for him.

"I will not leave with you believing anyone in the constabulary could—"

"But the thing is," I cut in, "we've got a pack of journalists — if you can call them that — following us around and asking some pretty awful questions. Surely you've seen the stuff they're putting online."

Glossop frowned and shook his head. "I can see how it would upset you. I won't look at that rubbish, and you shouldn't, either. You must pay them no mind, Ms. Lanchester."

Easy for him to say. "But the thing is, they must've got an idea somewhere about your accusation that Michael and Nick met."

"We made no such accusation," Glossop said. "But we must follow every lead. I'm sure you remember that."

"How can you even rely on an anonymous tip about Nick being there, and Michael turning down the drive?"

"No, now." Glossop held up an instructional index finger. "The anonymous tip about the body and the witness to Mr. Sedgwick turning into the drive are two separate items here."

It took me a moment to process this. An anonymous tip is a highly suspicious thing, but a witness is another matter.

"Someone saw Michael? Who?"

"At this time, I'm not at liberty to say."

"*No!*" I shouted, causing both of us to flinch. *Calm down — Natty Glossop is an ally.* "I'm sorry, Sergeant, but I can't let Michael be railroaded for something he didn't do on two bits of flimsy — well, not even evidence. Hearsay!"

"Ms. Lanchester—" the sergeant began in an injured tone, but he hesitated as a uniformed constable, a young woman burst out of the door and walked between us.

"'Evening, Natty," she called over her shoulder.

"'Evening, Moira," he answered, then glanced at me, straightened his already straight shoulders, and called out, "that is, *PC Flynn*."

PC Flynn pulled off her bowler hat and gave him a toss of her red curls in reply.

"Sergeant," I said. Natty tore his eyes away from the PC. "The witness, the anonymous tip."

"Yes," Glossop said, "what of this anonymous tip?" He seemed to have forgotten his mum and PC Flynn and stood with eyebrows raised.

He wanted me to take notice of something. *Think, Julia.* "Anonymous," I said, feeling out the word. "Anonymous. Ah! Why anonymous? What was this person afraid of?"

Glossop nodded, as if I had answered an exam question correctly. "Tips can be anonymous for a variety of reasons. Could be the person was where he or she shouldn't've been and is embarrassed about that. Could be the old 'I don't want to get involved' excuse."

"Could be it's the murderer giving you the tip," I said.

"Or someone close to."

"So, couldn't you make a statement or something to say that police do not believe Michael is involved in any way with Nick's death?"

"Although it appears *unlikely* that Mr. Sedgwick is involved, we must remain open to anything."

Unlikely. Glossop spoke the word as if he held it out at arm's length, afraid to get too close.

"And this is why we want to talk with Mr. Sedgwick further — perhaps you'll remind him of that."

In that moment, I saw my cottage waiting for me — empty and cold. I shivered. The DS must've read it on my face, for he hurried on. "Although perhaps it would be better if I rang him first."

"He's moved out," I said with a frown. I might as well come out with it — after all, Glossop was the police and so surely he'd discover it. "Only temporarily, until you find Nick's killer. They're after him, these journos, and he wanted to take the spotlight off Rupert. And me," I added in a tiny voice.

"That's admirable of him," Glossop said, shifting his weight from one foot to another and trying not to look at his watch.

"Thank you, Sergeant, and now off with you," I said. "You've a home to go to — and someone waiting for you."

CHAPTER 7

I drove back to the village and parked my car in its lockup behind Nuala's Tea Room. When I walked out onto the high street, I peered in the window, just in case Nuala had remained after hours washing down tables or something and I could spend some of my empty evening with her. But no, Nuala closed at five o'clock, and it was seven now. I contemplated my next move, but my feet made the decision before my brain, and I turned not left, toward my cottage, but right and walked up the rest of the high street and across the bridge over the brook. Straight toward the drive that led to Hoggin Hall.

I could hear the rookery even above the busy road traffic — a riotous noise as the birds began to settle for the night. I thought of Alfie and wondered if he was now safe at home with Tennyson and her mum. Had that been Alfie harassing the journos outside my cottage?

I stopped at the brick pillars that marked the entrance to the Hall and looked down the drive, which was straight before eventually curving to the right. A mix of horse chestnuts, rowan, and beech trees lined the way, with scrubby hawthorn filling in, and yellow cowslips blooming in the grass. The rowan had already leafed out, its clusters of tiny white flowers attracting a steady stream of bees. Other trees waited until spring was well and truly under way to show their new foliage, and their nascent leaves had barely begun to unfurl, turning the wood into a shimmer of fluorescent green that glowed in the last of the sun that peeked out from beneath the clouds.

I turned into the drive with no thought. Each step took me away from the noise of the road traffic and into a gloomy dusk with a heavy silence where no birds sang and the only sound was the echoing *crunch* of chipped rock under my shoes. Along the drive, an overgrown path took off to the left, leading down an incline before climbing up a hillock, where sat the summerhouse.

I paused and looked. The path was overgrown no longer. The ground had been trampled, the brambles pushed back and beaten down by police boots — I could smell the damp earth and crushed leaves on the cool air. And through the tangle of leaves and stems, I imagined I could see the blue-and-white police tape wrapped round the building. I took several deep, even breaths, my mind seeking something normal to settle on. *We should've started on the summerhouse before this*, I thought, grabbing for the lifesaver of everyday business. Refurb — repair the cracked steps up to the door, replace crumbled bricks. There was a fireplace inside, I believe — a summerhouse it may be, but even so, this was England, and July evenings could carry a nip to them. Windows on all sides of the octagonal building must've given a grand view of the estate before the wood grew up.

I heard the *crack* of a twig off to my right. I whipped my head round and squinted to where the wood opened up into grass and a ditch ran that emptied into the brook. I saw movement and my heart pounded in my chest. Then, I recognized a low brown figure with a black tail — a stoat with some small furry creature hanging limply from its mouth. It was the natural way of things and I had grown accustomed to such a sight long ago. Still, at that moment, I turned and ran.

You're such a coward, Julia Lanchester. But my admonition didn't stop my full retreat — I dashed across the road at the first break in traffic to the Stoat and Hare at the bottom of Church Lane. I paused for a moment under the swinging pub sign to catch my breath, glancing up at the fanciful depiction of the eponymous animals, both wearing waistcoats and sitting together over pints of ale, the hare's long legs crossed, the stoat's sinuous body draped over the chair. All things being equal, I preferred this fellow to the real thing.

* * *

My entrance into the pub hit the pause button on all conversation and activity. The crowd, usually light on a Monday evening, was chock-a-block. Two groups of locals stood stock still holding their pints — their only movement when they cut their eyes at me, then dropped their gazes to the floor. I stopped just inside and for one second wanted to step back out again, but instead I swallowed hard, put my chin in the air, and made my way through the crowd, nodding greetings to anyone who would actually make eye contact. My one consolation was that I saw none of the jackals from the press, which kept my feet moving.

"Julia, how lovely." Peg came out from behind the bar and met me halfway, as if I needed an escort. "We haven't seen you in a week or two. I'm so glad you've stopped." She glanced round the room, still silent. "Would you like to sit in the dining room. It's quiet in there on a Monday, you know, you'll have your pick of tables."

"No thanks, Peg. I'd like to take a seat at the bar if that's all right."

"It's more than all right — you can keep me company." She stripped the band off her ponytail and scraped her hair back before securing it again.

I chose a spot at the curved end where I could see the room, climbed up on a stool, and hung my bag on the hook beneath the bar.

Peg's eyes flashed toward the door, and I knew I had to say something.

"Michael . . . we . . . that is . . ." I should've planned this better. Peg's crestfallen look didn't help. "Business," I blurted out. "He'll be away on business for a bit — not long, really, but as I'm on my own this evening, I couldn't think of a better place to eat."

"Well, then," Peg said with such an expansive smile that I could tell she didn't believe a word of it. "Would you like to see a menu?"

We both laughed. I'd eaten at the Stoat and Hare once a week for the past year. Apart from the nightly specials, I could've recited the entire menu without a single prompt.

"I'll tell you what I'd like," I said. "One of Fred's massive beef burgers on a brioche bun. And chips. A pile of chips."

"Right you are," Peg said, reaching over and squeezing my arm. "That's the spirit. And a glass of wine?"

"Yes, lovely," I said, but with less conviction. Michael was the one who knew a great deal about wine, and he always ordered for us. I knew next to nothing. "Red. You choose for me, why don't you?"

I smiled at the crowd, but everyone seemed to be looking the other way, and so I took out my phone and went through the snapshots I'd taken at Southwold with Michael. Peg worked nonstop, serving pints and meals, but she kept glancing over my way. My burger arrived just in time, rescuing me before I tumbled into a morose pit of self-pity, and I'd just taken an enormous first bite when one of the local farmers came up to the bar. The farmer rocked on his heels for a moment and then turned to me.

"'Evening, Julia."

"Eh-ng, Ohng," I replied.

"Oh, sorry," he said, his eyes darting from bottle to bottle behind the bar. I heard him take a deep breath. "So, will we see Michael at the market setup?"

The food in my mouth turned to sawdust.

"And what do you mean by that, Tom?" Peg shot the question at him as she rushed over from serving plates of fish and chips.

"I—" He looked back at his friends, and they looked elsewhere.

"I don't expect you and your mates to come into this pub and hound my customers," Peg said as she jabbed a finger on the bar.

Tom sputtered, throwing another futile look to his group. "No, it's only that—"

I put down my burger. I couldn't chew. I couldn't swallow. I grabbed for my napkin.

Peg's finger drew an arc around the room and I froze, napkin midair. "All of you, listen to me," she said. "I want you to remember what this village was like before we had a tourist manager, before Julia arrived. We could barely get anyone from off the estate to stop. Who would you be selling your cheese to, Tom, if it weren't for Julia, I'd like to know — those expensive hay-wrapped parcels of Suffolk blue? Derry — who would buy your little potted herb gardens and rosehip wreaths if visitors didn't come out on the weekends from London? And you, Ben, you and your Apiary Arts — that honey's flying off the shelves of Akash's shop only because Julia here got you a mention in *The Guardian.* She goes above and beyond, and you all know that Michael, despite having his own work, helps out any time he can. And how do you lot respond? By believing a load of codswallop you read online?"

The silence in the room throbbed so that my eardrums hurt. I'd never seen this fierce side of Peg before. If I had further trouble with the asparagus farmers, perhaps I'd get her to sort them out for me.

Tom's face could've passed for a boiled lobster. "I didn't mean anything by it, Peg."

Peg huffed. "Too right, you didn't." She scanned the crowd. "We need to show our support where it counts. I'm saying this right now — Fred and I will not look at those rubbish websites. No scanning, no surfing, no nothing. And I expect the rest of you to do the decent thing and stay away from them, too. Now," she laid her hands flat on the bar, "what'll it be for everyone. Same again?"

A dozen pairs of hands dived into trouser pockets as the crowd shuffled up to the bar and ordered. The food in my mouth tasted like food again, and I chewed with relish as I gave Peg a quick smile.

"Honestly, Julia." Tom still stood next to me. "I don't believe any of that crap. I wouldn't even look at it, except someone showed me. You know?"

Someone showed you, and you looked. But I swallowed and said, "It's all right, Tom," with as much magnanimity as I could muster. "And yes, of course, Michael will be there to help set up. He wouldn't miss it."

I was left to finish my meal in peace. Eventually Peg caught up with the drinks orders and came back to me.

"Of course they would all know," I said. "You've seen it, too, haven't you?"

Peg leaned over the bar, dropping her voice. "They may have seen it, but they only needed to be reminded of the truth. Everyone thinks too much of you and Michael to really believe any of that rubbish. Here now, let me get you another glass of wine."

When she returned, I said, "My compliments to the chef. I particularly like this aioli sauce for the chips. Fred deserves a mention in *Suffolk Magazine*, I'd say."

"This can't be easy for you," Peg said. I sighed inwardly. I had to face it — this would be the number one topic of conversation until it was over. "Do you think," she said, "well, was your ex come back because he wanted to start up again with you?"

I shook my head. "The thing is, Peg, I've had no contact with Nick for five years. It was over long ago, and we weren't in each other's lives at all. Michael had never met him. And yet, all it takes is for the police to get some anonymous call" — was I spilling too much? — "for them to start in on us. And they say they have a witness who saw Michael turning into the drive to the Hall on Friday afternoon." I nodded toward the door where, outside and across the road, stood the brick pillars marking the entrance to the drive. "He's being set up. What kind of a person would say that?"

"Oh, God." Peg's face went white. "I said it."

CHAPTER 8

"A pint here, please, Peg."

Peg moved over to pull the customer a pint, but kept glancing back at me, her ashen face now flushed scarlet. I stared at the bar, listening in my mind to her words again — "I said it."

The witness to Michael turning down the drive to Hoggin Hall toward the summerhouse where Nick had been murdered wasn't some anonymous nutter or the murderer himself trying to pin it on Michael. It was Peg Phipps who, with her husband, Fred, ran the Stoat and Hare. A friend. I rubbed my face but couldn't rub out the frown I felt drawing up the skin on my forehead.

"They came round," Peg said, appearing in front of me. "The police. I spoke to a detective sergeant" — Natty Glossop — "he was here with a young thing in uniform and with red curls." PC Moira Flynn. My unwanted knowledge of the Sudbury constabulary continued to grow.

"It was Saturday afternoon," Peg continued, "and we had seen police vehicles going down the drive. I was afraid something had happened to His Lordship. Then after a while, here they came, talking to everyone in the pub. 'Where were you yesterday between one o'clock and five o'clock?' Where was I?" Peg clicked her tongue. "Where am I ever but here?"

"I don't think they meant anything by it," I said, reluctantly defending the police.

Peg nodded. "They kept it up, though — asking the same thing in different ways. 'Did you see anything unusual?' 'Did you notice any comings and goings?' until I remembered walking outside to collect empty glasses and seeing Michael in his green Fiat turn into the drive to the Hall."

"Peg?" Fred stuck his head out the kitchen door, his chef's skullcap snug over his short blond hair. "I can't lay my hands on — oh, hello, Julia, evening. You all right?"

"Evening, Fred. Yeah, I'm fine, thanks."

"I'll be right in, love," Peg said to her husband. Fred disappeared.

"But Michael only turned round and came straight out again," I said. "He forgot we weren't driving to Dunwich together until he got here, and then he had to find a place to turn round, reverse his journey."

"Yes, but you see, it isn't as if I have my eyes on that drive every minute of the day. I could only tell them I saw him go in, not come out again, because I came straight back indoors. The place was heaving on Friday afternoon, I could barely keep my head on straight."

I thought back and remembered driving by as I left the village and seeing the crowd of people on the pavement, the children playing. "Did you have a wedding?" I asked.

"No, funeral reception."

My eyebrows shot up. "But they all looked so happy."

"Funerals can be grand occasions when it's for one of the older folk. This fellow now was ninety-two. He'd moved away from the village a few years ago, into a care facility in Bury Saint Edmunds, but he was buried here and he'd loads of family and friends that came from all over. It's such a lovely time to gather and tell stories over a drink or two. It's a reunion of sorts."

"But weddings are happy occasions, too. Right?"

"You'd think," Peg said, wiping the bar with a towel. "I can't tell you the number of times I've walked into the kitchen during a wedding reception and found the bride collapsed in a corner crying her eyes out."

"Lovely," I said. "Makes one want to leap at marriage."

Peg smiled. "Not that we can't get a few strange ones in for a funeral, too. Gwen had to turf some wild thing out of the kitchen on Friday afternoon."

"Gwen?"

"Gwen Gunn — our new cleaner. She does a bit of prep in the kitchen, before she leaves for the day."

"Is that Tennyson's mum?"

"You've met the girl then, have you?"

"And her rook. How many jobs does her mum have?"

"Well, let's see now," Peg said as she looked up at the ceiling. "She's here, and does a bit of cleaning at Dot's, and takes in ironing. But she's always looking for more hours. They've had a rough time of it, apparently. The dad died when Tennyson was a baby, and the two lived with Gwen's mum, just eking by. Then the gran up and died. She was an old friend of Dot's and that's how they landed here. They were left with a load of debt, and Gwen's determined to see it through."

"Sounds like a lonely life for Tennyson — no wonder her best friend is a rook."

* * *

It took all my energy just to step inside my cottage, knowing what waited for me — nothing. Once in, I leaned back against the door and my eyes searched the sitting room and kitchen for some sign of Michael's existence. But he traveled light and had brought nothing beyond his clothes from his flat in Haverhill, and so had had little to pack up.

Upstairs, I noted glumly that he'd cleared out the two drawers I'd relinquished and emptied his side of the wardrobe. No, wait — my heart leapt. Here was the old stretched-out T-shirt he slept in. A giveaway from his family's PR business, the logo and name — HMS, Ltd. — were almost illegible it had been washed so often. He'd left it in a heap on the bed. I undressed and took up the T-shirt, burying my face in it before pulling it over my head. It came midthigh on me.

I'd read somewhere that one's bed should be used only for sleeping or sex. As I knew I'd be getting little of one and none of the other, I took my laptop to bed with me, propped myself up against a mass of pillows, and googled "Avian Institute of Learning."

No salacious headlines popped up — the scum news sites apparently had no use for Nick's work, his lifelong love of tracking vagrant birds. The AIL did have a website, but it offered nothing in the way of personal information about its staff, which numbered, as far as I could tell, three. No names appeared, as if they were a clandestine organization like MI5. Were the other two as antisocial as Nick, I wondered, preferring to spend their lives apart from the real world? The "About," "Our Work," and "Species List" pages were filled with copious amounts of data about birds, climate, seasons, ocean temperature, drift, and volcanoes. "Contact Us" included only an email address, but it wasn't the one Nick had used to email me.

* * *

I awoke to darkness. My laptop — sleeping better than I — lay open beside me. One tap of the space bar and I saw the time had just gone four-thirty. I closed my eyes, but my lids were spring-loaded, and popped open again, so I gave up, showered, and ate a piece of toast. I allowed myself only a brief glance at the work of those jackals — *Rupert Lanchester — His Daughter's Agony — Did She Plot with Boyfriend in Ex-Husband's Death?* — before heading to the TIC down an empty high street with not even Alfie for company.

Just as well I was at it so early — if I wanted to work two separate jobs, I would need every moment before and after the TIC opening hours. Even with Vesta adding to her work schedule and with Willow's support, it would be a miracle. Perhaps Willow could take the next farmers market meeting. No, that wouldn't work. Although I'd come to rely on her a great deal over the past few months, I wouldn't want to throw her to those wolves. Willow — what was it I should remember about Willow?

Just before nine o'clock, I'd almost got there, knitting together my two schedules all the way through the weekend. Marshy End film segment tomorrow morning — perhaps we could squeeze in filming two or even three segments for the program. Another filming Friday morning, and one on Monday out at the coast, at Minsmere. I shoved that to the back of my mind.

I had commitments to my TIC job during the week, too. Thursday lunch, I'd arranged to meet with a tourist manager from Lavenham, a village off the estate. Perhaps I could put that off for a week or so. Oh yes, and Saturday we had a mini-coach tour, and I usually gave a brief overview to the estate. But this visit, they'd be viewing an archaeological excavation that the University of East Anglia was carrying out around the remains of an Iron Age fort next to the abbey ruins. Did I need to be on site? Akash, who provided the boxed lunches, could also provide an introduction. Must check on that.

Really, if I could've added just three more hours to each day — in order to get any sleep at all — I believe this would work, as long as DI Callow and DS Glossop got busy and found the person who killed Nick before I keeled over from exhaustion. What a bother.

Vesta and Willow appeared before me, dripping. Behind them and out the window, I could see a sharp shower beating rain against the TIC window. I hadn't heard Vesta's key in the lock or the bell, because I had switched the kettle on. We really needed a new one — this old thing made so much noise we often had difficulty talking while it hissed, popped, and wheezed.

"There you are now," Vesta said, as if I'd been playing at a game of hide-and-seek. "Akash rang to say that the light went on here ages ago."

"Yes, well," I said lightly, "you know what they say . . ." *No rest for the wicked.* "The early bird, that's what they say. And

I've accomplished so much, you won't believe it." I stood, stretched, and heard my back *pop*.

"Oh, Julia, you are truly dedicated to your work, aren't you? Isn't the estate incredibly lucky to have you." Willow held a pink bakery box in one hand and in the other, a suitcase. At that moment, I remembered what I had forgotten. Willow was leaving.

"All packed, are you?" I said with such fake cheerfulness that I was certain Vesta would cotton on. I turned away from her to open the tea tin. "It was so good of you to stop in before you and Cecil left."

The details came flooding into my mind. Cecil had got on with an estate at the very northern tip of Northumberland. It would be a six-month internship, preparing him to come home and run his own family's estate. Cecil had asked Willow to accompany him, and she had secured a training teacher's position at a school nearby.

The couple had met the previous autumn, when Cecil had moved back to his family home. It seemed an unlikely pairing. Cecil had gone to the best schools and appeared to be looking down his nose at people even when he wasn't, and Willow, she of the batik-print skirts and layers of crocheted tops, was possessed of a free and artistic spirit. And yet, they delighted in each other.

We were all happy for them, and now that I'd remembered those details, I knew Vesta and I could manage quite well. In my mind, I began to pick apart my carefully woven schedule in order to stitch together a different pattern.

Vesta shed her coat and Willow removed the clear poncho she had draped over a vintage floral silk kimono. Peeking from the kimono opening, I could see her crocheted waistcoat.

"Cecil's taking a last look at accounts with His Lordship. Linus," Willow said, her face glowing pink at the use of the earl's Christian name, although he had been the one to insist.

"I certainly hope that's for us," I said, nodding at the bakery box. A savory aroma escaped from it, which made me quite faint, and I wasn't sure how long Willow would wave it around before revealing its contents.

She held up the box like a prize. "Cheese-and-bacon scones. I'd asked Nuala if she might possibly have them ready early today, for our little farewell tea." Willow's eyes cut to Vesta, who shook her head a millimeter.

I looked from Willow to Vesta and back to Willow. I knew what they wanted to say, but neither spoke. When the kettle switched off, we all jumped.

"See here now," I said, as I filled the teapot, hoping I could avoid the entire subject of a murder in the summer-house. "We'll miss you, of course, Willow, but the time will fly."

"Julia—" Willow began.

"Willow," Vesta said.

Oh, God, here it was. I'd have to tell them what I knew, what the police said, how I had no idea why Nick was here. I'd have to tell them that I'd taken over Michael's post and would need to rely on them — that is, on Vesta alone, as it turned out.

"Debra is pregnant!" Willow exclaimed.

I squinted my eyes at her, unable to comprehend the words.

"Isn't that the most wonderfully fabulous news?" she asked. "Vesta's over the moon, aren't you, Vesta?"

Vesta threw Willow a frown, mitigated by a broad smile. And the penny dropped — Debra was pregnant.

"Vesta!" I gave her a big hug. "How fantastic!"

This was indeed wonderfully fabulous news. Vesta's only child, Debra, was married and lived in New Zealand, just outside of Christchurch. In the year I'd known Vesta, I'd learned that Debra had had two early miscarriages, but retained hope that she could carry a baby full term.

"How far along is she?" I asked Vesta, who had reached into her pocket for a tissue.

"Eight months," Willow said. "And on bed rest. But everything looks good."

"Eight months?" I frowned. "You didn't tell me."

Willow opened her mouth, but Vesta cut in. "I found out only this weekend. They didn't want me to get my hopes up, you see."

"They want Vesta to go out," Willow continued as she opened the pink box and distributed the scones. "Be there for the birth. After all, she isn't just a granny, she's a home health-care nurse. Retired."

"It's a lovely idea," Vesta said, retrieving the milk from the fridge, as we settled at the table. "But the timing isn't best, actually. And they don't really need me. I'm not sure I should go."

"You *will* go," I said.

Vesta fretted over her scone. "It's a difficult time now, Julia — I shouldn't abandon you."

Her kindness stung my eyes. Vesta, always willing to fill in the ragged edges of my erratic life, always with a kind and understanding word that made me see my problems in a new light, offered to forgo the chance of a lifetime because of Nick's death. Well, I'd be damned if I would breathe a word about doubling my workload — I would stay awake for a week rather than have her miss her first and possibly only grandchild's appearance into the world.

"There is absolutely no reason for you to stay," I said. "I've got everything well in hand here. In fact, you'd better leave as soon as possible. This baby could come early. Go home now, pack. Wait, let's find flights for you."

"Akash sorted all that out for her," Willow said, smiling to reveal that little gap between her front teeth. "She flies out this evening. He's waiting for the word to hit the 'buy' button, and he'll drive her to Heathrow."

"Shall I stand out on the pavement and send up a rocket to signal him?" I asked. Instead, Vesta sent a text to him at the corner shop. We continued our tea in high spirits, Vesta describing how Debra and her husband had given her all their air miles to lessen the cost of what had to be an enormously expensive journey. I listened and reacted, but mostly stayed busy with my scone. I could feel Vesta's gaze on me, but I worried that if I looked up to give her a reassuring nod, she'd see the whole story in my eyes.

* * *

"What will you do if you need any time off?" Vesta asked as we stood at the door with Willow.

"I'll ask Thorne to fill in for me," I said. "Tourists would love to walk into the TIC and be greeted by the butler, don't you think?"

We had a good chuckle at the thought of Thorne, always in his dark suit that set off his cotton-ball head of hair, standing behind the counter. When Cecil's car pulled up to the curb, Willow walked out, but turned back abruptly, her face solemn. "Julia — will you be all right?"

"Of course I will. Be sure to let me know how you're both doing."

I stood at the window and watched as Cecil got out of the car and helped Willow with her bag.

When Cecil's car had disappeared round the bend, I turned back to find Vesta in my face.

"What about Michael?"

"It's fine, really," I said, edging past her to escape. "Not to worry."

"And the two of you?"

I walked over to the counter and pretended to straighten the tray of key rings Alfie had sorted. "We're fine, too. Everything's fine."

At that moment, I was saved from further questioning by the arrival of three of the archaeology students. I breathed a sigh of relief, gave Vesta a quick kiss on the cheek, and said, "Now, go be a granny."

* * *

Once alone, I rang Linus. As my employer, he needed to know the truth — or at least part of it. I told him Vesta's story, and about Michael's temporary sabbatical, but kept back the part about me now working two jobs. I needn't burden him with my problems, not with his own schedule so busy. Last year, the estate's financial situation had improved enough for Linus to hire an agent to oversee all the working farms and businesses. Sadly, that didn't last long for reasons I tried not to dwell on. Linus had decided not to fill the post, but rather to do the work himself until Cecil could take over the management.

"It's wonderful news about Vesta's daughter," Linus said. "But now with Willow off, too, how will you manage?"

"You know I love a work challenge," I said. "And it'll be good to stay busy."

"Julia, I'd rather you not be alone there in the TIC until the police catch the person who did this to Mr. Hawkins. They've been here, of course — the police — and questioned all of us and asked for descriptions of the visitors to the Hall that day, but I don't think we were of much help. See here, as Michael has taken time off from his work with Rupert, why don't you ask him to keep you company during the day?"

What a lovely idea — impossible, but lovely. The suggestion told me that Dad had not revealed to Linus that Michael had taken time off from me, too, and I wasn't about to venture down that road. No need to cause worry.

"I'll keep that in mind, but I'm sure I'll be fine here," I said breezily. "Really, Linus, what happened has nothing to do with me. And look — we've got a busy high street right outside the door. If I need anything, Akash is at the corner, and you are only moments away."

Next, I unraveled the schedules I had so successfully woven together and began to reweave. After that, it was on to Rupert's business. I attacked his summer schedule with a vengeance, hoping to clear off the emails that had come in since Friday. Dad loved to visit events around the country, insisting he stay in touch with his public, which offered him the best opportunities to teach about nature. Michael had suggested I should drop these small appearances, but the organizers of everything from the Brixham Pirate Days to the Green Man festival in Wales had questions about timing and crowds and which birds would they see that day and would Rupert be driving his old green Range Rover — as much a character of the television program as he was — that I knew Dad couldn't cancel.

Although the morning had begun wet, the afternoon turned off fine. Following the usual cause-and-effect, when the sun began to shine, visitors appeared from nowhere to interrupt my work with a constant stream of questions about footpaths, Boadicea, and did Queen Victoria ever visit the current earl's great-grandfather. I caught myself wishing they'd all just go away so that I could get some work done then gave myself a mental slap. These people were my work.

As the first visitors had come in and I rose to greet them, I had removed my nametag and tossed it in the biscuit tin. Who knew how many eyes had seen those horrible headlines, and I didn't want my identity to prompt them to ask questions unrelated to tourist activities on the estate. I smiled and welcomed each one, then gave a short overview of the estate, using the map on the wall. By the time I'd finished my mini-lecture, a crowd had gathered in the TIC.

None of them gave me a second glance, but instead concentrated on the map. Good — perhaps they didn't read the online tabloid press. The proper newspapers had printed a small account of Nick's death without implying any scandal. "Sudbury police are investigating a suspicious death on the Fotheringill estate . . ." That sort of thing.

At lunch, I nipped down to the corner for a sandwich to find old McKiddie minding the shop. McKiddie had run the shop before Akash and these days filled in for him occasionally. A tiny bubble of hope lifted my spirits as it occurred to me that Akash might fill in at the TIC the occasional morning or afternoon, because McKiddie could fill in for him. Akash knew a great deal about the estate. He had been my right-hand man in organizing the open afternoons at the Hall, which practically ran themselves now, because he had trained the docents so well. I hadn't even noticed the tightening in my chest until that moment when I saw McKiddie and the tightness eased, just a bit.

"It's awfully good of you to help Akash out like this," I said as I paid for my tuna and sweet corn, plus — remembering our stores were low — a packet each of malted milk, chocolate digestives, and shortbread fingers. "I know he appreciates it."

"I've not minded," McKiddie said. "But I've given my notice, so to speak. Today is the end of the likes of me in Smeaton. I'm moving in with my daughter in Shropshire, you see. So, it's farewell to the Fotheringill estate for old McKiddie."

He dropped my coins in the till as my heart sank with this news. "How lovely for you," I managed in a thick voice.

* * *

I ate my lunch as I prepared to ring the production staff of *A Bird in the Hand* to let them know I'd be on the set the next morning. Michael had suggested I'd need to contact Basil only and he'd pass the word along, but I knew that my news would go in one of Basil's ears and out the other before it had time to alight anywhere. Still, I did start with him, out of courtesy, and was surprised into silence at a female voice answering. It took me a second to think of what to say.

"Is . . . is this Basil's phone?"

"Yeah," the voice said. "Hang on. Baz — it's Julia."

"Be right there," a voice in the distance said.

I reflected on the familiar tone this woman took with both Basil and me. Who was she? I stopped myself just short of being miffed. Was it really my job to know? *Filling in, Julia. You're doing Michael's job here, not your own.* But perhaps this woman was a new crewmember. Perhaps I should go over staff changes with Michael.

I already had an ongoing debate in my head about our "no contact" order. Would those journos really care if we sent each other a text, or spoke on the phone? But the next minute, I would imagine the journos hacking into our private accounts, followed by screaming headlines: *Couple Continue to Plot — Are They Getting Away with Murder?* Right, no contact it is.

"Hiya, Julia."

"Hello, Basil. Listen, I'm ringing to let you know that I'll be producer for the next . . . oh, fortnight or so. Something's come up, and Michael—"

"No worries," Basil said. "We got wind of it. Look, I'm . . . er, I'm sorry about all that business. You all right?"

"Yes, I'm fine, thanks. I'll ring the rest of the team."

"No need, I'll tell them."

"Well, I'll see you in the morning then. Six o'clock — you remember that, don't you?"

"Righto."

I was not fine, and Basil's cavalier attitude toward work made me even less so. I could see it now — I'd be ringing him from Marshy End tomorrow well after six, asking where the camera guy was, the truck with the audio feed, the nest cams at the riverside. I couldn't trust him, and so I would ring each of the crew myself. I finished my sandwich, made myself a mug of tea, and started in.

But they did know. Every one of them, from camera guy to sound tech, had already received a text from Basil. I should've been relieved at this, because it meant one fewer thing to worry about. But in the previous twenty-four hours, I'd discovered that when a vacant space opened up in my brain, even for a moment, I slid sideways into dwelling on my current situation, and wondering — with a nauseating mix of guilt and resentment — how a brief, unemotional marriage years ago could still be affecting me. There's something to be said for a double workload.

Tap, tap, tap.

The sound broke into my thoughts and I glanced round on the floor, thinking I'd knocked a pencil off the table. Nothing.

Tap, tap, tap.

I realized it came from the front, but no one had come into the TIC, and I knew I hadn't left the door locked.

Tap, tap, tap.

I followed the sound to the front and looked out the window and saw no one on the pavement. I looked left, and my eyes dropped to the ground.

Tap, tap, tap. Alfie pecked at the glass door. And so I opened it.

"On your own today, are you, Alfie?" I asked as the rook picked up a small object near his feet and sauntered in. Tennyson came hurrying in behind him.

Alfie continued past me to the back as Tennyson leaned against the doorjamb, out of breath.

"He was so excited when I told him we'd stop and see you, that he took off ahead of me. Hello, Julia."

"Good afternoon, Tennyson. You're just in time for tea."

I stepped round the counter to the back, closing the lid on my laptop in case Alfie tried to check his email.

CHAPTER 9

"Alfie has exceptional face recognition," Tennyson said as she rinsed out our tea mugs, sounding as if she were giving a conference report. "And a good memory for events. He's a collector, of course. Most corvids are. In our flat, he hides things in one of Gran's old shoes that we brought along with us. I keep a list of the items. Data are important in species studies."

At that moment, Alfie had his head stuck in the pocket of my mackintosh, and I made a mental note to check later what treasures he'd left me.

"You're a citizen scientist, that's what you are," I said to Tennyson.

I was rewarded with an enormous toothy smile that made me smile in return.

At five o'clock as Tennyson gathered her schoolbag, I said, "I'm going your way, why don't I walk with you and Alfie?"

"Oh yes," the girl replied. "Are you going as far as the Stoat and Hare? You could meet Mum."

I'd like to say that had been my goal in suggesting it — to meet Gwen and introduce myself, so that she wouldn't have to worry about her daughter spending an hour in the late afternoon with a stranger. But there was another reason I felt myself pulled up the high street — what lay in the wood across the road from the pub. The summerhouse, like a siren's call, drew me to it.

Pulling on my mackintosh, I had a thought to change shoes, but then decided not to switch to my trainers — they were fine for an early-morning sprint to work, but not when I should still look like the TIC manager. So, I kept on my heels and left behind my bag and computer, because I knew I'd be back. I'd promised both Health and Safety and Highways England, because we would close off the high street for the event, a preliminary report and I had promised it for tomorrow. That was my evening sorted.

Tennyson and I walked up the road in a light shower, while Alfie flew ahead, waited, and then lagged behind before catching us up again. We waved to Dot in her dress shop. I pointed out where Sugar for My Honey would soon open, and Tennyson said she hoped that the shop would carry rhubarb-and-custard candy, an old-fashioned boiled sweet that her grandmother had loved. Just near Nuala's Tea Room, a small street took off to the right. Tennyson pointed out Sox in Box — the village launderette and post office.

"Mum says they need someone two afternoons a week to take in washing orders, and so she's applied."

We arrived at a quiet pub, and I followed Tennyson straight through to the kitchen.

"Hi, Mum," she said, dropping her bag on a chair in the corner next to a small desk where Fred and Peg did their menus and accounts.

At the sink, a slim, angular woman up to her elbows in suds looked over her shoulder. One moment her face looked a mass of worry — drawn, lined, with dark circles under her eyes — but in the next second, when her gaze fell on her daughter, she broke into such a smile there was room for nothing else.

"There's my girl. How was school?"

"Fine." Tennyson hanging her coat on a peg. "Teacher let me stay in at lunch today, and I wrote up my observations of Alfie's nighttime grooming habits."

I noticed her mother's smile falter for only a second. "That sounds lovely, Ten — will you read it to me this evening?"

"I will." The appearance of the big smile. "Mum, this is Julia."

"Very pleased to meet you, Julia. I'm Gwen. I'd shake your hand" — she lifted her arms and suds rolled off and plopped back into the sink — "but I don't suppose you need a bath right now."

"Lovely to meet you, Gwen" I said.

"I hope my girl and Alfie haven't been taking too much of your time these afternoons."

It had been only two afternoons, but at Gwen's words, I could see that this might easily become a daily event. Could I tell Tennyson I was too busy for her to stop at the TIC for a visit? I subtracted one precious hour of sleep from my schedule and added it to "tea with girl and bird."

"Certainly not, we have a lovely time."

Gwen grabbed a towel, dried her arms, and then ran the back of a damp hand across her forehead. She dislodged a tiny clip from her chestnut hair, which was the same shade as her daughter's. She caught the clip before it hit the floor and stuck it back in to rejoin about a dozen that kept her short, straight-as-a-rail, layered haircut at bay.

"Don't worry about telling the two of them they need to be on their way," Gwen told me, then turned to her daughter and gave her a hug and a kiss. "Look now, you, Peg wants us to have our tea here today. Fred has offered egg and chips. What do you say?"

"Will Fred do chips for Alfie, too?"

"He will," Fred answered as he pushed in the door. "All right there, Julia?"

"I am, Fred, and you?"

"Grand, now that I see this one's here." He nodded at Tennyson. "Did you wow them at school today?"

"I did my best," Tennyson said with a grin.

"Your Alfie's out there complaining about something." Fred jerked a thumb behind him, in the direction of the yard between the pub and storage shed. I could hear a faint *caw*.

"He likes you, Fred," Tennyson said. "He thinks your chips are smashing."

"Ah, I see it now" — Fred wagged a finger at her gently — "buttering me up, are you? But first, I've chicken to prepare for the menu tonight. Gwen, I still can't lay my hands on those shears. Any sign of them?"

"I've not seen them, Fred, sorry. Right, you," Gwen said to her daughter, "better get to your homework."

"Thanks for tea, Julia," Tennyson said as she settled at the desk. "I'd say Alfie will see you home."

"Right. Bye now."

Gwen followed me out through the pub area and to the door. I raised my chin to say goodbye at Peg, who stood at the bar serving the late-afternoon customers.

"Really," Gwen said as we stepped out on the pavement. "It's so kind of you to take time for Tennyson, but I don't want her to be a bother. It's just that we're new here, and she hasn't made any friends at school yet."

"She's a lovely girl, and I quite enjoy her company," I said. "And she's smart — already with university plans."

"Oh God," Gwen said, laughing, despite her furrowed brow, "and here I am having trouble paying for her school uniform."

My mind ran at top speed. Scholarships. Hadn't the Rupert Lanchester Foundation been created for just such a purpose? Grants to institutions were all well and good, but how about helping a promising student whose passion matched the goals of Rupert's organization?

"Look, Julia, it's a terrible thing that happened."

Gwen's words brought me up short, and I didn't reply.

"Sorry," she continued, "it's only that — Peg told me he was your ex." She shrugged as if apologizing. "I'm sure it's terribly difficult. He didn't think you two . . ."

"We'd hadn't been in contact for years," I explained for what seemed like the millionth time. "It truly was over. Nick would never have wanted to start up again."

I remembered Gwen had been working during the afternoon in question, and she could hold some vital piece of evidence. "You were here on Friday, weren't you? You don't remember seeing anything unusual?"

Gwen scrunched her face and shook her head. "No, sorry. I was stuck in the kitchen most of the time. It was a fair crowd here, too, and they were everywhere. I went out to collect glasses and had to step over a few old fellows sitting at the bottom of the stairs singing 'We'll Meet Again,' and when I came back, I found a woman in the kitchen. Said she couldn't find the loo. She'd a bit of a wild look to her." Gwen waved her hands round her head. "Big hair. It looked as if she'd been crying, poor dear. Mind you, I did listen for clanking when she ran out, in case she'd had a mind to nick the soup spoons."

* * *

Gwen asked for my mobile number, which I gave willingly — I understood that mums needed to keep track of their daughters — and she responded with hers before she returned to work. Then, Alfie made his presence known by flapping over and landing on the roof of a car nearby. He turned his head to look at me as I stood on the pavement watching the traffic on the road, busy now in the late afternoon. I should go back to the TIC. I'd work to do — a great deal of it. And an early morning tomorrow.

For a full minute, I stared across at the brick pillars that marked the drive to Hoggin Hall before at last walking across the wide verge to the road edge. Waiting for a break in traffic, I stuck my hands in the pockets of my mackintosh, and encountered — what? I pulled out half a shortbread finger and a small twig with a bit of moss stuck to it. I dropped the treasures back into my pocket, and looked up to see Alfie, who had a much easier crossing than I, soar over my head. He landed on a low branch of an oak next to the drive and waited.

CHAPTER 10

I stood once again at the precipice, the toes of my shoes on the recently beaten path to the summerhouse, my heels in the gravel on the drive. Alfie had followed me, but now, as I hesitated he went ahead and sailed off between branches. I gazed down at the track and its thick layer of leaves. The beech trees held on to last year's dried foliage through the winter, waiting until spring to drop them as the new growth emerged, and so in the last week or two, the wood had been provided with its own fresh blanket of mulch. I stepped off, my heels punching through the leaves and sinking into the soft earth. *I should've worn my trainers*, I thought. Now I'd have a devil of a time cleaning these, and I'd have to wear my older pair tomorrow. Thus, keeping my mind on mundane matters, I approached the place where Nick had been murdered.

The path bottomed out, then rose. I climbed the hillock, picking my way over low branches and vines, my heart pounding, my face hot and, at the same time, cold with sweat, as if a five-minute walk could take it out of me. The summerhouse appeared, wrapped up like a birthday present with the blue-and-white police tape. I stopped at the bottom of the steps, reached out my hand to touch the white stone cap that sat atop the newel, but then jerked my hand away. Fingerprints.

The wood — quiet but for a distant birdcall of *chiffchaff, chiffchaff* and the rumbling of traffic — had reclaimed its own. Brambles snaked up the cracked steps of the summerhouse, and ivy crept in and out of the broken windows. The bricks had held firm — no crumbling masonry as I had expected — and the shape of the domed roof and octagonal building could be made out easily. The door had either come off or had been pushed open, and I could see indoors. At that moment, a light breeze set the surrounding trees atremble and created a shimmering green pattern inside on the walls and floor, as if the place had come alive just for me. I caught the scent of new growth and damp earth.

The tape stretched across the steps, barring my way, but Nick had been inside the summerhouse, and I was determined to see the spot for myself. The least I could do, right? I touched the tape, thinking to duck under it, but my movement set off a deafening screech as Alfie flew past so close I felt the wind from his flapping wings. I stumbled sideways and grabbed hold of the newel, fingerprints be damned. He made a beeline through the trees, and I heard a thrashing in the thicket. I watched as he deftly avoided branches while he banked to the left and was lost from view.

"God, you gave me a fright, Alfie," I called after him. "Mind you don't mess with that stoat!" I thought a full-grown rook too large to be taken by a stoat, but caught unaware, you never knew.

Behind me, I heard a car on the drive. The engine cut off, and a door opened and closed. A pricking sensation danced up my arm. I shouldn't be here. Murderers return to the scenes of their crimes — that's what they said, wasn't it? I should run. If I dash through the wood, and jump the drainage ditch, I could make it safely to the front door of the Hall and throw myself on Thorne's mercy. Why hadn't I put my trainers on?

I crept forward, hoping I could dive across the path and through a gap in the hedge I saw about five feet ahead, but I froze on the spot when I came face-to-face with Detective Inspector Callow.

"Ms. Lanchester," she said, pausing in her climb up the trail. "What are you doing here?"

I thrust my chin out. "It's the Fotheringill estate, Inspector. I work here." She raised one eyebrow and waited — such an irritating police maneuver, as if the simple act of keeping quiet would force me into spilling all my thoughts and motivations and reasons.

"I wanted to see where Nick died — where you found his body. It isn't as if I'm trespassing." With a backward glance to the summerhouse, I added, "I didn't go in."

Callow walked past me, took hold of the police tape, and pulled it up. "Go on, then. We've finished here, and officers have searched the area."

Permission to enter didn't cause me to hurry. I ducked under the tape and made it up two steps, but my feet were like lead, and it took all my energy to continue, both drawn to and repelled by what I might see.

"What did you find?" I asked as Callow came up beside me and we continued to climb the stairs — much easier, I found, with a companion.

"Why would Mr. Hawkins choose the grounds of the Hall to meet Mr. Sedgwick? And would he have known of this summerhouse?" she asked.

Yes, fine, don't answer. But don't expect me to give up asking.

"Michael's never been to the summerhouse. It's mentioned on the estate's website. And it's indicated on maps, but we put it in small type with an asterisk and a note that says, 'Not open to the public.' I've no idea how it got into Nick's head."

We'd reached the small terrace at the top of the stairs, and I stopped. I may have even backed up a step or two, because Callow asked, "Are you sure you want to go in? It's been gone over" — cleaned up, she meant — "but it still can be upsetting to—"

Afraid she was about to say, "to loved ones," I strode ahead without her and into the room. First, I was struck by the cold. With the tree cover, the stone and the brick had little opportunity to absorb heat from the sun, and so the mild spring had yet to penetrate. But I could still see what a pleasant place it must've been when well cared for — the white walls would have made it a bright and cheery place. For a moment, I even could see past the ivy that had twined itself round the sconces on the walls, the brambles tumbling in through the broken windows, and the weathered dining table in the center of the room that looked as if one place setting would cause a sudden collapse, and I saw long summer evenings and cold suppers and watching the sun sink behind the undulating farmland to the west.

"We found him here."

Callow had moved to the north side of the room. I took in the scene from where I stood. Police had done what they could, I suppose, but an extremely large dark spot covered the white stone floor below one of the windows. Nature had taken advantage of any opening, but here the brambles had been swept back like a stage curtain.

The DI took on a neutral tone, as if describing plans for a new traffic control system. "It appeared that Mr. Hawkins had fallen into the vines and become tangled, the thorns catching at his clothes. We've taken a sample of the stems and sent them away for blood analysis."

I swallowed hard.

"Mr. Hawkins would've lost consciousness quickly," Callow said. I detected a kind note in her voice that I wished she would keep out. I blinked rapidly as she continued. "If he didn't become entangled on his own, the murderer may not have realized how severe the wound was and wanted to make any escape attempt more difficult."

Nick and I may have been the world's worst match as a couple, but I knew him well enough to know he could never have done anything so bad as to deserve to die for it.

"Did you find anything — fingerprints or footprints?"

"No, not even in here with all the blood. The killer was careful. And the ground's thick with leaves. That's not good material for shoe impressions. A car on the drive wouldn't show in the chippings. But." Full stop.

"But?"

"Someone met him here, not far off the drive where he told Mr. Sedgwick he'd be and on land where his only tie was to you."

I knew her next words. *Why did he come here? Why did he want to meet me and to talk with Michael? Why?* The question ran on a loop in my head, and I had no way to stop it.

"Have you thought further about it? Have you thought of any reason why he would be here?"

"I don't know!" I shouted at her. "How many times can I say that?" I clapped my hand over my mouth as my voice bounced off the stone and brick. Out the broken windows, I heard a rustling. *Calm down, Julia — no need to frighten the wildlife.* "Sorry," I whispered.

The DI put up her hands. "All right, fine," she said. "Would you like me to leave so you could be on your own?"

God, no. I shook my head, and we walked out together, dipped under the tape, and continued single file along the path, down from the knoll and then up to the drive.

"There could be something or someone that you haven't remembered," Callow said behind me, but cautiously. "An acquaintance from when the two of you were married. Someone from your circle of friends."

"Nick and I didn't have friends," I said as we came out on the drive near her black Volvo. "I'm not trying to sound pitiful, it's just the way it was. I had my friends. He had birds." I crossed my arms. "Peg told me that she's the witness you have to Michael turning into the drive here. But just because she didn't see him again, doesn't mean he didn't come straight back out. She had her hands full that afternoon."

"Yes," Callow said, scanning the drive. "And now PC Flynn has hers full, tracking down and interviewing everyone at that funeral."

We stood quiet for a moment. The grounds of Hoggin Hall were familiar territory to me and I knew why I had visited the summerhouse, but if police were finished with the site, what was Callow doing here?

"Were you looking for me?" Surely her internal DI radar didn't beep every time a person neared a murder scene.

"No." Callow looked back into the wood. "I find it helps my concentration to stand alone at a site. Impressions, thoughts, bits of evidence, can sometimes all come together."

"And I got in your way."

Before Callow could agree or disagree, a swoosh and a single *caw* from above caught our attention. I looked up and searched the highest branches of an oak before I spotted Alfie.

"So there you are," I called.

Callow followed my gaze and squinted. "Do you have a pet bird?"

"He's a rook. And no, he isn't a pet. He's a friend of a friend."

I caught a smile from Callow just before she turned away. It reminded me of the only other time I'd seen her smile, the autumn before. Michael and I spent the night at a lovely country hotel near Colchester when we happened upon Tess Callow in a remarkably short cocktail dress that was most un-DI-like. We weren't the ones who made her smile, of course, she had reserved that for her girlfriend, Chloe, an elegant woman with dark skin who glided across the floor. It seemed Callow and I were becoming quite chummy. Maybe I should ask after Chloe.

"Once again, Ms. Lanchester, I want to remind you to refrain from acting the cowboy — we need no other investigators on this case but the police."

I sniffed. Perhaps I wouldn't ask about Chloe, after all.

Alfie cawed loudly from his perch and dropped something — a folded sheet of paper. It drifted, scraping by a twig or two, but got stuck in the fork of two branches. The rook floated down after it, nudging the paper with his beak, setting it free to sail the rest of the way like a paper airplane. It hit the ground not six feet away.

Callow and I approached and bent over Alfie's prize. The paper had been rolled and squashed, crumpled as if held too tightly in someone's hand or it needed to be crammed in a pocket. The corners were torn and a few holes punched in it, but I could easily read the title: *Birds of Hoggin Hall.* I reached for it.

"Don't," Callow commanded.

My hand stopped midair. "But it's just one of our leaflets. Visitors can print them out online. That's where this one came from." I swept my gaze left and right. "Although they should know better than to litter. I wonder should we put a rubbish bin along the drive."

Callow paid no attention to my TIC musings, but pulled a thin blue glove from her pocket and, using it like a potholder, picked up the paper. She dug in her suit pocket, came up with a key and popped open the boot of her car.

I followed her over and continued to explain the paper's appearance. "It's only a leaflet. I wrote it. It's sort of a crossover promotion with Dad. Visitors can follow the trail, use a special online code for tickets, and watch extras from the television program. They can get discounts for bird feeders and seeds and the like."

Those words — discounts, codes, tickets — smacked into each other like bumper cars causing minor collisions. They were a reminder that I needed to take care of something but couldn't remember if it had to do with my job or Michael's. I began at the beginning, stacking up my own schedule and responsibilities against my temporary post as personal assistant to Rupert and looking for the snag.

"Ms. Lanchester?"

I jumped, surprised to find myself standing on the drive with Callow. She held up a clear plastic bag in one hand and in the other, the leaflet.

"Would you mind?" She nodded at the bag.

"Right, yes." Obediently, I opened the bag. Callow dropped in the leaflet and only then did she smooth it out, so that I could see, deep within the folds, a reddish-brown stain that had soaked through. It was a sight with which I was becoming disturbingly familiar. I stepped away.

Callow got on her phone and called for two PCs to do what she called a "fingertip" search. "Tomorrow," she said, "no stone unturned."

"But you already searched, didn't you?" I asked when she finished.

"Yes, well." Callow held up the bag as she sealed it. "Either we overlooked this or it's been left since."

Good luck to those poor sods. "There's no reason for Nick to have that leaflet with him," I said, putting up a weak argument, but hurtling on regardless. "He didn't care for birds in their proper places. Mind you, if he'd spotted a sparrow on the cliffs of Hirta, he'd be delighted, but here — where a sparrow should be — he wouldn't give it a second glance."

"Perhaps the murderer printed it out."

It gave me the creeps to think of murderers printing out our estate leaflets. I continued to search for another explanation.

"That" — I stuck my hands in my pockets and nodded to the bag — "that could be rabbit blood. Yesterday, I saw a stoat hunting just there. He'd caught a baby rabbit."

"Was it the baby rabbit or the stoat that had been birdwatching using one of your leaflets? And referred by your friend the rook, no doubt."

CHAPTER 11

At four o'clock the next morning, the alarm went off, sending spasms through my body as if I were being electrocuted. I'd chosen the loudest, most obnoxious sound I could pull up on my phone, in case I entertained any subconscious thoughts of sleeping in. Job done — with the result of eyes open, nerves jangled.

A shower and a cup of tea and I was away on my forty-five-minute journey. I flew up the empty, early-morning A14 outside Bury Saint Edmunds. Where was a roadside service when you wanted one — at least a petrol station with a Costa Express or even a tea caravan in a layby. Nothing. *They're missing a great business opportunity here*, I thought, *serving all of us who are up early and off to work*. Me and — I scanned the empty road and in the mirror saw headlights in the distance — me and that fellow back there. I tried to take my mind off food.

The evening before, after stopping at my cottage for a quick omelet, I'd had a productive five hours at the TIC, managing to whip out both reports for Smeaton's Summer Supper as well as sorting out upcoming interviews for Dad on Cambridgeshire and Norfolk BBC radio stations. Twice I'd picked up my phone to ring Michael on the pretense of clearing up some small detail. But I didn't ring, didn't text. He had been quite clear on the parameters of this "stepping away" business. Was he even thinking of me now? What was he doing, apart from banging out bird quiz questions on Rupert's website? I had seen him only two days ago, but at that moment, it felt as if eons had passed. Perhaps he would return to his old life, working for the family PR firm. Perhaps he would never come back again.

My sister had rung — a distraction I had desperately needed, although while we talked I had continued on Rupert's schedule, writing him an email with interview dates and times.

"Jools, are you even listening to me?" Bianca had asked.

"Of course I am," I said, hitting "send."

"And so, how many hours has Vesta added?"

I'd had a vague notion that I could avoid telling Bee and my dad that Vesta was gone, just as I could avoid admitting to Linus — who knew where Vesta was — that I had taken on Michael's job. I knew it would require a bit of juggling the truth, and I had thought myself prepared, but when put on the spot, I hesitated, as my mind had darted about looking for a useful lie. My sister heard the nanosecond of silence loud and clear and pounced.

"Jools — you've asked Vesta, haven't you? You said you wouldn't do this all on your own. You can't."

I suppose the truth would have to do. "Right, well, here's the thing." And I had, in bright and cheery tones, related Vesta's happy news and how everything was ticking along perfectly well, and I had it all in hand.

"How're you doing with Nick's death?"

I took a sharp breath. God, she's good at the sneak attack. When we had played draughts growing up, I often had thought myself on the verge of winning when I'd cornered one of Bee's remaining pieces, but she'd suddenly appear from nowhere, jump four of my men, and cheer her victory.

My defense in a shambles, I confessed, "I went there today. I saw the place."

"Why?"

"To see if it would hurt."

"And what good did it do?"

"It was sad to think of him there. And then Callow arrived and found one of our TIC leaflets nearby. Well, Alfie found it."

"Alfie? Is he police?"

I laughed, and told her the story of my new friends, and was thus able to lead her to more pleasant chat.

"How're the children? How's baby Estella?"

Before we had finished our conversation, I begged, "You won't mention to Dad about Vesta, will you? Because I'm doing fine, really. I've got all events, meetings, and tours in hand." As I had said this, I pulled up my merged schedule one more time to make sure all was well. "Everything's under control."

* * *

When I reached the other side of Mildenhall, I turned down the lane to Marshy End just after five o'clock, and a thought came to me — I'd send Basil out to collect breakfasts. That's the sort of assignment that suited Basil Blandy, general dogsbody that he was. That is, whenever he arrived.

I bounced along the drive — really, we should get this leveled out — with scrub willow and blackthorn obscuring my vision until I turned the last bend and stepped on the brake. The yard, surrounded by our cottage and a couple of outbuildings, buzzed with the crew stringing cable, carrying ladders, and stacking logs against the low stone wall. That's right, Dad had wanted to build a hedgehog haven. Hedgehog populations had dropped dramatically, and creating shelter for the little lovable creatures would be a fantastic living-with-nature segment. But it hadn't appeared on the schedule. Who had taken this initiative?

I marveled at the activity. We would have no Rupert this morning, but instead concentrate on selecting positions for motion-activated cameras at various nest sites, testing the feed, and choosing segments long enough for Dad to do a voice-over.

"Good morning, Julia," one of the tech lads called. A couple of others I recognized, with their hands full of equipment, raised heads in greeting. I spoke with each and introduced myself to the two I didn't know.

Basil wandered out of the cottage, headphones round his neck and computer tablet in hand. His ginger hair had gone a bit long on top, and it suited him.

"Hiya, Julia, 'morning. You're just in time. We're about to record the dawn chorus. Well, a bit past." Basil looked round the yard. "Phones!" he called.

Every single crewmember pulled a phone out of a pocket. Basil looked at me. "Sorry, Julia — it's the only way we can get a clean sound. I don't even mind the Lakenheath boys flying over, but those pesky mobiles. We switch them off completely. You all right with that?"

"Certainly," I said, reaching for my own mobile and thinking I needed to institute that rule when Dad was on a phone interview. Even a vibrating mobile could spoil a recording or a live broadcast.

Basil lifted his finger, pointed to several trees where I could see he'd installed the audio equipment, and we all stood silent and let the birds have at it for about ten minutes. Songs of blackbirds, chaffinches, robins, wrens, and dunnocks filled the air. Those early birds dug into the ground for their food and so took advantage of the soft soil in the morning. I breathed in the sweet, cold scent of spring and closed my eyes for a moment. What a peaceful way to begin a day.

When he gave the cut signal, the crew moved with new energy. "We've just installed the cameras at the swift boxes, there under the eaves," Basil said, nodding to the shed. "We'll have a look at positioning on the monitors in about two ticks."

I had no reply for a moment. Basil had never greeted me with the news he'd actually accomplished something on time.

"Right, well, Basil, that's lovely," I said, looking down at my clipboard to the morning's schedule and ticked "swift boxes" off the list. "Trap cam for the moorhens in the reeds?" I asked. "At that slow bit of the river near the bridge?"

"Done and dusted — they've built a fine nest, easy to see and all. They've a total of nine eggs, so there could be two rounds of egg-laying. Do you think?"

"Yeah," I managed to say. "They'll often lay twice. We'll keep an eye out for the early hatchers." Tick. Next?

"Oh, and we spotted a wren nest in the back garden in that raspberry patch," Basil said. "She's all tucked in nicely on the eggs now, and so we set a camera just in front to catch the action."

Michael had been right. All it had taken was to show confidence in Basil, and Basil had responded — not only doing what he should but taking initiative. "That's fantastic," I said, chagrined at my former lack of belief. "Everyone loves a wren."

"Not 'we,'" a voice behind me said. "You found her. You were the one who spotted the wren's nest."

I looked over my shoulder to find a young woman about my height with a knit cap pulled low and a tiny, sparkly earring in one nostril. She had a fleece zipped up to her neck and wore fingerless gloves.

Basil's face took on a pink shade. "Here we are. Julia, this is SaraJane. SaraJane, Julia. SaraJane's production assistant for us now."

"Two days a week, at least. Hiya, Julia." SaraJane stuck out her hand, and I shook. She had a good firm grip — I admired that in a woman. Had it been she who answered Basil's phone for him? Perhaps Basil's newfound confidence wasn't only Michael's doing.

"Lovely to meet you, SaraJane," I said. "And good on you, Basil, for spotting that wren's nest. Children love the little birds. I'll let Rupert know that's been added."

"Righto," Basil said, typing something into his tablet. Basil's fingers hovered over the tablet. "I could" — he cleared his throat — "send the details off to him, if you like."

"Yes, Basil, would you?" I smiled at him. "I believe you're just the man for it."

We were on a roll. As SaraJane was called away by one of the crew and Basil typed, I moved to the next item on my list. "Have you got the trap camera on the kingfisher nest? The first brood can hatch early — might already be showing."

Basil's face went from a pleasant pink to puce. "Well, that's the thing — no one's been able to tell me where to position the camera. Rupert wanted to do it, go down to the river. It takes patience, he said, sitting and waiting and watching. He was to come out on Sunday and spot the nest for us, but . . ." Basil kept his eyes on the ground.

Poised to blame Basil for this lapse in production schedule, I found instead that I was the one who had buggered up the works. On Sunday, Dad had been trying to track me down to tell me about Nick. Then, he and Beryl had been at the police station in Sudbury to meet Michael and me. The rest of that day and the next was a blur of sensationalist journos and Michael's departure.

"No, it's fine, really," I said. "I tell you what, you've everything in hand here, and I know where they often nest. I'll just nip down there now and have a look, shall I? And once spotted, you can get the camera in place."

* * *

I took a path quite familiar to my feet — one that led off our Marshy End property and through a thicket of willow and thorn until it came out on the bank of the Little Ouse. The memories of growing up at Marshy End and calling the river our own were overshadowed by the thought of the spring before, when Michael and I had run down this trail in search of Rupert, who had gone missing. My mind deftly skipped over the details of what we had found and landed directly on how it felt when Michael put his arms round me as I fainted. We'd only just met, and I had decided I didn't like him, although I didn't mind those arms.

Avoiding a patch of nettles, I settled near the edge of the bank with my back against the trunk of an alder, lifted my binoculars, and scanned the opposite bank, about twenty feet away. The holes kingfishers make in the sandy bank are quite small — not even three inches across — and can be difficult to spot until a parent is seen entering or leaving. We always had kingfishers nesting somewhere round here, and so I would only have to sit and wait.

I heard a light rustling just after I'd homed in on the nest across and up the river a few feet.

SaraJane appeared, holding two steaming mugs. "I saw a tiny flash of color just then — orange and blue. Was that a kingfisher?"

"Yeah, they're gorgeous, aren't they?"

"Thought you could use a cuppa," she said, handing me one of the mugs. Settling beside me, she pulled off her knit cap and scratched her head until her short hair — brown with pink tips — stood out like a bristle brush.

"Cheers, thanks." I breathed in the steam. No food, but tea would do for the moment. "You and Basil — you're . . . ?" I raised my eyebrows.

She had a wide mouth but thin lips, and so her smile created a long, upswept line across her face, like a child's simple drawing. It was a happy smile.

"He's very kind," she said, "and I needed that. We met about six months ago through a class I teach at the community center in Brandon — 'Find Your Passion, Seize Your Life.' It's all about seeing yourself where you want to be, how to visualize your success. Baz, he's seeing his way to what he wants to do, and he's ready to take on a challenge. I've learned a massive amount about editing film from him. And, well, he's more than that, of course."

That was the beauty of a well-suited couple, I thought as I swigged my tea. You became a power equal to more than the sum of your parts. Basil had met SaraJane, and they both had grown. Michael and I had our own version of that story. He had learned from me that the devil is in the detail, and I had learned from him how to come up with Grand Schemes. We were a good match — and yet look where we had ended up. I felt a pang of hunger that went well past my empty stomach.

"Rough going at the moment, is it?" SaraJane asked.

Of course she would know. I nodded, as the tears blurred my view of the kingfisher perched on a low stem over the water. "Yeah, it's a bit of a mess."

"Exes," SaraJane said and shook her head.

"I don't know why he was here," I said, almost automatically. Perhaps I should have that tattooed on my forehead. "There wasn't much to the marriage," I added. "And it was ages ago. We'd both moved on."

"I'd say you've found a good one now." SaraJane kept watch on the bank across the river but gave me a sideways glance. "Michael barely stops talking about you, you know."

"Really?" I whispered, wiping my nose on my sleeve. I dug in my pocket and managed to locate a tissue — one that had seen better days.

"Yeah, really. So, you just hang in there."

I thought perhaps I should sign up for SaraJane's "Find Your Passion, Seize Your Life" class. She had a good way about her.

"Look, I've got a packet of stuff for Michael that he wanted last week, but not everything had arrived, and so I printed it out yesterday. I'm with Rupert's crew only two mornings a week. Shall I give it to you?"

"That'd be great, thanks," I said. "My car's open — you could toss it in the back."

"Well, you take your time here," SaraJane said as she left. "I'll let Basil know about the kingfisher."

* * *

Nest cams, trap cams, swift boxes, sparrow boxes, and, for good measure, a bat box. Everything installed and tested. We hunched round the monitor and gasped when the kingfisher appeared like a streak of blue electricity. We even got a great piece of footage of mother wren sticking her head out of her delicate, woven nest. I was on my third or possibly fourth cup of tea, when I stood up from the table in the kitchen of the cottage a bit too fast and had to grab the chair before I went over. I was starving. The cupboards were bare here at Marshy End — I'd already checked that before we sat down to review camera angles on Basil's laptop — and I had a thought to go out to the car and rummage through my bag, in a vain hope that Alfie had deposited a biscuit in the outer flap. As I reached the door of the cottage, a motor scooter puttered up the lane, and before the rider could even dismount, the crew had crowded round. SaraJane snatched a large paper bag from him and opened it.

I could smell the bacon from ten feet away and swooned. SaraJane tossed small, wrapped parcels to the crew as if she were feeding penguins at the zoo, and I crept forward, ready to dive for my own.

"Bacon roll, Julia?" Basil asked. He had emerged from the shed and joined in the distribution.

"Oh well, yeah, sure," I replied, wiping the drool from the corners of my mouth. "If you've enough, that is. Thanks."

The roll was fresh and soft and the bacon still warm. This was possibly the most delicious thing I'd eaten in my entire life. So good that it made my jaw hurt.

We stood about in the yard, making short work of the bacon rolls. I'd heard there was another pot of tea going and thought I'd better track down my mug.

"It's good you can take time off your tourist job to help out," Basil said, triggering such a rush of adrenaline I almost levitated.

"Tourist, yes, center, open—" I glanced at my watch and continued to sputter as I ran to the car.

"I'm terribly sorry — must fly," I called over my shoulder as I popped the last bite in my mouth and jammed my hand in my trouser pocket, searching for the key before jumping in.

"Julia!" SaraJane shouted and ran up to my window. "Look, we've a few left. Would you like one for the road?"

I snatched the bacon roll out of her hand as I shifted into gear and stuck my head out the window as I stepped on the gas and took off. "Cheers, bye!"

For the first half of my journey back to Smeaton, I dutifully slowed down every time I saw the warning for a speed camera, but after I'd made it through Bury Saint Edmunds, I put my foot down and finally screeched to a halt round the corner from the TIC at seventeen minutes after nine o'clock.

Unlock the door, turn the sign, switch on lights — thank God no rambler had been waiting on the pavement, tapping his foot impatiently for a map of footpaths on the estate. I dashed behind the counter, stripping off my trainers, trousers, shirt, and sweater as I went, while at the same time, managing to reach over and start the kettle.

Not that I'd planned to work in the nude. I'd stashed my second uniform here at the TIC so that I could — like a superhero — transform instantly from *A Bird in the Hand* producer to TIC manager. I reached for my skirt, cardigan, and blouse, hanging on the loo door.

My phone rang and I dived into my bag and came up with it. My sister. I put her on speaker as I hopped on one foot, pulling tights on.

"Bee, are you checking up on me?" I asked.

"Julia, what's that noise? Are you in the middle of a construction zone?"

"No, I'm at the TIC, it's only the kettle. I ran a bit late is all, but we got through a massive amount of work this morning, and Basil Blandy has turned into a budding television producer. Michael was right about him." That gave me pause. "I wish I could tell him so."

I lost all interest in dressing and stood in my knickers and bra with tights stretched up one leg, and the other leg bare as the bleakness of my existence overwhelmed me.

"What in God's name are those police doing?" Bianca demanded. The kettle switched off and the background noise fell to nothing. "They can't still be suspecting Michael, can they? And what was Nick up to, lurking round the estate. What did he want with you?"

In the din of the kettle, I hadn't heard the bell above the door, but looked up now to see a tall thin figure standing by the counter. She wore layers of drooping clothes, all in varying shades of beige, and her hair — beige with a wide swath of gray — was pulled back into a low bun. Her face held no expression. I had seen her only once in my life for all of five minutes, but I recognized her at once. Kathleen Hawkins, Nick's sister.

CHAPTER 12

"Jools?" Bianca's voice, on speaker, bounced off the walls of the TIC. "Listen, Nick had no business—"

"Bee, I've got to go," I cut in, taking the call off speaker. "I'll ring you later."

In a weak attempt at modesty, I held my cardigan up in front of me. "Hello, Kathleen."

"Hello, Julia."

Pleasantries over, I gathered up the rest of my uniform and said, "Excuse me for a moment, will you? I'll be right out."

Our loo at the TIC was not designed to be a changing room. I hit my head bending over to pull up the other leg of my tights, and banged an elbow into the mirror as I stuffed my blouse into the waistband of my skirt. At last, I yanked the shoulders of my cardigan into place and ran my fingers through my hair. The bacon rolls in my stomach churned, and when I cast a quick glance at my reflection, I saw dark circles under my eyes. Must be the lighting.

Kathleen hadn't moved an inch from where she stood, but had at least occupied herself by picking up a copy of *Who Are the Fotheringills?*

"There," I said, smiling at her. "All sorted. Sorry about that. I had an early appointment and thought I'd be back before this." Kathleen folded the leaflet and returned it to the holder. "Would you like a cup of tea?" I asked.

"I don't want to disturb you," she said.

The agenda for tomorrow's organizational meeting for Smeaton's Summer Supper should've been sent out yesterday, and I had repromised it for this morning. I still had two interviews to set up for Dad, and the higher-ups at BBC Two expected next month's production schedule by five o'clock. But Kathleen's only sibling had been murdered and, although I hated to admit it, I was her last connection to him.

"You aren't disturbing me," I said. "Please come round the counter and sit down."

She did as she was told, and I poured up the tea, set out mugs, spoons, and milk. I noticed the well-spent tissue had tumbled out of my pocket and onto the floor. I picked it up.

"When did you arrive?" I asked.

"Yesterday," Kathleen said.

I poured our tea and we sat stirring milk in silence. My hands in my lap, I began shredding the tissue.

"Are you staying locally?" I asked.

"I found a guesthouse near the police station, but Sudbury is so congested."

Sudbury was a small market town of about thirteen thousand people, hardly London. Still — I took a deep breath.

"One of our pubs here in the village has rooms — the Stoat and Hare. You might find it a bit quieter there. Would you like me to ask if something's available?"

Kathleen gazed out the window of the TIC and onto the high street. Now that the morning commute was finished, only the occasional car passed by.

"If it's no trouble."

I reached for my phone and at last said what I should've started our conversation with. "It's a dreadful thing that happened to Nick. I'm so very sorry."

"Thank you." Kathleen took a sip of tea and set the mug down.

"Did the police explain what happened?" Perhaps the police told her more than they told me. Perhaps Kathleen would share. I almost laughed aloud.

"They told me as much as they could. They said they are following several lines of enquiry," Kathleen said.

Were they indeed? They were no lines of enquiry to follow as far as I knew.

"Kathleen, I have no idea why Nick was here." That was a fact, although I wondered if she'd heard about the email. "You do know I didn't see him again after he moved away from Cambridge?"

She gave a slight nod, and the silence enveloped us again.

"Had you heard from him recently?" I asked.

"At the new year."

"Did he ever mention the people he worked with? Was there anything he was concerned about? Any worries?"

A slight frown arose on Kathleen's face — the first sign of emotion I'd seen. "The police asked me these same questions. I understand gathering this information is part of the investigation."

"Yes, well," I said, hearing her implied question to be *why the hell would you want to know*. "We're all concerned about how this could happen to Nick."

"I don't know who his co-workers were," Kathleen said. "Two men, I believe. Perhaps a woman, too. They were merely seasonal." She sighed and stared out the front window. "To think he came here to his death. He should never have left St. Kilda."

I should never have unlocked the door this morning.

"The police have released his body," she continued. "I'm having him cremated. I'll take him back with me."

"Where are you living now?" I asked politely, thinking it sounded as if she were taking Nick off on a holiday.

"On a small island up the coast from Halifax. It was left to me. You may remember I was employed for many years as a personal secretary to a man whose business was manufacturing gaskets for ship boilers. He was working on his memoirs when he died four years ago. He had no family, and left everything to me, with the instructions to complete his work. And so I've continued the project."

That would be a riveting read.

I asked a question I believed I could already answer. "Do you live alone?"

"Yes," she said, and a small smile surfaced — emotion number two. "I see no one, apart from the woman who takes a ferry out three times a week to cook and clean. And the occasional odd-job man. It's quite peaceful. It reminds me of our family home."

The Hawkins siblings had grown up with their parents in a remote valley in Cumbria, so, although the topography may have been different, I knew what Kathleen meant. It was the isolation they loved. Easy to see where Nick and his sister had acquired this need to be far away from people.

We returned to silence. I longed for a load of ramblers to burst in or Alfie to tap at the door. Anything to break up the somnambulant atmosphere before my head dropped to the table and I began to snore. I lifted my mug to find it empty.

"More tea?" I asked.

* * *

Thank God she declined. I rang Peg to book a room. When I gave Kathleen's name, I heard a significant pause, and so I filled in quickly with, "And let me ring you back directly about that other business — about the farmers. Shall I?" hoping Peg would hear the subtext, *I'll explain later.*

"Well, Kathleen," I said once that business was done, "I'll look in on you. Please let me know if you need anything." I thrust one of my cards in her hand and prayed she wouldn't use it.

As she stood at the door, she looked round the TIC. "You've made a life for yourself here, Julia. I hope it's to your liking."

* * *

I began work with a vengeance. *Yes, my life bloody well was to my liking, thank you very much.* As if I needed to prove my worth, I completed the meeting agenda and the rest of my tasks all before lunch — and that, despite the guide leader from the local Brownies troop appearing unannounced to talk about earning nature badges. I rang Bianca back to explain why I ended our call so abruptly.

"She didn't hear me, did she?" Bee asked. I changed the subject.

After that, I rang Peg, who whispered, "Yes, she's gone up. She's very quiet."

Late morning, I found my fingers dancing lightly above the keyboard as if waiting for permission. I granted it to myself and typed in Dad's website on the pretense of checking that Michael continued to maintain it as he said he would do. It was one thin thread of connection that remained between us. I had taken a look the day before, too. Allowing myself this indulgence every twenty-four hours didn't seem excessive. New articles and videos posted, schedule updated, and interesting bits of bird trivia stuck round the page had all refreshed. I had a picture in my mind of Michael huddled in the dark in his tiny Haverhill flat, computer screen setting his face aglow as he tapped away at the keyboard. I longed to be there with him.

At lunch, I locked up and nipped down to the corner shop.

Akash always dressed the part of grocer with panache, wearing a bib apron over his coordinated shirt and tie — a lovely rose shade, gorgeous with his dark skin and hair, which was threaded with silver. When I walked in, he glanced up from restocking the dairy shelves and I could swear he did a double take.

"Julia," he said, eyebrows raised, "everything all right?"

"Yes, of course," I replied, but gave my clothes a quick check to make sure I hadn't missed a button on my blouse. "And how are you? Any news from Vesta?"

"Only a text from one of her stops — it's a long journey, she won't arrive in Christchurch until five o'clock tomorrow morning, British time." He took the empty milk crate to the back of the shop and came out wiping his hands on his apron. "I saw a woman at the TIC this morning just at nine, but she didn't go in."

"Yes, right." I thought about where to begin and how carefully I needed to step. Akash needn't know about my double life, because Vesta might hear of it, and I didn't want her feeling guilty from halfway round the world. I went about my shopping — sandwich, tea, milk, biscuits. I wondered if Alfie liked custard creams. "That was Nick's sister, Kathleen. She's come from Nova Scotia. And I was running a wee bit late."

I deposited my shopping on the counter and made a show of searching my little coin purse for money so that I wouldn't have to look him in the eye.

"You can always give me a ring if you're held up somewhere," Akash said, dropping my coins into the till. "Remember I have a spare key to the center — it's right here behind the counter. I could open up for you."

"Oh Akash, how lovely," I said, full of gratitude. "But you can't leave the shop — you don't have McKiddie to cover for you any longer."

"True," Akash said. "And I've no one properly suited to replace him yet." He scanned walls, shelves, and displays in the shop. "In truth, I need someone that can do more than fill in. I feel I'm getting a bit stale with my displays. The whole place needs . . . well, I'm not sure what. Still, if you are caught again, I wouldn't mind keeping an eye on both places for a short time."

As I stepped out of the shop and turned my head to catch the April sun, a blast of screeches broke out ahead of me, just in front of the TIC. I saw Alfie diving at a cluster of people who fled down the pavement and dashed off into the narrow spaces between shops. Alfie tilted a wing and soared away.

I stormed up the high street. I may have seen only their backsides, but I knew who they were — those journos. The jackals. I held up when I reached the center. They'd disappeared, and pursuit would be pointless. I stood outside the TIC for a moment, breathing hard and daring them to return, but I saw only Lottie from Three Bags Full step out of her shop and look round. She waved when she saw me, and I could see a hopeful look on her face as if she thought we might have a chat. I didn't believe I could muster the energy to explain yet again that I had no idea why my ex-husband had come to the village. I waved back and beat a retreat into the TIC.

* * *

Throughout the afternoon, I remained on high alert, checking the high street outside the TIC, flinching each time the bell above the door jingled, and thankful for a steady stream of visitors who kept me well occupied. Near four o'clock, I glanced out the window, thinking I'd see Tennyson and Alfie coming along to tea. Instead, I saw that they'd regrouped — the hydra — all five of them loitering across the road and down a bit. The big one, the twins, kitten woman, and the little weasel, all accounted for.

My jaw clenched and I ground my teeth. Enough of this. I dug in my bag, edged up to the front window, and slowly lifted my phone just high enough to get them in sight. My fingers shook as I snapped, but when I checked the photo, I saw that my phone had steadied my hand. Trembling, I typed, "They're back," and sent the text to Michael. I longed to add, "It didn't work, please come home. I miss you," but held myself in check. As much as I wanted to plead, I would not guilt him into returning to me.

I turned my back on them and next time I looked, they had disappeared. Traffic had picked up — perhaps the queue of cars didn't suit the journos. Instead, I was met with the sight of Tennyson. I opened the door and Alfie appeared from behind her, flying straight past me to my mackintosh with something large in his beak. I made a mental note to clean out its pockets before it overflowed with gifts.

Tennyson dropped her school bag at the counter. "I stayed after in the library today to watch a video on the ecology of wood warblers," she explained. "There's been a rapid decline in their populations, and the RSPB is studying the problem. I thought I should keep up on the latest results."

Not what I remembered doing with my after-school hours, but there you are.

"I enjoyed meeting your mum," I said to her as we sat over our mugs of tea and the opened packet of custard creams. Alfie had placed his biscuit in the seat of a chair and was in the process of reducing it to a pile of crumbs.

"Mum says she'd like to have you to tea sometime. You could come to our flat."

"Do you live here in the village?"

Tennyson nodded. "Dot said we should live with her, but Mum didn't think it was a good idea with Alfie and all," Tennyson said. "So we're in a place above the garden shop. Loads of room, and Derry, in the shop, didn't mind a bit."

Derry ran The Holly and the Ivy, the garden and gift shop. As far as I knew, the rooms above her shop — although fitted with kitchen and bath decades ago — had been used only for storage. But the place must provide Tennyson and Gwen with what they needed — room for a rook and an ironing board — at the right price.

"Would you like to see how good Alfie's memory is?" Tennyson asked. "We've an exercise we could show you."

"I would love to see that," I said, switching on the kettle.

"Right," Tennyson said. "We'll need five objects."

* * *

Tennyson and I collected and lined up five random objects on the table — the key to my cottage, a spoon from the sink, a purple crocheted beret left on the coat rack by Willow, a pencil from the counter, and a tiny ceramic figurine of a red squirrel that sat in the front window. The girl pointed to the objects one at a time, following each indication with a bite of shortbread for the bird. Alfie watched carefully and snatched up his treats. After that, Tennyson distracted the rook while I swept the objects into a large basket and mixed them with an assortment of paraphernalia, including an unopened packet of tea, one of Tennyson's shoes, a pair of gloves, and a butterfly-print scarf. I set the basket on the floor under the computer desk. Tennyson then tapped the table and said, "All right, Alfie. Get to work."

The girl and I leaned against the sink and watched. The rook hopped up to the back of a chair and paced, muttering to himself and looking at the empty table. Then, he cast his gaze wider, stopping when he eyed the basket. Down to the floor he went, stuck his head in, and rummaged round. One by one he found what he sought and lined each item up on the table. When he'd reclaimed all five, I could see that he'd switched the order, setting the squirrel before the beret. Alfie took toll, touching his beak to the table in front of each object, but gave a squawk when he saw his mistake, and corrected himself. He shook out his feathers.

"Well remembered, Alfie," I said.

Tennyson offered the rook a shortbread finger as reward. Alfie accepted it but placed it on the table and set to returning each object to its proper place.

On his way back from returning the squirrel figurine to the front window, he swept by the wall of leaflets and maps, picked one out and came back, dropping it on the table and eyeing me. I glanced down at his choice. *Birds of Hoggin Hall.*

"Well, we'd best be on our way," Tennyson said, slinging her school bag across her shoulder. She hesitated at the door. "Mum says Alfie and I shouldn't take up too much of your time."

"Not a bit of it," I said, tearing myself away from Alfie's leaflet. "I look forward to your visits — be sure to tell your mum that. You and Alfie are always welcome here."

A smile spread across Tennyson's face. "Well, that's good news, because you see, I met Ms. Darke at the tearoom this morning on my way to school. I introduced Alfie and told her we knew you, and Ms. Darke said that if I stopped there tomorrow afternoon, she'd have two wedges of chocolate cake I could bring to tea."

"Perfect," I said as I saw them out. Pitiful, I thought, that a wedge of chocolate cake for tomorrow's teatime could very well be the high point of my week.

I stood with my back to the door and my eyes on the leaflet Alfie had left for me. Not possible that he picked *Birds of Hoggin Hall* out of a wall of leaflets because it had been the one he'd found near the summerhouse. Not possible.

I heard a jingle. Drat, gone five o'clock and I hadn't locked the door.

"Hello, welcome to Smeaton-under-"

I choked on the greeting when I saw who it was. Just inside the door, with two cameras round his neck, his wispy hair awry, and his faced flushed, stood the little weasel.

CHAPTER 13

"Get out!" I shouted as I advanced on him. "*Get out this instant!*"

His hands flew up in front of his face. "Wait, no, please, Ms. Lanchester," he stuttered.

"Out! Do you hear me?" I towered over him and shrieked in his face as he backed up and bumped into the door, which rattled and jingled.

"I only want to—"

"I'm ringing the police. You'll pay for this harassment!"

"All right, yes, I'll leave. It's just I thought you should—"

I pulled the door opened and shoved him out. He stumbled backward and out onto the pavement, landing against my Fiat. Across the road, Alfie marched back and forth along the gutter, turning his head to eye the situation.

As the little weasel scurried down the pavement, I looked over at the rook — a silent witness.

"You're neglecting your duties," I said to him.

Alfie shook out his feathers and returned to sentry.

I stepped back in, threw the lock on the door, and stood trembling. After a few moments, I saw Alfie casually beat his wings, rise, and fly off. I swept up the rook's crumbs from the chair and washed out mugs before sitting down in front of the computer to consider my evening. I would work at home. I needed to outline the filmed segments for Dad. He refused to work from a script, but I would hit the highlights for him so that he would know what to talk about. He excelled at off-the-cuff introductions and spontaneous narrations, although we'd still need to do some editing. Yes, that's my evening sorted.

When my phone rang and I saw the caller, I pounced.

"Hi," I said, out of breath as if I'd just come in from a 10K run.

"I'm sorry, Julia, I am," Michael said, his voice full of irritation. "I just saw your message. I thought they'd leave off by now."

"It isn't your fault. But, it hasn't worked, has it? You wanted to draw them away, yet here they are."

"They can't find me, that's why. I'm away in Exeter doing a bit of work for Miles."

My heart dropped through the floor. My suspicion had been confirmed. He'd returned to the family PR business, which his brother ran. Michael hadn't taken a step or two away from me, he'd moved home.

"That's . . . lovely."

"How are you doing?" he asked. "Ah, that's a stupid question to ask, I know, but you know what I mean. Are you all right?"

God, where's an old tissue when you need one? I had no pockets in my uniform, and so I wiped my nose on my sleeve.

"Fantastic. Everything's ticking along with no problems at all." Should I have said something about Nick?

"The journos — they aren't trespassing, are they? Coming in the TIC to bother you?"

"It would hardly be trespassing, would it? We are open to the public." The little weasel had ventured into my domain, but no need to mention that.

"Any word from the police?"

For a moment, I was transported to the summerhouse — the smell of the wood in spring, Alfie finding a TIC leaflet soaked in blood.

"Nothing. I don't know what they're doing."

"Julia—"

"You were right about Basil," I said brightly, wishing I'd kept my mouth shut one second longer to hear what Michael was about to say. "He's doing quite well. And I've met SaraJane."

The silence between us grew heavy.

"It's too much for you," Michael said.

Well, then, come home. "No, really, I'm quite able to keep up."

"I'll be finished here by late Sunday," he replied. I imagined I heard longing in his voice — an unspoken desire to be together again. I've always had a vivid imagination.

* * *

I gathered up my things, slung my bag over my shoulder, and stepped out of the TIC and locked the door. The traffic had started to let up. It made it quite easy to hear, above the noise of engines, the voices calling to me from down the pavement.

"Julia, what did Michael do with the knife?"

"Did he give it to you? Did he hide it?"

"Will you give it up to the police, Julia? Will you give Michael up?"

Stunned, I could do nothing but stare at them, until they hurried toward me. I dug for my key and leapt in my car, pulling away just as the kitten woman held her muff-covered recorder out toward my window.

I tore off and made straight for Sudbury and the police station. No one, I said to myself, shaking violently as I shifted gears, no one has a right to treat another person that way. Callow, Glossop — somebody must put a stop to it. Had they been at Michael in the same way? Is that why he'd left — deserting me for good, as far as I could tell.

Making a wide turn into the car park and narrowly missing a black Volvo, I slammed on the brake, lurching forward with the momentum. I took a moment to compose myself before walking into the lobby of the station and asking for Detective Inspector Callow.

"Please tell her it's Julia Lanchester," I said, meek and mild and in no way in anyone's face. I would save that for when it mattered.

Three minutes later, Callow emerged. She caught me pacing between desk and door, a journey of seven steps.

"Ms. Lanchester?" she asked.

"Do you know what they're saying?" I hissed at her from across the room. "Do you know what they have the nerve to ask?"

Callow cut her eyes at the desk sergeant as she crossed the room in three strides.

"What's the problem?" she asked.

"The problem is when I walk out of my place of business I'm met with those journos shouting at me, saying 'What did Michael do with the knife?' "

She caught me by the elbow. "Shall we go back to an interview room so that we can talk about this?"

"I won't," I complained loudly, pulling my elbow away. "I won't go back there and look as if I'm guilty of something. You tell me what you're going to do about this leak you have in the police department. Those leeches aren't supposed to know about a . . . a *knife*," I whispered.

"Yes, yes, all right," Callow said, quiet but intense. "Can we talk about this elsewhere? Why don't we go back to your village?"

"No," I said, hearing a whinging tone in my voice and hating it. "Villagers look at me out of the corners of their eyes and talk behind my back. They think I haven't noticed, but I have." I straightened myself up. "Can't we act like normal people and go out for a coffee? There's that place on Gainsborough Street — it's quite close."

Callow's frosty gaze softened. She looked past me, and I could almost hear her mind sifting through possible places to interview a hysterical woman.

"There's a pub at the bottom of The Street in Foxearth — do you know it?" she asked.

A pub? Foxearth?

"You mean The Den?" I asked.

Callow nodded. "The Den."

Foxearth, a hamlet just down the road from Smeaton-under-Lyme, had only the one pub that I knew of. It sat low in the landscape on a busy bend in the road and was almost indistinguishable from the concrete storage buildings nearby except for the glaring neon signs in the small, high windows. Motorbikes usually packed the car park. I'd thought it was some sort of club bar.

"Yeah, I know it."

"It's off my patch, you see, and it's also away from your estate."

"Ah, neutral ground."

"I'll meet you there," she said. "Thirty minutes?"

"All right," I said, and she disappeared behind the door that led to the inner workings of the station. I looked down at my TIC uniform. I wasn't going for a drink at The Den looking like this. And then I remembered my trousers and trainers and pullover sweater I'd worn at Marshy End early that morning. They were stuffed in my bag in the car. I retrieved it, came back into the station, and changed in the public toilet.

* * *

I pulled into the car park at The Den and squeezed my little Fiat between two enormous black motorbikes, the sort you can hear rumbling down the road long before you see them. No sign of Callow's Volvo.

Inside, the place was heaving with bikers, pensioners, couples, and a few groups of young women seated out of the fray along the wall. Two children dashed past me and into a larger room. So, just a family pub after all. And they must do food as well — I detected a hint of curry in the air. My tummy growled.

"Julia?"

Adrenaline shot through my veins. They must've found me, those journos. I backed up and bumped into the door, thinking to flee. I should've waited in my car until Callow arrived.

"Julia, over here."

I cut my eyes left, afraid to acknowledge I'd heard my name. A tall, slender woman wearing a snug black turtleneck sweater, skin-tight denims, and knee-high boots — her short silver hair swept back on the sides — stood by a table in a corner. She nodded me over, and I obeyed.

"Um," I said, not sure how to talk to a detective inspector who wasn't in her usual black business suit and who called me by my Christian name. "Hello."

"I'll get us drinks, shall I? What will you have?" Ah yes, now I recognized her — brusque, efficient, a let's-get-on-with-this attitude.

"Thanks. A glass of wine, please."

Callow raised an eyebrow.

"Oh. White?"

I sat with my back to the wall and watched as she went up to the bar. My gaze shifted past her, and pride swelled in my chest as I noticed a line of bottles on the shelf. That's Bugg's Best Cider — our cider, grown and bottled on the Fotheringill estate by Adam Bugg.

"Wait!" I got up just as a swarm of extremely large men all wearing leather vests and no shirts took a position directly in my path. "Excuse me," I said. They didn't move. "Do you mind?" I stuck an elbow in the middle of a protruding stomach and bumped my way through, finally squeezing my face between two bare, hairy arms. "Wait — Tess!"

She turned and frowned.

"I'll have a cider instead." I pointed to the bottles. "Bugg's Best."

I returned to our table, eyeing a server who passed by carrying two steaming plates of curry. Perhaps I'd order a meal when Callow and I were finished.

She returned with a bottle of Bugg's Best and a pint of ale.

"Right, who is it?" I asked as she sat on the bench next to me instead of across the table. I didn't blame her — I wouldn't want my back to this room either. "Who's the leak?"

"No one on my team is leaking information about Mr. Hawkins's death."

"Then how do they know?"

Callow took a long drink of her beer. "The general manner of a death is difficult to keep quiet, because there are too many people and departments involved. The forensics team, following leads, uniforms, all the questioning of potential witnesses."

"Yes, but they said what did *Michael* do with the knife. Why did they say his name?"

"Speculation," Callow said. "Unscrupulous, but not unheard of. They look for the worst possible scenario, stretch it past its limits of believability, and try to put those words in your mouth."

I disagreed, but silently. There was something particularly evil about how those jackals were going about this, as if their real goal was to destroy Michael's reputation and our relationship. They'd mentioned Dad in their headlines, but Rupert, the celebrity associated rather tangentially with the murder, didn't seem to be the focus of their unwelcome attention. My mind returned to wonder what Nick had wanted with me and with Michael. Was that why he was killed?

A shadow fell across the table as a tall man leaned far enough over us that I could see the top of his head where his greasy blond hair had been pulled up into a ball of a ponytail. He had a few wiry hairs on his chin and thick eyebrows that joined in the middle. He leered at Callow.

"How are you this fine evening, Tess?" A cloud of whisky fumes stole all the breathable air from our space.

Callow smiled and shook her head. "I've nothing for you tonight, Tommy. I'm only having a drink with a friend."

Tommy's head swiveled so that he now loomed over me. "Good evening, Tess's friend. You've chosen a fine establishment in which to enjoy that bottle of . . . cider, is it?"

"Push off, Tommy," Callow said in a friendly way.

"Right you are," he replied amiably. "You ladies enjoy yourselves."

My mind swelled with questions. Not a police officer. Not a boyfriend — even if Callow had been interested in men, I don't think she'd be interested in this one. That led to only one answer. He was an informant. I tried that annoying police technique — I looked at the DI, smiled, and said nothing.

"Police business," she said at last.

Ah, I was right. Wouldn't it be handy to have someone on the inside feeding you the details you needed in order to solve a case? I wouldn't mind an informant about now who could explain just what I was doing in the middle of an investigation into the murder of a man with whom I hadn't shared a life even when we were married.

"Have you talked with Nick's co-workers?" I had a long list of questions, and although I knew Callow would not answer all, perhaps I could annoy her enough that she would answer one or two.

The DI took another drink of her ale and leaned forward, arms resting on the table. "We've yet to find them. Emails to the Avian Institute of Learning's website have not been returned. The few year-round residents verify Mr. Hawkins was one of them, but kept mostly to himself. Two additional men spent summers there. The residents say Mr. Hawkins left Monday week, five days before he was killed. There was no mobile phone on the body. We've asked police from the Western Isles Area Command to go out and search his digs."

I frantically updated my mental list, amazed that Callow would rattle off answers to questions I hadn't yet asked.

"We can find very little on the AIL," the DI continued. "These days, every man Jack is able to set himself up as an institute. I want to talk with your father about this. I've told him so."

"Rupert isn't a suspect."

"No, we've confirmed his whereabouts for Friday, but he may be able to shed light on the Cambridge end of Mr. Hawkins's life."

Dad could tell me if he'd found anything. Next topic. "Can you do something about those jackals?" I scrambled for my bag. "I can show you what they look like — I snapped a photo through the TIC window this afternoon." I found the photo, held it out to her, and pointed. "It's the same group all the time. It's that large fellow, the twins — they aren't really twins, of course, but they wear the same windcheaters. That's one is kitten woman—"

Callow cut her eyes at me. "You've named them?"

"Well, she has this hand-held recorder with a muff on it to reduce wind noise and her . . ." Perhaps I wouldn't mention that the scratches on her hands made me think she'd been playing with a kitten. I sounded daft enough as it was. "This one — he's the little weasel." I pointed to the last one, cameras round his neck, waistcoat covered in Velcro pockets. "Today, he actually came in the TIC."

Callow's frown was deep. "Did he harass you?"

"I didn't give him the opportunity. I told him to leave or I'd call the police, and that got him moving. Here now, let me send this photo to you."

"No need, we already have it," Callow said, and my hand froze mid-search. "From Mr. Sedgwick."

My heart *thump-thumped*. "Michael sent it to you?"

"We've CCTV from Sunday afternoon outside the station, where you first saw them," the DI said, "but these are no local journalists we know of."

"Michael's gone away," I said in a voice so weak even I had trouble hearing it.

“Yes, and I can tell you firsthand he is frustrated at not being here to sort this out for you to the point he thought he could order the constabulary around, demanding a police guard at your door, insisting we get a no-contact order from the courts.” She picked up her glass and just before taking a drink, added, “He sounded fairly miserable.”

“Did he?” I flushed with pleasure at the thought of Michael as miserable as I.

“I warned him off getting involved, but he wouldn’t hear of it. He insisted, saying he could use his family’s PR firm and its connections to try to track down their identities.”

“And so, you’ve crossed him off your suspect list, right?”

“He’s a suspect until he isn’t,” Callow said. “We continue to look for evidence to show he left the village only minutes after driving in. Yes, he is being helpful, but” — she leaned back and stuck her booted legs out, crossing her feet — “there have been cases where the murderer is most eager to assist the police and therefore send them off track. Of course it’s more common in arson, but not unheard of in this situation.”

I leaned forward. “You can’t be serious? Are you telling me that you actually think that Michael or I am capable of this?”

Her gaze shifted to me, and I saw a bit of iciness melt. “No,” she said. “I know the two of you well enough by now and I have enough sense that I don’t believe that. Too bad, though. We’re remarkably short of suspects.”

My emotions, a tangled-up ball of rubber bands, lodged in my chest. I couldn’t sort out what I truly felt. Michael’s and my conversation had been stilted and caused me such pain, but he’d gone to the police and now was helping them to try to stop those jackals from attacking us me. He’d tried to draw them away and it hadn’t worked, and so he would find another way to protect me.

“Julia?”

I blinked and remembered where I sat — in a pub with Tess Callow.

“He’s concerned about you.”

Please don't be nice to me, I thought, blinking again several more times so that reality came into sharp focus. "Not concerned enough to come home," I said to the table.

Tess looked into her glass as she said, "Sergeant Glossop told me you and Mr. Sedgwick are separated."

"We are not separated," I said hotly. "We're just not . . . he thought this would be better until you find out who killed Nick. But it isn't better at all."

"Might it have been at all possible that Mr. Hawkins had gone to the estate seeking a reconciliation with you?" She kept a close eye on me but leaned back ever so slightly, as if expecting the explosion.

I bit my tongue to keep control, but I despaired at the number of times I'd had to answer what amounted to the same question: *Had Nick wanted you back?* Each time, for a split second I would feel a sliver of sheer terror that perhaps they were right, but common sense followed quickly on. The people asking me this question — Tess, SaraJane, Peg, Gwen — they had not known Nick Hawkins. I had, and I knew better.

"I don't think I explained myself well enough. My marriage to Nick was not . . ." I wondered how I could put this in words that wouldn't make me sound like a person deficient in human emotions.

"Happy?" Tess offered.

"It wasn't happy. It wasn't unhappy. It was a five-year period of nothingness." I shrugged. "Look, I may not know who will win the next World Cup, but I am certain about this — Nick did not come down from St. Kilda to profess his undying love and win me back or to challenge Michael for my affections. His life lay elsewhere."

"Relationships can be complicated," Tess replied and drank her beer.

"How's Chloe?" I threw the question out there more to deflect than to inquire.

She cut her eyes at me and away. I steeled myself for a police rebuke, but she softened. "I wouldn't know."

And now I felt like a heel. “Oh, I’m sorry,” I said. “She seemed quite nice.”

Tess shrugged her shoulder and glanced toward the pub door when it opened. We heard the rumble of a motorbike.

At the sound, I made the connection — why there was no black Volvo parked outside. “Is one of those enormous things out there yours?” I asked.

“I keep meaning to sell the thing — it’s a holdover. Chloe’s favorite way to travel.”

How odd. I could almost be having a fun girls’ night out, commiserating about relationships. My nose went on high alert as another plate of food passed by. I took a tiny leap of faith.

“Look, I’m starving. How’s the food here?”

“All right, I suppose, but I’d steer clear of the curry, if I were you.”

* * *

I ordered two fish suppers at the bar and returned with a second pint for Tess and another cider for me. We began a cautious conversation, which sounded remotely like two new friends.

“. . . And just about the time I moved back home after Nick and I split, Dad had reached an agreement with BBC about the television program, so I added producer to the list of responsibilities as Rupert’s PA.”

“Do you think Mr. Hawkins’s co-workers are also from Cambridge. That he met them at university?”

Tess asked this casually as she popped the last chip into her mouth, and I realized that the conversation had been heavy on my end and light on hers, and that this counted as just another form of questioning. DI Callow couldn’t put work down even when she wanted to.

“Possibly,” I said, “or from one of his bird groups. They were all scientists, and a bit too intense for me, so I didn’t participate.” The only other person I’d known as extreme about birds as Nick was Gavin Lecky, a twitcher — someone who would go to the ends of the earth for a rare sighting. But Gavin was far from the emotional void that described Nick's entire personality. Gavin was hotheaded and passionate about his desires.

* * *

I arrived back to my Pipit Cottage and ignored the silent cold, instead making myself hot cocoa and pulling out my laptop. I swore to myself I wouldn't look at the tabloid headlines, I only wanted to be sure I hadn't missed anything from Dad's schedule before I sent it to him. I would be strong. I would not look.

Boyfriend Runs from Bloody Scene!
Did Julia Set Her Lover Up?
You'll Never Have Her, Cried Murderer!

Well, maybe for only one second.

When, eventually, I found it difficult to lift my hands to the keyboard, I remembered that I'd been awake since four o'clock that morning. I dragged myself up the stairs and stripped. Pulling on Michael's T-shirt, I fell into bed.

But my mind had other ideas and began assembling my to-do list. Smeaton's Summer Supper — organizational meeting tomorrow evening. Update the estate's website. Review film Basil — now associate producer extraordinaire — had sent me. Was the studio booked for Dad's voice-overs?

Michael was looking out for me.

I slept.

* * *

We walked the dunes at Minsmere, the wind off the sea bending the grass, sending the hood on my mackintosh up, and Michael's hair into his eyes. Clouds scuttered across the sky.

With the sea on our left and the sluice ahead of us, we walked in and out of the line of enormous concrete blocks left over from East Anglia's coastal defenses during the Second World War. We meandered along, observing a flock of lapwings soar inland toward the scrape, pausing to watch the konik ponies graze at the edge of the reed beds. Michael wrapped his arms round me from behind and whispered things in my ear. Lovely words.

I awoke to the darkness of my cottage and a sound. What sound? I listened and heard a *thunk* and a scraping. Last year, the cottage door wouldn't open well and the bottom scraped across the stone floor, but it had been repaired. Would the door make that sound again?

"Michael?"

Silence. I held my breath, crept out of bed, and stood on the landing. Below me, nothing moved. I could see the entire place — the outline of furniture, the kitchen, the French doors to the back garden. I could see the front door, closed and chained as I had left it.

A car motored by and I jumped, then sank weakly onto the top step, pulling Michael's T-shirt over my knees. I had been dreaming of Michael and when I awoke, I thought he'd come back. But no, I was still alone. I dragged myself back to bed and stared at the ceiling, waiting for the blackbird to begin its predawn song. At some point I fell back asleep, only to be awakened at six o'clock by actual noise — someone beating on my door and shouting my name.

"Ms. Lanchester! Julia? Are you in there?"

I ran down the stairs. The beating continued, but I paused with my hand hovering over the chain, the stone floor cold underfoot and a chill creeping up my bare legs.

"Who is it?"

"Sergeant Glossop, Ms. Lanchester. Are you all right? Can you open the door?"

"Of course I can open the door," I said, but my voice shook. I dropped the chain and turned the latch as the worst possible events crowded into my mind, each vying for top billing. Dad, Michael, Linus — who, what?

I pulled open the door, and Glossop put his hand out like a traffic cop.

"Don't come out, Ms. Lanchester. Step back."

The door swung in wide and I saw, protruding from its center and covered with an all-too-familiar reddish-brown substance, a long, slender knife.

CHAPTER 14

Police poured in — Glossop, Callow, PC Flynn, and three other uniforms. I didn't move and watched as if from a distance, like one of those out-of-body experiences you hear about. I saw two plainclothes men stop at the door, pull on gloves, and begin to examine the knife. I shivered from the cold air that came in with them, and Callow tried to lead me away, but I refused to budge when I heard one of the men suggesting they remove the entire door and take it with them. I heard myself shouting something about destruction of private property and how this was a Grade II-listed building and I'd have Historic England down their throats in a second if they touched a single hinge. That was when Tess suggested I go upstairs and dress.

PC Flynn stood at my bedroom door when I came out, straightening the skirt on my uniform. She smiled encouragingly, then dropped the smile in favor of a neutral police face. Just like Natty Glossop — how sweet. Those two were a pair, weren't they?

"You've been questioning the people at the funeral, haven't you?" I asked her. Her eyes darted down to the kitchen. "It's all right. DI Callow told me that."

"Oh, yes, ma'am, I have. And door-to-door as well. Asking if anyone saw something unusual. Showing everyone a photo of the vic — Mr. Hawkins."

Door-to-door meant the Stoat and Hare plus the line of cottages that ran up the lane to the church, as well as Hoggin Hall.

"Have you found out anything?"

She wrinkled her nose. "I'm afraid not. Seems everyone had a grand old time that afternoon but didn't pay much attention to anything else. Sorry."

"Yeah, thanks."

I peered over the banister at the crowd in the kitchen and sitting room. It looked as if we were trying to best the record for the number of people crammed into a red phone box. Linus had arrived and stood examining the hole in the door. Police had removed the knife, but left the door, thank God. Commuter traffic on the high street crawled by, giving everyone a good view into my cottage.

Nuala busied herself in the kitchen making tea. She looked, as always, like a dancer, wearing black flats and long, full skirt, her wiry black hair streaked with gray and somewhat secured in a bun. Sergeant Glossop guarded the table which held two plates of hot cross buns studded with sultanas. Other sundry police loitered nearby.

"Julia." Linus rushed up to me. "You're all right, aren't you?"

"Yes, thank you, I'm fine."

Tess finished a phone call and came over.

"Who did this?" I asked her. "Is that the knife that killed Nick?"

"The knife fits what we're looking for, but we won't know for certain until we've examined it further." Tested the blood, that's what she meant. "I need you to tell me what happened."

"Tea's ready," Nuala called over in a stage whisper.

I looked at Tess, and she nodded. "The rest of you are finished here," she said to her team, checking her watch. "I'll see you at the station for the briefing at nine o'clock."

I noticed a bit of foot dragging and I knew the reason. "Why don't you all take a bun with you," I suggested. "That's all right, isn't it, Nuala?"

It wasn't that I was being overly generous. I had counted buns and counted police and knew that those of us staying behind would come out ahead.

Nuala passed a plate, and the rest of us settled at the table. When I took my first sip of tea, I felt the world begin to right itself. I tore open a bun, breathed in the scent of cinnamon orange peel before stuffing a piece in my mouth and licking off the icing that remained on my fingers. I felt eyes on me and glanced up to see Callow, Glossop, Linus, and Nuala standing silently. Waiting.

I took another drink of tea before I began. "I woke up in the night, about three-thirty, because I'd heard a noise. I thought it was the door. I thought" — I had thought it was Michael — "and so I got up and looked. I'd put the chain on and all. There was no one there." I tore off another hunk of roll, but before I filled my mouth, I asked Callow, "How did you know about it?"

"We got a tip," she replied. "At 4:23 this morning."

"Another anonymous call?"

"This time a text. From Mr. Hawkins's mobile."

* * *

Although I went over my story again, we gained no new information. I saw nothing, no one who passed saw anything, the village had no CCTV — that was a modernization Linus had resisted, insisting, "I will not spy on my tenants." I could see that changing soon.

In return, DI Callow told me that they'd not yet been able to trace the text from Nick's phone. Whoever used it had switched it on and then off again.

"Julia, why are you wearing your uniform?" Linus asked as Inspector Callow and her sergeant examined the French doors, and I boxed up one of the remaining buns for my morning tea break and one more, just in case. "You can't think of going into work today."

"I can and I will." I attempted to sound confident, not defiant. Linus was a dear friend who had put up with a great deal and he was my employer. "How could there be any safer place than in plain sight — in public with ramblers and picnickers and archaeology students continually streaming in and out of the TIC?"

"Well . . ." His hesitancy told me he saw the logic in my argument. Then he continued. "I want you to come stay at the Hall."

"I'm perfectly safe here. Really, Linus, I live on the high street. This was only someone trying to scare me, that's all." Someone with the murder weapon, I added to myself. I so wanted to blame this on the journos and get them out of my hair for good but couldn't quite figure out how to turn it on them. And then an idea struck.

"Tess?" I called and saw Sergeant Glossop take note of my casual tone.

"Inspector," I corrected myself, "wouldn't it be just like one of those journos to do something like this? Perhaps it's all a prank, and it won't be the actual knife. Or if it is, maybe one of them ran across it. If they found evidence and kept it from you, that would be a crime, wouldn't it? You could arrest the lot of them." I liked this idea.

"Or perhaps the murderer left you his own message," Tess said. "You've thought of that one, too, haven't you?"

"You see there, Julia," Linus said, pouncing on this. "The inspector is right." He turned to Callow. "I believe Julia should move into the Hall for the time being."

"*No!*" I took a deep breath. As fond as I was of Linus and the butler, Thorne, and housekeeper-cook Sheila Bugg, I had no desire to reenact my residence at the Hall that had lasted for months the previous summer and autumn. "I'm sorry, Linus, but I won't. I live here. I won't be frightened away."

We both looked to Callow to act as judge. Her eyes moved from us, around my cottage, out the window to the street. I followed her gaze and saw Alfie on a chimney across the road. Tennyson must be in school already. It was time for me to open the TIC.

"Right," Tess said. "I'll put a foot patrol on in the village during the day, and a patrol car will come through regularly overnight."

"Well, if the police are on it," Linus said, looking defeated.

"Thank you, Inspector," I said, relief rushing through me, because I wouldn't be put in a cage and watched. "Thank you, Linus. We can't let our visitors down. It's spring, the estate has so much to offer, and I've loads of work to do to get ready for upcoming events. The farmers market is less than a week away. Oh, and there's a meeting in the church hall this evening for the summer supper."

All eyebrows rose. Linus opened his mouth, but before he could speak, Tess filled in. "We'll have someone there."

"Yes, right, good idea," I said. "You never know what those chefs might get up to."

I took up my bag to leave, but stopped at the centuries-old oak door, which still stood open with a PC on guard outside on the pavement. I took a close look at the gouge the knife had left.

"We'll need to get some wood filler," I said. Dad loved these DIY projects — perhaps I could ask him to do it. Dad.

"Linus, Inspector — you won't say anything to Rupert about this, will you? There's really no need to worry him, because I'm all right. Everything's fine."

They exchanged glances, and Tess gave a single nod, conceding my victory.

"For the time being," she said.

* * *

I unlocked the TIC door and turned the sign to Open. I had left the cottage only when satisfied that the DI would keep this incident from not only Dad, but also Michael. Tess pursed her lips at this but hadn't said no, and I left the cottage with the conviction that, if Michael were watching out for me, I would do the same for him. He was away in Exeter, and there was no need to make him worry from afar. Although, I knew the absence of worry wasn't enough. Michael had taken action to protect me. I should take action, too. But what?

The morning started just the way I liked it with the sun shining and several phone calls easily taken care of — people asking about campsites over the Easter holiday, which seemed to be flying toward us, only the next weekend but one. I switched the kettle on, feeling almost optimistic until I remembered the knife sticking out of my cottage door.

I shook the thought out of my head, and when the bell jingled, looked up in happy anticipation of greeting a rambler. Instead, Thorne walked in.

The sight of the butler in his black suit and with his cotton-ball hair caused me to lose my train of thought. I couldn't recall that he'd ever set foot in the TIC before, and I was poised to take an immediate leap to the conclusion something else had happened. But he smiled at me — a reassuring, "don't-worry-a-fig" sort of smile.

"Good morning, Thorne," I said, coming round the counter. "This is a lovely surprise. What brings you to the TIC?"

"Good morning, Ms. Lanchester," he said as he admired the wall of maps and leaflets. "As it happens, I needed to collect an item from the chemist and I thought, as I was so close to you, I would put my head in and say hello."

I didn't buy it for one moment.

"Linus sent you, did he?"

Thorne's shoulders stiffened slightly. "You are quite important to us, you know," he said. "To everyone here on the estate."

"Yes, all right," I said. "Would you like a cup of tea and a hot cross bun?" I knew the extra one would come in handy.

"I wouldn't want to disturb you," he said with a hopeful tone.

"Nonsense, come round." Out the window, I saw two uniformed PCs stroll by across the road. Right, everyone on duty.

As I poured out our tea, I glanced at the computer screen and noticed six emails from the BBC had come in, two others with "Rupert speaking engagement offer" in the subject line, and one with "problem with electrics for farmers market."

I closed the lid and, over tea, Thorne and I caught up on all the estate gossip, nimbly avoiding any mention of Nick Hawkins.

* * *

I waited until ten thirty to ring Dad, beginning the conversation cautiously. But there was no need, because I could tell from his tone he knew nothing about the early-morning events. We settled into our meeting but had made it only halfway through the agenda when the five-year-olds class from the village school trooped in looking adorable in their uniforms. They came bearing gifts — crayon drawings titled "Our Walk with Willow in the Wood," the results of an outing the previous week. I ended my conversation with Dad and spent the next hour taping up pictures of copper beeches that looked like enormous clouds of pink candy floss, robins bigger than sheep, and, in one case, what I was told was a boa constrictor.

Before lunch, while I engaged in a rather heated phone conversation with someone at Health and Safety about hand-washing facilities at the farmers market, Sheila Bugg arrived, her brown hair swept up into an untidy bun, and wearing her usual quasi-uniform of plain dress in a dark hue. She carried a large brown paper bag.

"I've been cooking such a heap of food these last two evenings — I've not quite adjusted to the fact that the young master and Willow aren't sitting down to dinner these days. I was hoping you could help me out." She held up the bag.

"Well, you've come to the right place to leave extra food, haven't you?" I took the bag and couldn't resist a peek. "There's certainly a fair bit."

"Just a beef sandwich for your lunch and chicken and the rest of the roast potatoes. And a bit of rhubarb crumble."

We sat down over mugs of tea, and Sheila reached over and patted my hand. "You've had a terrible shock."

"I'm all right. Really," I said, my voice catching in my throat.

"And you're working too hard to cover it up," Sheila said. "You look a bit . . . peaky."

I couldn't continue to blame the lighting for the dark circles under my eyes.

"I'll be fine. Linus doesn't need to order you all to keep an eye on me, you know."

"His Lordship doesn't order us anywhere, you know that. It's only that he wanted to look in on you himself, but realized he had a meeting up near Diss today. He nearly canceled until Thorne said we'd pop round and see how you're doing. I think it eased his mind." Sheila glanced out the window to see the PCs stroll by outside the window. "And that'll ease his mind as well."

* * *

My sister rang, but swamped as I was with a constant stream of visitors, I couldn't talk. Good thing, too, because I always told Bee everything, but I couldn't tell her what had happened at my cottage. Not yet.

Amid the normal visitor foot traffic into the TIC, the cavalcade of Linus's spies continued. Midafternoon, Akash walked down from his shop to tell me Vesta had arrived in New Zealand and Debra was doing fine, which he could easily have done by text. Nuala returned my cottage key. Between friendly visits and PCs on patrol, I was beginning to feel claustrophobic.

It was a relief when Tennyson and Alfie arrived in the late afternoon. She held the door open for the rook, and he flew straight past me to my mackintosh with a beakful of something dark. My pocketful of treasures could wait. Tennyson carried a pink bakery box, and I knew what lay within.

I switched the kettle on and dropped tea bags into the pot while the girl told me about Alfie's latest triumph.

"Mum writes out her ironing schedule for the week on a card and she'd set it on the fridge, but it slipped off and fell behind. She couldn't reach it, but Alfie had been watching, so I said, 'Let's see if Alfie can get it,' because, you see, I'd watched a video online. We had a bit of wire that had been holding one of the windows shut. I gave the wire to Alfie, and he took it and bent it so there was a hook on the end. He put it in his beak and dragged the card out from behind the fridge. Along with a bit of my toast from breakfast that he'd hidden there."

"That's quite good problem-solving, Alfie," I said to the rook. He nodded his head and dropped a custard cream into his tea.

I finished up my chocolate cake while I took a call from one of the chefs canceling out of the meeting that evening, because of an emergency at his upscale bistro in Stoke-by-Claire. He begged me to keep him on the list and made abundant promises to bring samples of his wild mushroom risotto to the next meeting. I told him I'd allow it this time, just as the bell above the door jingled and Gwen walked in.

Tennyson ran to her mother, who hugged her, losing one of her tiny hair clips in the effort. That sent a short, straight hank of hair across her forehead. Alfie skipped out to the counter and chortled.

"These two keeping you from your work?" she asked, one arm around her daughter, the other holding an enormous cloth bag stuffed with fabric.

"Not a bit of it," I said. "I enjoy their visits."

"Look now, Ten," Gwen said to her daughter, giving the bag a shake, "curtains and sheets from Mrs. Collier on Mill Street. How do you like that? A new customer. Now then, Dot's waiting for you. She's got a few things her granddaughter has grown out of and they might just fit you. Let's leave Julia to finish her work. On your way now, you and Alfie, and I'll nip down to the shop and catch you up in a bit."

Girl and bird said goodbye, and I stood out on the pavement with Gwen to watch them as they walked and strutted off in the spring sunshine. They stopped and looked carefully both ways when they came to the corner where the road that led to their flat above The Holly and the Ivy before crossing to continue up the high street.

"Tennyson told me of Alfie's latest feat — retrieving lost items lost from behind the fridge. He's a smart one, that bird."

"Mmm," Gwen replied. "Although he gets funny ideas in that brain of his. Lately, he's taken against any of us that go into the shed out back of the pub. He perches right on the corner of the roof and complains something fierce when we haul a bag of rubbish or kitchen peelings out that way to the bins. Today, when Peg opened the shed door, Alfie flew straight in."

"Maybe he's a hoarder and that's where he keeps his trinkets. He's left me a few," I said.

Gwen laughed. "Yesterday, I found five acorns stuck in the middle of a stack of bedsheets. But he's a good companion to my Tennyson, and she needs that right now. Although I dearly wish she had a few human friends as well."

* * *

Gwen continued to the shop, and I returned to work, jotting down a note at the bottom of my agenda with Dad. Truly, he would love this whole Alfie business, and what fun it would be for Tennyson to see her own rook on the telly.

I stared at the computer screen, hoping to get my brain back in gear, gazing at the long list of emails to return and attempting to refresh my memory on the topics for the Smeaton's Summer Supper meeting. It had grown quiet — the TIC, the high street — and given a moment of quiet, my energy level plunged to the floor. I let my mind drift. Nothing from Callow or Glossop about the knife. No journos today. Perhaps the presence of the police had scared them off. Had

Michael identified them? Michael was looking out for me. What would I do for him?

My phone rang and I jumped.

"Hello, Julia, SaraJane here. Baz has sent you the link to all those segments. Sorry it's late, but he wanted to edit the film of the kingfisher nest down to the best bits."

"Fantastic, please tell him thanks. I'm talking to Rupert later, and we'll get back to you both about what else is needed. Basil is doing such a fine job."

"Yeah, he is, isn't he? Right well, we'll see you in the morning, won't we? Basil's hoping for sun. We think there are adders about, and wouldn't it be fantastic to get some film?"

"It would indeed." Adders — there's one bit of wildlife I would prefer to see on film rather than in person. Perhaps the adder would wait until I'd left Marshy End to make its appearance.

"Look," SaraJane said, "did you have everything you needed in that packet I gave you? Michael told me what to print off, and I know I was supposed to give it to him, but as you've taken over . . ." Her voice drifted off as she no doubt remembered my troubles.

Packet. Yes, SaraJane had given me a packet the previous morning at Marshy End. Just drop it in my car, I had said, and then I had proceeded to forget all about it. What was it — filming schedule? Crew lists? Potential sponsors for workshops?

"I'm sorry I haven't had a second to go over it, but I'll do so immediately and let you know."

"No worries," SaraJane replied.

Plenty of worries.

Ten minutes to five, I nipped out of the TIC and to my car, parked just round the turn in the road. I saw nothing at first, but after practically standing on my head, I at last spied the corner of a large brown envelope, which had slipped under the driver's seat. It had some heft to it, and I managed to tear off a corner as I pulled it out. A sharp shower came out of nowhere, and I hugged the envelope to my chest to keep it dry as I dashed back round the corner to find the two PCs on foot patrol standing in front of the TIC, one of them talking into a radio clipped to his shoulder.

"Hello!" I called, running up to them. "Here I am — were you looking for me?"

"Cancel that," he said to the radio. "She has been located. Repeat, Julia Lanchester has been located. She appears unharmed."

The rain did nothing to cool my burning face. I sounded like a lost dog.

"I'm sorry, I only popped round the corner to my car."

"Ma'am, you shouldn't leave the door unlocked with no one attending," the other PC said. "How long were you away?"

"A minute — two. Really, it's nothing." I made to pull the door open, but he barred my way.

"Let us to take a look round, first. All right?"

"Yes, fine." The rain caught in my eyelashes. The high street was just beginning to fill up with traffic, and I could see the woman who ran the chemist shop across the road peering through her window. I smiled and waved, hoping she would think this a community awareness event or something. The PCs walked into the TIC, and I followed. "Don't worry," I said when they turned abruptly. "I'll stand here and wait."

After one minute, the first PC said, "The area is secure, ma'am." Of course it was — I could've told them that from the front door. The only place that couldn't be seen at all times was the loo, and they'd checked that. Twice.

"Thank you. And again, I'm sorry, but I did only step away for a moment."

"You must be aware of your surroundings at all times. It's really the best way to stay safe."

Oh God, not a safety lecture, please — I had work to do. "Yes, right, well then, it's closing time." I nodded to the clock. "I'll lock the door right after you, shall I? Unless you'd like a cup of tea?"

They declined, although regretfully, I thought, when they saw the shower gathering strength, raindrops bouncing off the pavement. I threw the latch and turned the sign to Closed as I watched them make their way up the high street toward my cottage.

I shook out my damp cardigan and laid it on the back of a chair, then switched on both the kettle and plug-in radiator, before opening the envelope. SaraJane had gone to the trouble of giving me the packet, and the least I could do was to sound coherent about it next time I talked with her.

The envelope contained papers that really had nothing to do with me. Michael had asked SaraJane to print off the applications received for the first grant to be awarded by the Rupert Lanchester Foundation. Michael had worked so hard to get this going. Not that Dad's foundation was the Heritage Lottery Fund by any means, so it wouldn't be awarding millions of pounds. But the foundation would give up to one hundred thousand pounds for the first grant — an amazing sum, and all down to Michael's tireless work. I remembered that he had not wanted to look at any one application without seeing them all at once, and he'd expected to have them in hand at the meeting he'd scheduled on Friday last. The day we met at the coast. He'd been quite put out that all the paperwork hadn't been ready. It hadn't been SaraJane's fault it wasn't, but some last-minute updates. Is that what he had said?

I forgot about the work in front of me and settled at the table with a mug of tea to peruse the applications. Each sounded worthy of the money — a learning lab hut for Boy Scouts; a hedgehog flyover on a busy roadway; a wildlife biology teacher's salary; a new ornithological research station near St. Margaret's at Cliffe in Kent. My eyes passed over and then shot back to the requester.

Avian Institute of Learning — AIL. Nick Hawkins's very own institute.

CHAPTER 15

My heart stopped and restarted with a *ka-thunk* as I stared at those letters. AIL. That was Nick's invention, the reason he'd left for St. Kilda, the reason we'd put our marriage out of its misery — a marriage so boring I had felt half-asleep for its entire, albeit brief, lifespan. Now I understood why Nick had been here in Smeaton. He had wanted money from Rupert.

That wasn't an unfamiliar situation, but one I had never wanted to examine too closely. I turned to the first page of the grant and began reading again. After a moment, I frowned, and went once more to the beginning.

Where was Nick's name? Amid all the requirements of the grant application — statement of purpose, intent of use, signatories and references and qualifications and promises — I found two names: AIL Directors Terry Fisk and Sam Redman. I crawled through the pages again, setting my finger on each word so not one would escape, yet I found not a single mention of Nick Hawkins.

I began yet again — I'd have the thing memorized soon — this time attending to the application itself. Perhaps this was a different AIL. Nick certainly hadn't been living in Kent all these years, far too populated for him. At last, I saw the phrase "relocate from St. Kilda to . . ." I got no further when my phone rang. For a moment, I couldn't remember where I was until I saw the caller. Dad.

"Jools, will you take a look in my study when you're at Marshy End tomorrow morning? I thought I'd brought my journal from autumn 2004 away with me, but I can't find it anywhere, and I need to check on migration dates for sand martins. Ring me from there, and I'll walk you through it."

"Righto," I said.

"And listen, I'm ready for the phone interview with Radio Norfolk tomorrow morning, but I'd prefer they ring me first. I want to make sure I've got my broadcasting setup ready to go."

This was good — Rupert launching into business meant he hadn't heard about the knife in my cottage door. He didn't know both Vesta and Willow were gone and I was doing two jobs at once. I scrambled to bring up the agenda on my computer, shifting the grant applications out of sight, but certainly not out of mind. Should I tell him? Should I ring Callow first? Should Michael know?

"Jools?"

"Yes, Dad, I'm on it. I'll let them know to ring you ten minutes before. How's that?"

"You're doing all right, aren't you?"

"I'm fine, of course. It'll be no problem." Had Nick lost his job with the institute? But how could he lose his job if he'd started the bloody thing?

An email popped in as Rupert started on another topic. I glanced at the subject line, and my blood ran cold — "Final number for your Walking Festival event."

I had made sure Smeaton-under-Lyme would not be left in the dust of the Suffolk Walking Festival. I had offered to lead a birding walk around Hoggin Hall beginning at eight o'clock and ending at eleven, to be followed by a breakfast in the Hall. Nuala had offered to open the café early, especially for the event. The email confirmed I would have thirty-two people in my group and everyone looking forward to it.

It was taking place tomorrow morning.

How did I forget this? I had been so careful to merge the TIC schedule with my duties as Rupert's PA. True, I had initially counted on Vesta to be here to catch all the hours I had to be away. But Vesta was gone, and somewhere along the way, the fact that I was to be at both Marshy End for filming and at Hoggin Hall on a bird walk at the same time had become lost in my brain.

No, wait. Make that three places at once, because who would open the TIC in my absence? Not Vesta, not Willow, not Akash.

I envisioned the Closed sign on the center and a queue of potential visitors that reached all the way to Sudbury, each person tapping an impatient foot on the pavement and complaining about Lord Fotheringill, titled gentry, thinking he could do this to the public. I couldn't breathe.

". . . I'm prepared to admit I'm amazed as you are about Basil. Michael has really brought him along, you know. And so, what do you think?"

Dad's comments had entered my ear but not my brain. A few words stumbled out of my mouth, incomprehensible words.

"Julia, what's wrong?" The alarm in his voice brought some sense to me.

"Fine, I'm fine. Really." Not fine. "It's only that, I may have made a little slip-up."

He was my dad, after all — who else could I tell? I spilled the beans, and then toward the end, tried to clean it up a bit.

"But you know, it's all going quite well otherwise. This is only one little mistake I made." My voice shook, and I cleared my throat to regain control. "I'll have to keep the TIC closed until eleven. I'll explain it all to Linus tomorrow. And as for Marshy End . . ."

Rupert was, shall we say, not happy that I'd kept the news about Vesta from him. He demanded to know how I ever thought I could carry on with two full-time jobs while also carrying the burden of what happened to Nick.

"Have you talked with Michael?" I asked.

Dad sighed, and I heard a scratching sound. He was rubbing his hand over his face — I knew the gesture well. "Michael wanted to give you time to get through this, Jools. He didn't mean for you to wear yourself out."

"I thought Michael left to keep those journos away," I said. "Are they still hanging about?"

I didn't have the strength to continue this dance, and besides, I'd just seen the time — almost seven o'clock. *Get a grip, Julia.*

"Look, Dad, I'm going to let Basil take the filming and I'll keep the TIC closed until I return from the walk. There — all sorted. Now, I've got a meeting tonight for the summer supper."

"You can't keep this up, Julia."

"Did you see the film Basil made of the wren nest?"

* * *

The showers had passed, and it was a dry walk to the church hall. As I hurried up the lane past the Stoat and Hare, I rang Basil and told him of his windfall — an opportunity to be executive producer for the morning. He was chuffed, as well he should have been.

As I approached the church hall, I saw ahead of me a figure waiting. My feet slowed, but my pulse sped up, until I realized who it was.

"PC Flynn," I whispered. "I forgot someone would be here." I noted with relief that she was out of uniform, wearing dark trousers and a smart, teal-colored sweater that set off her red curls.

"Hiya, Julia," a voice behind me called. Here came Fred from the pub laden with an enormous box out of which wafted a scent of lemon and garlic.

"Fred, let me get this door open for you." I found the key and shoved it in the lock. "Oh, and this is . . ."

"Hello, good evening," PC Flynn said with great cheer. "I'm Moira Flynn."

Fred peered at the PC. "Are you the PC who came asking about . . . ?" He stopped and cut his eyes at me.

"I'm only giving Julia a hand this evening," Moira said. "Can I help you with that?"

"Yeah, thanks."

And so PC Flynn adeptly sidestepped any impression of a police presence, and she'd get a free meal out of it and all.

Our Smeaton's Summer Supper organizational meeting at the church hall could've been subtitled the Great Suffolk Cook-Off — five chefs came with examples of their dishes, explaining that by August, the asparagus would be replaced by courgettes and the tomatoes wouldn't be from Israel. We ate and talked menus and logistics, and PC Flynn became quite taken with the idea of pork roulade and asked about how to roll up the meat.

Throughout the meeting, although I ate and talked and made notes, I was truly elsewhere. Half my mind lay with my bollocksed morning and the other half with the grant application from AIL that made no mention of its founder Nick Hawkins. Who were these other two men, and did they have something to do with Nick's death?

Past ten o'clock, we all said good night, and Moira and I walked back down into the heart of the village.

"Thanks for not making a big thing about why you were here," I said.

When we came to my Pipit Cottage, Moira stopped, but I kept going.

"I've only a bit more to do at the TIC," I explained. "But you can go on. I'll be fine, really."

She followed me down the high street until we reached the tourist center. A police car with its blue-and-yellow Battenberg squares painted on the side pulled up to the curb.

"We don't mind waiting until you're safe in your own home with the latch thrown and the chain on. And I believe they've installed a security bar on your French doors. Just to put your mind at rest."

It hadn't occurred to me that someone would go the effort to run through the field behind the terraced row of cottages, leap over the back hedge and crash through my French doors. It seemed a bit extreme.

"Right, well I won't be long. Just tidy up my workspace."

PC Flynn got in the police car, and I made a show of locking myself into the TIC so they'd see. I grabbed the stack of grant applications and looked at AIL's proposal again in case Nick's name had magically appeared while I'd been away. No, only Terry Fisk and Sam Redman. I went through every sheet of paper to the end and saw that an email had been tacked on.

"We will be staying locally while you consider the application and would be available at your convenience to answer any further questions and discuss our plans. We appreciate this opportunity to re-focus our efforts on climate change and its effects on migration."

They shouldn't have done that. The grant application guidelines called strictly for no personal contact — this might look as if the applicant wanted to try a bribe or some other form of persuasion. And yet, here were Terry Fisk and Sam Redman offering themselves up to be questioned. They'd included a mobile number — the same one as in the application.

The police were looking for the AIL, and I had found them. I should hand this over directly to Callow. But Michael had gone out on a limb to protect me. He'd talked the police into letting him investigate the journos. I needed to participate in this effort. I wanted to do something for him — something to make it easier and quicker for him to return.

I reached for my phone.

Don't lie about who you are, I told myself as I punched the code that would hide my mobile number. I couldn't be that deceptive, because I wouldn't have the nerve to keep it up. No, I couldn't lie.

"Hello," a male voice said.

"Hello, good evening, I'm SaraJane from the Rupert Lanchester Foundation. Am I speaking to Terry Fisk or Sam Redman?"

I heard scuffling, voices in the background, the sound of a glass scraping across a table and the general din of a pub.

"This is Terry, yeah. I'm here with Sam right now."

"I'm sorry to be ringing so late, it's only that we'd like to move things along, and as you'd offered to answer any further questions 'at our convenience,' I believe you said, I was hoping we could get these things sorted out."

"Sure, yes, of course, we're happy to talk with you."

"Great, lovely," I said, thinking Terry Fisk sounded a bit too eager. "Well, obviously not at this late hour. Why don't we meet tomorrow, say" — it would take me the better part of an hour after closing to get to Cambridge — "six o'clock? And let's make it someplace casual. Do you know The Eagle?"

If they had been students at Cambridge along with Nick they most certainly would know the pub.

"We do, yeah. That's great. We can bring along the stats we've gathered on migration changes of five species for the past three years. It's only a beginning, but—"

"Ah, no thanks, Terry. Not this time. This'll be just a casual chat over a pint. See you tomorrow."

I ended the call before he could start in on a lecture about the migratory patterns of cuckoos and sat tapping my mobile against my chin.

Why had I done that — rung them and arranged a meeting? Because I was uniquely qualified to interview them, that's why. It certainly couldn't hurt anything, and I'd turn all information over to the police after. I pulled over a pad of paper and began making notes, my energy and power growing with each point.

Terry Fisk and Sam Redman made no mention of Nick Hawkins. Why?

Did Nick know of these plans to move the AIL from the Outer Hebrides to Kent?

Had Nick tried to put a stop to it by coming to tell me or Michael?

When Terry and Sam got wind of it, did they put a stop to Nick for good?

If Nick had wanted to blow the whistle on his AIL pals, why didn't he just ring Rupert?

When I met them the next evening at The Eagle pub in Cambridge, would I be SaraJane or Julia?

CHAPTER 16

When at last I emerged onto the pavement, Moira hopped out of the patrol car. She waited while I taped a sign up on the door of the TIC, apologizing profusely that the center would not open until eleven o'clock on Friday, and then escorted me up the high street as the car crept along behind us. The PC took a quick look round the inside of my cottage and showed me the security bar on the French doors before walking out and standing on the pavement.

"All safe now," I said. "Good night," I waved at the car before closing the door and sliding the chain.

I made myself a half mug of cocoa with the last of the milk, washed out a blouse and two pairs of tights, and left them hanging in the kitchen to dry.

* * *

Sleep came in tiny doses. I awoke at every noise, imagined or not, and spent my waking moments wishing I'd brought the AIL grant application home with me. I had, instead, stashed it under our desk at the TIC. When before dawn, I heard the blackbird start up, I rose, went downstairs, and peered out the front window to see a strip of red light along the horizon in the east. The beginning of the day, and plenty of time to iron my blouse and set out my uniform for a quick change between the tour and the TIC's late opening. I had switched the kettle on before I remembered I had no milk, and so switched it off again, after which I struggled to get the security bar off the French doors so that I could get into the back garden and refill the feeders. After that, I checked my watch to find my excess time had vanished.

The walk to the Hall took twenty minutes, but I made it in fifteen, hoping I'd have enough energy left for a two-hour stroll and talk. I could've driven, but whereas my feet took me to a path that led around the back of the Hall, my car would've taken me down the drive and past the trail that led to the summer-house. I'd no desire to return there. I had a triple layer of clothes on, because it was always a bit chilly first thing in the morning in mid-April. We had a clear sky and the air smelled clean. I pulled in a deep breath as I came out of the wood at the bottom of the garden and saw the walkers had already begun to gather.

Behind us, a hedgerow held the promise of chaffinches and robins and perhaps returning whitethroats if we were lucky. Impossible to schedule the birds to appear, but I would fill the time with talk about habitat, and we'd enjoy the sun. I'd count it lucky if we heard a green woodpecker. God, I was dying for a cup of tea.

I chatted with each arrival, smiling and ticking their names off my list, until, just after eight, it was time to start.

"Hello, good morning," I said to the group. "I'm Julia Lanchester. Welcome to the Fotheringill estate and the grounds of Hoggin Hall. Lord Fotheringill makes a special effort to encourage our native wildlife here on the estate, and I hope you'll enjoy our walking tour today. Please let me know if you have any questions as we go along. Just shout them out."

"Will we be taking a tour of the entire grounds round the Hall, or is part of it off-limits?"

I froze, and a thick silence fell on the group. Here it was — the one thing I'd hoped to avoid. But I wouldn't let them draw me in. I would take the high road.

"We've lots to see this morning, and I certainly hope to cover as much—"

My words faltered when a commotion at the back drew everyone's attention. Had the journos shown up? I plunged my hand into my pocket to call the police when I saw a hat — wide-brimmed, beaten-up leather — and the person wearing it.

"It's Rupert!" exclaimed an older woman, sweeping the knit cap off her frizzy gray hair and waving it round as if a royal procession were passing by.

"Good morning," Dad called, smiling broadly. "Welcome, good morning." He shook each person's hand as they all drew forward. "Glorious weather, isn't it? Will we see a yellowhammer today — what do you think? How are you? Lovely to see you here."

And so he made his way to me and I could only watch, as taken in by the magic as the next person. Although I couldn't keep the smile from my face as he walked up to me, I had to point out "You're meant to be talking to Radio Norfolk right now."

"I put them off until Monday and promised an autographed bird box." His jovial demeanor faded as he scanned my face. He put his hand to my cheek, and said, "My dear daughter, you cannot do this alone."

My nerves were that shot, that tears filled my eyes and overflowed within a second. I turned my head away, and Rupert spread his arms to the crowd.

"Well, I hope we've given you a pleasant surprise. You're probably already aware of what my daughter Julia Lanchester, does here on the Fotheringill estate. You've heard about the big plans for the second annual Smeaton's Summer Supper — just try saying that three times fast. Did any of you attend last year? Tables down the high street, the top chefs in the county, the best wines — and to top it off, the earl uses all the proceeds for renovations on the pensioners cottages."

"I'll take two tickets," someone called from the back to general laughter.

"Steady on," Rupert replied. "Tickets on sale—" He looked at me.

"June first," I said, hoping that would be true.

"So, now, although Julia is well able to lead this outing herself, I begged her to let me step in. That is, if you'll have me?"

There was a round of cheers and clapping, followed by a woman saying, "But Julia, you'll come along, too?"

More clapping, and I waved them quiet.

"You know, I believe I'll leave you in Rupert's hands this morning, if that's all right. But mind that you don't let him have first go at the baps when you've finished with the walk, or there'll be no breakfast left for the rest of you."

They chuckled and began speaking to one another and popping the lens covers off their binoculars. Rupert hadn't taken his eyes off me.

"I'm all right," I said quietly. "It's only that I haven't had my tea." I threw my arms round him, and he gave me a kiss on the cheek. I heard applause. "Thanks, Dad," I whispered.

* * *

I blew my nose and fluffed my hair before I tapped on the kitchen door at the Hall. Sheila looked out the window, smiled, and nodded toward the door.

"Now why ever would you need to ask permission to come into this kitchen?" she asked as I walked in. But one swift glance and she took my arm. "Here now, you sit down."

"Why is everyone treating me as if I'm an invalid? I'm not ill, I'm fine." Still, I did as I was told. Sheila set a mug of tea in front of me.

"Have you taken a good look at yourself lately?"

My hand went up to my bob. "I need a haircut," I suggested.

"You're exhausted," Shelia countered. "You look as if you're carrying the weight of the world on your shoulders."

"I had no milk this morning," I insisted. "I only need a cup of tea. And maybe a slice of toast?"

And a plate of scrambled eggs, followed by a second cup of tea. The morning had taken a turn for the better, rescued by my dad and a good breakfast. After that, I still had plenty of time to stop at my cottage, change clothes, and get to the TIC in time to open. I was a renewed woman.

* * *

The first round of visitors had been sent on their way walking out to the abbey ruins, followed by a stop at Adam Bugg's cider orchard, which opened on one Friday afternoon a month. I wrote up notes from the summer supper meeting, finishing just as the bell jingled and Dad walked in.

"Look now," he said, holding a paper bag out, "Nuala wouldn't let me leave without sending these rock buns along. How about a cup of tea?"

"Fantastic." I led him round the counter and positioned him at the table with his back to the window — and just in time, too, as the PC foot patrol strolled past. I wouldn't want him asking what they were doing in the village. Rupert leaned back in the chair with his legs stretched out. His relaxed manner told me Linus had remained silent about the knife incident, and I didn't see any point in setting Dad off on a worry jag.

"How was the tour?"

"I'd say it was worth the price of a ticket," he said. "We spotted a firecrest. I believe they're nesting in that ancient apple tree toward the brook. I took Thorne out after the breakfast so he could see."

"I had wanted to show Michael a firecrest at Minsmere." I set our mugs of tea down and slid into a chair as my spirits sagged. "He's in Exeter. Did you know he's working for Miles again?"

"Jools, he isn't gone for good."

"Why wouldn't he be? He's only just realized what an unfeeling person I am — barely showing emotion at Nick's death. Doesn't speak well of me, does it?" I broke off a hunk of rock bun and tossed it in my mouth, ashamed at my exhibition of self-pity.

"I won't have it." Dad wagged a finger at me. "I won't have you thinking this of yourself."

Yes, stop with the wallowing, Julia. I grabbed the sugar bowl and held it out with a smile. "I do sound ridiculous, don't I? Here you are. Let's enjoy our tea."

I saw emotions fly over his face like clouds in a sturdy wind — his brows furrowed, his mouth set in a hard line, his eyes shone, and at the end, a clearing. He plopped three spoonfuls of sugar into his mug and stirred violently. "Now," he said, "what are we going to do about you trying to carry out your own work plus everyone else's?"

"It's fine now. It was only this one little snag. And it's good for me to stay busy."

He took a long drink of his tea and nodded. "We're going to sort this out."

I couldn't see that there was anything to sort out and thought it best to head into safer waters. "I've met a girl who has a rook for a best friend," I said.

I caught the keen look in his dark eyes. "Has she got him trained?"

"I'm not sure which one of them does the training," I said, and told him the story of Tennyson and Alfie.

"Remarkable, really," he said. "We'll work up a segment on the two of them, shall we? A girl and her rook — I look forward to meeting them."

"Why don't you pop back round tomorrow afternoon? I'll ask Tennyson's mum if that would suit. Saturday afternoon, no school. You could get to know them. Bring Beryl and we'll go for a drink at the Stoat and Hare after I finish." I regretted the offer the moment I'd extended it — what would I say when he saw the gouge in my cottage door?

"Tomorrow. No, that might not work out. How about one afternoon next week?"

We agreed on it and finished our tea. At the door on his way out, Dad encountered a covey of pensioners from the estate who'd got wind of his whereabouts. I gave him a stack of *Birds of Hoggin Hall* leaflets to autograph, and he sent them on their way happy.

* * *

I lunched on the cold chicken Sheila had left me the day before while reviewing Basil's film, which he had got to me incredibly quickly, and after that, I sorted out the rubbish removal plan for the farmers market. Alfie and Tennyson came and went and there it was four-thirty and I found I had thirty minutes on my hands — plenty of time to work myself into a state of high anxiety over my impending meeting in Cambridge with Terry Fisk and Sam Redman of AIL. What had I got myself into? I should just ring the police right now.

No wait now, I said to myself. *Not yet.* No need to let the police in on this until after I'd faced Nick's co-workers and they'd answered a few questions. Then Tess could have at them.

* * *

On the drive to Cambridge, I struggled with how to begin. Who would I be? As Julia Lanchester, they may know me as Nick's ex-wife and keep their traps shut. I barked a laugh that echoed round my car. I doubt Nick had divulged much personal information to his co-workers. I thought it more likely they'd know me as Rupert's daughter rather than Nick's ex. But I'd been SaraJane on the phone to them, and part of me wanted to continue that. After all, with SaraJane, a stranger, they might feel freer to talk about the grant, their hopes and aspirations, and why they'd squeezed out their partner. They might let slip some vital detail that would break open the entire case. I turned into the stacked car park at the center of town and began winding my way up, looking for an empty bay, and thought, yes, SaraJane.

The Eagle, a rambling, frenetic pub near King's College, had two bars and several rooms all filled with both tourists and students at almost any time of the day. Now, just gone six o'clock, the garden seating in front was brimming with smokers. I skirted the bulk of them and walked through a few rooms, scanning the crowd and wondering what sort of fellows I was looking for. I made my way to the RAF bar, searched the room, and saw them at a table against the far wall.

What gave them away? I'm not sure I could say, except perhaps that they oozed unease. I watched for a moment, halfway hidden behind drinkers crowding up to the bar. They sat unspeaking, staring into empty pint glasses on the table in front of them. They looked about Nick's age — fortyish — one barrel-chested, with a full face and coppery hair pulled back into a ponytail. The other, thin, caramel-colored skin with his tight curly hair sheared, and thick black glasses. He had a pinched expression. He leaned over and spoke to the first fellow, who nodded. They checked their watches and looked round the room. At that moment, the crowd in front of me parted and my TIC uniform must've caught their eye.

I slapped a smile on my face and raised my hand in acknowledgment as I worked my way to them, stepping round tables. I told myself to breathe, to relax. I clutched my bag with both hands to stop them from shaking.

The men remained seated when I arrived at the table, looking at me with raised eyebrows, but without recognition.

"SaraJane?" asked the one with the ponytail.

"No," I said, "I'm not SaraJane. I'm Julia Lanchester."

CHAPTER 17

Terry Fisk and Sam Redman leapt off the bench, knocking into the table and sending their glasses dancing across the surface. A sense of calm, controlled power flowed through me, and I reached out and stopped the glasses just before they tumbled to the floor.

"Oh lovely, are you getting the drinks? Thanks. I'll have a pint of the bitter."

"Yeah, right." "Yes, of course." "Let me." "No, I will." They fairly fell over each other to get out from behind the table, avoid me, and rush to the bar.

"Don't forget these," I said, holding out their empties.

I took one of their seats so that I could continue to watch them. I don't know what made me come out with my right name when I saw them, but it seemed to have made an impression. They kept trying for casual glances over their shoulders — they must've hated having me stare at their backs.

The barman approached them, smiled, and said, "Don't you two have homes to go to?"

The two men collected the drinks and made their way back, the cream head overflowing and running over their fingers before setting the glasses on the table. I don't really drink beer, but I feared that if I'd ordered a glass of wine, it would be gone in two gulps, and then where would I be? At a disadvantage, that's where. But I could make a pint of bitter last forever.

"Well, now," I said after a sip. I put my hands in my lap and looked at the men pleasantly. "Which one of you is which?"

"Oh, sorry — I'm Terry Fisk," the one with the ponytail said.

"Sam Redman." The fellow with the glasses put his hand out for me to shake, but then took it away.

"Lovely to meet you, Terry and Sam." And after that, I shut my mouth. I also clenched my teeth, because what I really wanted to do was to shout questions at them. No, I'd do this interview the proper way. The police way.

They each took a long drink of their beers. Sam must've swallowed wrong, because he coughed. That seemed to spur Terry to action.

"We thought . . . SaraJane rang us. We thought she was coming here."

"SaraJane couldn't make it," I said. Did they deserve a further explanation? I didn't believe so. I waited.

"This is a bad thing," Terry said to his beer, "what happened to Nick."

I logged my observations. He hadn't begun with "We're here to talk about the grant application and what do you have to do with that process, Julia Lanchester?" His offering — akin to "I'm sorry for your loss" — made me believe they did indeed know that Nick and I had been married. And perhaps most important, they knew that I knew that there was a connection between Nick and AIL.

"Yes, it is," I said. "When was the last time you saw him?"

"Last summer," Sam said, and took another drink.

"Last summer?" I couldn't keep the disbelief from my voice.

Terry nodded. "Sam and I go up to St. Kilda only two months in the summer — it's difficult enough to arrange that much time away."

"Where do you live?"

"I live in Southampton," Terry said. "Sam's in Birmingham."

"And so, you're staying locally? Where?"

"With a mate from uni."

"Do you work at nature reserves or something?"

Sam shook his head. "Microbiology lab," he mumbled, "for a food company in Malvern."

"Quality control for chocolate-covered pineapple bites, that's Sam's specialty." Terry smirked and Sam drank.

"And you?" I asked Terry.

Sam's turn to smirk. "Terry's your man for urine analysis, aren't you, Ter? Grand work, that — and he's on nights." Terry's face flushed.

"Neither of you is an ornithologist?"

"We *are*," Terry said loud enough for the foursome at the table next to us to glance over. "But we bloody well don't have to live in the middle of nowhere to prove it."

"And so, you saved the ornithology for your summer holidays in the Outer Hebrides?" I asked. "Was it only a lark to you? Not like Nick, of course. He stayed up there year-round. He devoted his life to birds." I could attest to that.

They exchanged glances and frowned.

"Dreary, desolate place," Sam said, shaking his head. "Terry and I stayed an extra month the first year but couldn't make a go of it."

"Isolation doesn't suit us," Terry said. "Nick lived like a monk up there."

"Not like a monk lately, he didn't." An impish smile popped up on Sam's face. "Not with Daft Doris as his shadow."

Terry chuckled, glanced up at me, and swallowed it, grabbing for his pint. Did they think it inappropriate news to reveal to the ex-wife? Think again, boys.

"So, Nick had a girlfriend on St. Kilda. That's good, I'm glad."

"Daft Doris, a girlfriend? I might not go that far," Terry said. "There's a small canteen on the island for the ones who live there, and she came up to cook last summer. But she set her cap for Nick, and decided to stay the winter, too."

"Set her cap?" Sam asked his friend with his nose wrinkled. "You sound like my granddad." Terry ignored him. "Mind you," Sam continued, "I wouldn't have minded if she had worn a cap — that massive amount of hair she has. I was forever pulling a long, dark strand out of my food." Both men shuddered.

I took a swallow of my bitter, and found I'd managed to finish half of it. At the tables round us, servers set down plates of haddock pie and sausage and mash. My tummy growled, but I ignored it. I had yet to learn anything of substance apart from the fact that Nick had a girlfriend. Hope she enjoyed the sex, because I was pretty sure that was all she'd got from him.

"Why isn't Nick's name on the grant application?"

Both men stared at me for a moment, and then shifted their gaze, their eyes darting about like damselflies. Terry looked at Sam. Sam looked at Terry. At last, Terry shifted in his seat and jabbed his finger on the table.

"We wanted to include him on this. We tried to tell him it would be for the best to move, but he wouldn't hear of it."

"We've an amazing opportunity in Kent," Sam cut in, "a good space shared with the Kent Ornithological Society, all the support we could ask for. Think of the data we could amass. It would really make a difference. Not only for vagrant species, but also to record the fallout during autumn migration. It's fantastic."

"Nick said, go if we wanted to." Terry thrust his chin out. "And so we did."

"Nick is the one who created AIL, wasn't he?" I asked. "Wasn't it his money that carried you through?"

"It was not." Sam slammed his glass on the table. "At least, it was at first, but that ran out. Terry and I, we spent our own money on it. We're the ones who carried Nick through these last few years."

And so these two thought they owned the institute.

"But still, Nick had started it. Didn't he didn't mind you taking the name with you when you left?"

A millisecond of silence split the air. It echoed in my ears.

"Well, what was he going to do with it?" Sam asked.

"And we've published under that name," Terry said. "It has some cachet attached to it. That's important for continuity."

"When did you have this discussion with Nick about moving the institute?" I asked.

"Over the winter," Sam said. "By email."

"Why was he here?"

Terry kept his eyes on the table, and Sam stuck his hands in his lap.

"Dunno," Sam mumbled.

"We didn't have any idea he'd come down." Terry looked away as he spoke, and Sam's glasses were so thick, I couldn't see his eyes.

"Did he want the grant money for himself?" I asked. "To fund the St. Kilda work?"

They didn't answer. I moved not a muscle, except shifting my glance slowly from one to the other. Not even a minute passed before they broke.

Terry crossed his arms over his chest. "Nick said that you . . . Rupert would never . . . the foundation wouldn't give us the grant. He was sure of it."

"He said, go ahead and apply," Sam added. "See for ourselves."

And in that moment, I could see it. Nick had used up his own money and had let these two fund AIL for years. They wanted to move the institute to suit themselves, but to Nick, it felt like thievery. He had left his precious, isolated existence — isolated apart from Daft Doris apparently — to come down here and tell both Michael and me that AIL, his true love, was being hijacked and that he wanted the grant for himself. He had confronted Terry and Sam and they had stopped him. They had followed him to Smeaton and down the drive of Hoggin Hall to the summerhouse and they had . . .

I needed to get out of this pub. I needed to phone the police. I finished off my pint in one long drink and grabbed for my bag. "The awarding of the grant has been delayed. The announcement won't be made for another fortnight. I'm sure the committee will be in touch with you as soon as possible. Good luck to you both."

I stood, and they both shot up out of their chairs.

"But aren't you on the committee?" Sam asked.

"I represent the interests of the Rupert Lanchester Foundation," I said, looking down my nose at them. "The administrator, Michael Sedgwick, oversees selection." Did Terry blink at Michael's name? "And of course, Rupert himself."

"Naturally," Sam said under his breath.

Before they could ask me why I was taking a personal interest in their grant application, I pushed off through the crowd. Out on the pavement, I was hit by a thick mist that swirled round, slapping me in the face, landing heavily in my hair, and settling on the shoulders of my cardigan. I rushed down the street, but kept glancing behind. I felt the beer slosh around in my empty stomach as I dug out my phone on the way.

I got connected with DI Callow's voicemail.

"Tess, it's Julia Lanchester. I found them — I found the two fellows who worked with Nick in the AIL." My excitement, my speed, and dodging the Friday evening crowds caused my voice to quaver. I rounded the corner of the Corn Exchange and took the concrete staircase to the car park entrance.

"I think they were squeezing him out of the group," I continued, "and he must've put up a fight and came down here to blow the whistle on them and they found out and . . . Well, look, I'll explain more when you ring back."

As I reached the top step of the outside landing, Terry caught up with me.

"Wait, Ms. Lanchester," he wheezed as he caught me by the elbow. I pulled away and backed up against the concrete wall. Rivulets ran down my face, mist mingling with a fearful sweat.

"Get away from me," I pointed my phone at him. "Don't touch me or I'll scream."

He held his hands up in surrender and shook his head violently. "No, no, I'm sorry, I only wanted to . . ." He stopped to cough and catch his breath. While he did so, I peered over the barrier. The mist grew heavier, but street-lamps illuminated the road below, and I could still see plenty of people rushing about their business. Surely he wouldn't try anything here.

"We've put a lot into this application," Terry said. "We're counting on this new start. We just don't want anything to . . . you know, get in the way of being considered."

"Are you saying Nick got in your way?"

Terry slapped a palm on the concrete barrier. "Look, I have no idea who would want to do this to him."

"Apart from you, you mean?"

God, Julia, can't you just keep your mouth shut?

"We would never . . . we didn't even know what happened to him until . . ."

Until they'd seen it online? Or had they murdered Nick and then started feeding information to those journos to take the spotlight off themselves. There had to be a connection between these two and the jackals. Tess would find it.

"We're sorry about what happened to Nick, but it had nothing to do with us."

"Did Nick know you were going ahead with this?"

"He—" Terry broke off. He looked past me and down to the street, squinting. "What the—" He asked leaned over the balustrade and then leapt back against the concrete wall.

A childish attempt to divert my attention — did he think I would look, too?

"You'd better go, Terry. Any further contact could jeopardize your application."

"We'll wait it out. We know you . . . the committee will give us serious consideration. Have you seen our website?" he asked weakly. "Sam did that. We've put a lot into this. We'd like a chance to work at what we love. Is that so bad?"

He didn't wait for an answer, but left, shuffling down the concrete stairs. I watched as he stopped for a moment and gazed in the direction where something or someone had caught his attention. I kept my eyes on him until he'd given up and left, walking off toward The Eagle. I didn't move until he was out of sight.

* * *

I pulled in at the roadside service off the A1307, too buzzed to drive — and not from the beer. I'd done it — I'd found Nick's co-workers, and at the same time, I'd found his murderers. High spirits crashed round inside me like waves during a storm carrying with them an undercurrent of fear. Also, I was starving. Tess had returned my call, but I had been driving and didn't answer. I circled round the car park looking for an empty spot and finally found one in the back overflow area — really just a grassy spot against a hedgerow. I dashed from my car through a steady rain, longing for my mackintosh, which still hung at the TIC.

Sadly, my food choices at this service stop were limited to Little Chef. I stood back from the order line and watched as people with indiscriminate palates carried trays of food off to plastic tables with plastic chairs bolted to them. I eyed the burgers — dismal when I thought of what Fred could create. I ordered chips, doused them with vinegar, and took possession of my own plastic chair and table. I stuffed a few chips in my mouth as I readied myself to ring Tess back, but she beat me to it.

I chewed quickly and swiped the grease from my fingers on a paper napkin that dissolved into nothing at first touch.

"Hello, yes."

"Where are you?"

From the tone of her voice, I'd say we were back on Inspector Callow and Ms. Lanchester terms.

"At a Little Chef."

"I'm standing outside your cottage door, where I've met the patrol whose assignment it was to assure your safety.

They say they have not laid eyes on you since you closed the TIC. There was no sign of you at your cottage, and so they rang me. Their call came in just after I received your message. I rang you back — or tried. You're meant to stay in touch."

"Am I under house arrest?" My throat constricted, and my voice jumped. "Am I to report my every move? You might as well force me to wear an ankle bracelet like every other criminal let loose on the unsuspecting public." At the table next to me, a couple picked up their trays and their toddler and moved off.

"Your safety is the concern of the police, Ms. Lanchester."

See — I knew it. Detective Inspector Callow back on the case.

"Do you want to hear what I've learned?"

"Yes, of course." Her words were clipped.

"Why don't I meet you at the station in Sudbury? Or" — perhaps this would put her in a better mood — "or we could meet at The Den?"

"No need," Callow said with ice in her voice. "You may as well come back here to your cottage. We'll be waiting."

"You won't leave the police car outside my door, will you? That blue-and-yellow Battenberg paint job is so obvious." I rushed on, afraid I'd pushed it too far. "Right, I'm on my way back now. No need to worry. I'm in no danger."

Standing over the rubbish bin, I crammed a few more chips in my mouth before dumping the rest and sprinting through the rain to the far reaches of the car park, where it was too dark for me to see the deep puddle until I was up to my ankles in it. Inside the car, I took my shoes off and tossed them in the back, fired up the engine, and set the heater on full blast, hoping to dry off before I arrived back in Smeaton.

I put the car in reverse and checked the mirror, but I couldn't see out the back. I whirled round to take a look and saw the back window had been transformed into a silvery spiderweb — cracked into a million tiny pieces that held together and emanated from a single starburst in the center, a round hole as big as a fist.

CHAPTER 18

"I might be in a bit of danger after all."

It hadn't taken much more than those words on the phone to Callow to result in a swarm of police cars pulling into the car park, blue lights flashing. The DI had called on Cambridgeshire police, who arrived in fifteen minutes with the Sudbury contingent showing up in thirty.

I stood just inside the building watching it all and talking to the relevant parties, telling my short tale over and over. Sergeant Glossop had brought me my shoes and my bag with my phone in it. I hadn't given them a thought when I'd bolted from the car, running into the grass and tripping on a stone curb, which landed me smack in the middle of the brambles. The thorns pulled at my cardigan, tore my tights, and scratched my hands and neck. I just barely kept my face out of it as I shouted and struggled. My calls for help had gone unanswered, and I'd at last extricated myself, saw no one — which was a relief — and had run straight back into the Little Chef. I'd had to ask a cleaner for a phone to use. She didn't speak English well, but she understood my mime.

"Polis?" she had repeated when I'd finished the call. "Come sit?" I had shaken my head. I'd desperately wanted a cup of tea but punished myself for my stupidity by standing and waiting like a brave soldier — wet, cold, and in tatters.

* * *

I knew I was in for a scolding, the way Callow marched in the door of the Little Chef. I felt just as I had at school on the rare occasions I'd been in trouble and was called to the head mistress's office. Possibly not so rare as I remembered.

Fair play to her, the first question the DI asked was "Are you all right?" although that was followed quickly by "You look dreadful, sit down." Once I was seated, the barrage began.

"Did you see anyone follow you out of Cambridge? Do you know where these men are staying? Does the grant application list their home addresses? Did you feel threatened at all by them? Do you have anything one or both of them touched? Did you take a photo of them?"

Callow shot questions at me, and so I returned fire with my answers, pausing only when PC Flynn appeared at my shoulder with a cup of tea.

"Oh thank you, Moira." I held it with both hands for a moment, letting the steam rise into my face. I'd at least got warm after the PC had draped a crinkly silver blanket over my shoulders. We sat off in the corner of the large room. Foot traffic had tapered off, but my alien garb still drew attention from departing customers.

"How did you get those?" Callow asked, nodding to my scratches.

Right, I could hear Tess's voice again. I wonder did she know she had a split personality? I glanced down at the thin lines of blood, now smeared over my wrists and hands, and at the red blotches on the tissue I'd used to dab my neck.

"When I ran out of the car, I tripped and fell into the brambles." I caught my reflection in the window, my hair standing on end. My God, I looked like a madwoman.

"I don't see how they could've followed me," I said. "Terry didn't see what sort of car I was driving, and they wouldn't have had time to catch me up. I watched him head back toward the pub."

"Still, we will need to talk with them." I waited while her brain whirled along. "Sergeant Glossop and PC Flynn will take you home."

"But my car—"

"We'll take it back to the village for you. You won't want to be going anywhere tomorrow, regardless."

"I'll be going to work," I said, but added meekly, "of course I don't need my car for that."

I saw a challenge in her eyes, but she must've decided better of it. "Right" was her only reply.

"Could you have them put my car in my lockup? It isn't a great advert for the estate to see a vandalized car on the high street, is it?" A thought lifted me ever so slightly. "Because it could be only vandals, don't you think?"

"Possibly vandals," Tess said. I had parked too far out for the building's CCTV to capture anything useful, but she didn't need to add the rest of her thought — all those cars in the lot, and mine was chosen to have its back window smashed the day after a knife was found in my door?

"About the knife," I said, as if she had spoken those thoughts aloud.

"We found no fingerprints, but yes, the blood on the blade is Mr. Hawkins's."

* * *

Saturday morning began nonstop. Between visitors and triple-checking Rupert's schedule I couldn't catch my breath or make a second cup of tea, but that suited me just fine — I would rather be busy than be alone with too much time to think. Even so, events of the past two days made regular appearances in my mind — images of knives and smashed windows popping up in the middle of offering leaflets and suggesting footpaths to the steady stream of visitors.

It had been past eleven o'clock when we'd arrived back at my cottage the previous night. DS Glossop and PC Flynn had driven me home and they'd even stopped at a petrol station market and bought a pint of milk. We said goodnight to Natty at Pipit Cottage, because Moira would be spending the night. She'd given me a scolding — albeit a mild one — when she'd noticed that I'd neglected to replace the security bar on the French doors. I'd had a shower — the water stinging the scratches on my arms and neck — and a mug of cocoa and had gone straight to bed. Moira had camped out on my sofa and I'd cooked porridge for our breakfast.

PC Flynn had gone on her way and I had started out my workday refreshed, but as the hours wore on, my anxiety grew. I watched the foot patrol stroll by on a regular basis and waited for Callow to ring to tell me Terry and Sam had been apprehended. Wouldn't that be the polite thing to do?

Now, the sun streamed through the window of the TIC, throwing a spotlight on the dust motes that swirled into mini whirlwinds each time the door opened. A group of ramblers had only just left, chatting about the bluebells in the wood and how if the fine weather kept up, the cow parsley would bloom early. Now, I stood near the window, my face to the sun and my eyes closed for a blessedly quiet moment. In my heart I followed those ramblers out the door.

Oh, to be lying in a field of cow parsley next to Michael. We would watch the sparrows dash out of the tall grass and flit about, catching insects on the wing. I could almost hear the drone of the bees, and feel Michael's lips, soft and warm on mine. My knees went quite weak as I imagined he—

Jingle-jingle-jingle!

My eyes flew open.

Kathleen, Nick's sister, dressed in either the same or quite similar shapeless layers of drab colors from Wednesday, looked even paler than before, with her eyebrows so furrowed that they collided in the middle, and rose to a peak. Her downturned mouth quivered as she clutched a black Grecian-style urn with two curlicue handles and a gold motif that included a row of women in togas holding baskets of grapes over their heads and standing on one foot as if caught midstep dancing a conga line around the middle. On the lid, a winged figure with a beard struck a poetic pose.

"They made a mistake," she whispered.

My eyes flew from the urn to Kathleen's face and back to the urn.

"You mean that isn't . . . ?"

"Oh, not with the remains," she said. "Those are Nick, but the crematorium . . ." She looked down at the ornate object as if she had hold of an alien. "I asked for a plain ceramic urn, no decoration. That's what would be appropriate. They got it wrong."

I'll say. I stifled a giggle and blushed with shame.

"Kathleen, come round here." I led her to our back table, filled the kettle, and switched it on. Kathleen took a chair, still clasping the urn handles, and so I pried the vase from her. Although made of rather thin metal, it had a heft to it and *clunked* when I set it on one of the few available surfaces in the TIC, next to the computer. There you are, Nick.

"I couldn't take him back to my room at the hotel," Kathleen said, shaking her head. "Not like that. It didn't seem right. But I couldn't leave him at the crematorium, either, could I? They have ordered the proper container and said when it arrives, I could return and they would . . . change it out." She shifted her chair slightly, so that the urn wasn't in her line of sight.

"Well, then, it'll all be settled," I said, pouring our tea and setting out shortbread fingers. "I'm so sorry I haven't checked to see how you are doing."

"I brought work along with me, and the room is quite adequate. Thank you for arranging it. I do need to leave each morning for the cleaner, but I walk up to the church, and have had a pleasant chat with the vicar. The food in the restaurant is suitable."

Adequate. Pleasant. Suitable. Never let it be said that a Hawkins was overly effusive.

We drank our tea. The dust motes drifted.

"I hope you've had a chance to look round the village," I said.

"Yes, I have." Kathleen took a bite of shortbread.

"Have the police been in touch?" I asked. "Have they told you anything?" The chances were slim to none that Kathleen knew more than I did, but it couldn't hurt to ask.

"I'm told the police continue their lines of enquiry."

Right.

"Julia" — Kathleen's glance hit and ricocheted off the urn — "I have a small predicament this afternoon."

"Is there something I can do? What do you need?"

"I've arranged a lunch meeting with a man in Chelmsford as part of my research into the history of ship-boiler gaskets. But you see, I don't feel as if I can leave it" — her head bobbed toward the urn — "in my hotel room alone. And naturally, it isn't as if I can take it along with me."

Was I now a minder for my ex-husband's ashes? Would this be my punishment, to stare at a tarted-up Grecian urn the rest of the day and dwell on its contents?

"I tell you what," I said, accepting my sentence, "why don't you leave it here with me? You can come and collect it on your way back through the village. How's that?"

A bit of color brought life to Kathleen's face. "Yes, thank you for offering. It's kind of you."

* * *

She couldn't get out of there fast enough, and I couldn't settle on what to do with Nick. I didn't think he should stay next to the computer, because I just might accidentally elbow him onto the floor, and although I knew that the remains were well-packaged within the final decorative container, I didn't want to push my luck. I tried everywhere — next to the sink, on top of our small fridge, in the loo. I set the urn on the table and went out to the front to get the visitor's view. No, much too prominent. He'd just have to put up with the floor. But before I could get it there, the door jingled, and a cavalcade of visitors streamed in.

The rest of the morning passed, and I had only just sent a family on its way loaded with stories about the Viking invasion when a fellow walked up to the counter offering to give a free talk on his new book about Suffolk Druid settlements, including the one located on the Fotheringill estate near one of the hamlets. Druids could be a big draw and at once I envisioned a solstice celebration. I wanted to ask the author if he might be available for that, but the phone rang and I had to answer, because it was the president of the local Women's Institute. The chapter would have a tea tent at the farmers market in four days' time, and it had come upon them suddenly that they needed an extra, adjoining stall space just next door for tables and chairs.

"I did offer you that spot to begin with, Maevis, don't you remember? But you declined it, and Solly's Sausages took it up. Hang on a moment, can you?" I said to Maevis, and then whispered to the Druid author, "I'll be in touch about the details, thanks!" I waved as he left, before returning to the WI. "I tell you what I can do, I'll let you have a space directly opposite your stall. Surely people can carry their tea and cake a few feet." Maevis then started in on trying to wrangle two spaces instead of one just as the bell jingled again, but not a visitor this time. "Lord Fotheringill," I said, "what a lovely surprise."

Linus nodded at the phone, a sign for me to continue. He balanced a large pink bakery box in one hand, while he slipped his bicycle clip into the pocket of his jacket and looked round the TIC, his gaze snagging on the urn. Nick.

"I must run, Maevis," I said into the phone. "One extra space is all I can promise — let's see how it works out after the first week or two. Bye now." I set the phone down as Linus set the bakery box on the counter.

"I say, Julia, you've worked miracles with this little space, you truly have," Linus said. "And such enticing information for our visitors." He idly picked a map out of a wall pocket and then put it back again.

It had been two days since the knife in my cottage door, and although Linus had sent emissaries to check on my well-being, I suspected he needed to see for himself. Right. I'd play the game that this was only a casual visit.

"We try our best — Vesta, Willow, and I. What brings you into the village this morning. Time for our weekly meeting?" A small joke. We'd begun my tenure as TIC manager with a regular sit-down, but after Linus had seen I could handle my responsibilities and as his time had been consumed with other duties, we'd let that go by the wayside.

And so he gave up the pretense, and leaned forward, giving me a close look. "How are you, Julia?"

"Fine," I said, "I'm fine." Although if I had to say that many more times, I thought my head would explode. "Really fine." He looked concerned but not alarmed, and so I didn't think he'd heard about my smashed car window. And why should he hear? Vandals at a distant roadside service had nothing to do with the Fotheringill estate. "It's good of you to stop in. Would you like a cup of tea?"

"No, thank you." Linus smiled again — a smile that appeared full force, but then faded a bit. He tugged at the hem of his jacket. He was nervous, and that made me nervous. He took a deep breath. "I've come to ask you . . . I've come to tell you that it's my decision that you are to leave the TIC."

CHAPTER 19

"Leave the TIC?" I asked Linus, too stunned to think. "You're letting me go? Making me redundant? Why?"

Linus blushed. "No, Julia, that isn't what I meant. I meant that I want you to take the afternoon off."

This modified request was no less shocking to me. "But Linus, I can't do that."

"This is all getting to be too much, and I can't stand to see what it's doing to you."

I put my hands behind my back, afraid he'd seen the scratches, although I knew they were just as evident on my neck. Also, I'd braved the mirror that morning and knew those pesky dark circles under my eyes remained. I had smiled at my reflection, hoping that would vanquish them, but that seemed only to accentuate the sadness in my eyes. I didn't know how to make that go away.

"It's only temporary," I said. "And I'd so much rather stay busy."

He took a deep breath. "Still, I want you to take the afternoon off and go to Cambridge. Spend the evening with Rupert and Beryl. They're expecting you."

"But Linus, it isn't possible. Here it is Saturday afternoon, and we're far too busy. Remember, I've no one to replace me."

"Yes, you do." He lifted his chin. "I'll fill in."

"You?"

"You need a rest. I'm suggesting this as a friend, but I'm perfectly willing to force the issue if need be. I am your employer, after all." He set a hard look on his face.

I tried to muster all the courage I could to refuse, but at his words, a wave of longing swept over me to go to my family home, drink a cup of tea in my mum's back garden, take a nap in my old bedroom. But I couldn't. I shouldn't.

"I—"

"After all," he said, his face softening, "if I can't talk about the Fotheringill estate, who can?"

"But—"

"And you're to take that with you." He nodded to the pink bakery box, although he hadn't needed to draw my attention to it, because I'd caught the scent of chocolate the moment he walked in. "Nuala insisted."

I took a peek. "An entire cake?" I asked. "For only three of us?" Not that I couldn't take care of a fair amount of the layered beauty myself.

"We don't argue with the baker," Linus said. "Now, off with you."

"All right, I give in. But I'll be here to open tomorrow afternoon." I dashed behind the counter to get my bag, afraid that if I waited, my common sense would take over. But then I came face-to-face with the Grecian urn. "Oh dear. Linus, there's just one little thing." I briefed him on the situation. "And so, Kathleen will stop back by later and collect it. Is that all right? I'll set it over here." I took hold of the handles and moved Nick to the floor on the other side of the fridge.

As I opened the door to make my escape, I remembered something else.

"Also Linus, you might have a rook visit this afternoon. He's Alfie, and a girl named Tennyson will be with him. But Alfie may arrive first and peck at the door. You can go ahead and let him in, it'll be fine. They're lovely, the pair of them, and don't worry, Tennyson comes equipped with her own bottle of Dettol, so she'll see to any . . . you know. Oh and — Alfie likes shortbread fingers."

Linus raised his eyebrows, but no further explanations were possible, as I was met at the door by a family of five wearing short trousers and hiking boots with rucksacks slung over their shoulders. I gave Linus an enquiring look. He nodded me off, and so I left, cake box cradled in my arms.

Out on the pavement, another problem, more severe than Nick's ashes or a rook in the TIC, stopped me in my tracks. I had no car. Now what? A taxi to Cambridge would cost a bob or two, and the bus would take forever. *Think, Julia.* Should I ask Linus for yet another favor? But no — a solution was at hand. Instead of turning left toward my cottage, I took off right, across the road and to the corner.

Akash stood at the counter of his shop, chatting with two women while he packed a basket with cold chicken, salad, rhubarb tart, and a bottle of wine. He rang them up, and they walked away smiling.

"Good afternoon, Julia," Akash said.

Next to the counter, a stack of wicker baskets rose from the floor, topped with a notice that read: "Your picnic sorted! Choose a main, salad, pudding — buy the basket and you'll get a free bottle of wine today and another on your next visit!"

"What a fantastic marketing idea," I said.

"You know, I've had these baskets for a year," Akash replied, "in the back there, near the sandwiches. I've sold one in all that time. Gwen suggested I move them up by the counter and put them on offer, and I've sold six of them in one morning."

"That's Gwen, Tennyson's mum?"

"She's the one. She's got an eye for display. Do you think she'd be interested in giving me a few hours a week, helping me spruce the place up?"

"I'd say she'd be delighted." If she could find any more hours in her day. "Say now, Akash, I'm in a bit of a pickle at the moment. My little Fiat is having some repairs done, and I need to get to Cambridge."

I'd borrowed Vesta's car on two previous occasions, so I knew it wouldn't be a problem. Akash, keeper of the keys, produced the one for the red Citroen from a drawer below the counter.

"Parked in front of the cottage, as usual. She'll be happy it's being driven."

I dashed off to Vesta's cottage, only two streets away, and drove the car back to my Pipit Cottage. I sat low in the driver's seat as I crept up the high street, searching for any signs of the jackals. I found none, although I did meet the PC foot patrol when I parked and dashed in my front door. That reminded me I was indeed being watched, but in a safe way, and so as I changed clothes, I rang DI Callow.

"Hello, it's Julia Lanchester. I'm taking the afternoon off work. Well, I've been told to take the afternoon off — it was Linus's request. I'm going to Cambridge this afternoon to my dad's. Dad's and Beryl's. And I wanted you to know, in case the foot patrol reported me missing or something, because I won't be missing, I'll be safe." I paused as I pulled on my trousers. "It's all right if I go, isn't it?"

"Of course it's all right, Julia." Tess sounded not cold and unfeeling, but a wee bit exasperated. "You are not, as you reminded me, under house arrest. But thank you for telling me. Why don't you text me when you arrive? And I wanted to let you know police were unable to locate Mr. Hawkins's laptop at his digs on the island. He must've brought it with him. Either the person who murdered him has it or it's been left wherever he had been staying."

This held promise. "Terry Fisk and Sam Redman might know. What about them — did you find them?"

"Yes, I spoke to both of them by phone. They had no suggestions for us but offered up a list of fellow students from their time at uni. And, just to let you know, they left Cambridge soon after talking with you."

"They escaped?" I stood clutching my socks to my chest. This was my fault — I'd let two murderers go. Why didn't Callow sound angrier with me?

"They had returned to their homes — Fisk to Southampton, Redman to Birmingham. They had no need of escape. They've said they were both at work last Friday, and we are in the process of verifying their alibis."

Disappointment surged through me. They were the ones who murdered Nick, I had been sure of it. After all, they had the motive. I didn't want to believe them innocent and so I didn't.

"Aren't you even going to take them into the station for questioning?" My voice sounded reedy even in my own ears, like a little girl not getting her way.

"I see no need for it. We know how to get in touch with them."

"But they've been in Cambridge since just after Nick's murder. They could've put the knife in my door."

"The blood on the knife was a match for Mr. Hawkins, remember. Fisk and Redman were not here when that happened."

"And so, you believe what they told you."

"Until we find evidence to the contrary."

* * *

I drove to Cambridge under bright sunshine, although inside the car I was enveloped in a cloud of annoyance. If Terry Fisk and Sam Redman had killed Nick because he had objected to their taking over the AIL, they'd've been locked up and this whole business would be finished. That is, I meant that Nick's killers would have been apprehended and punished as they should be and the rest of us could get on with our lives. That didn't sound much better. And after all, how far would nabbing the murderer go to fixing what's wrong with me? No, even that resolution wouldn't change me from the soulless human being that I was.

Fisk and Redman hadn't even been in the area the afternoon Nick was killed — or so they told police. And they said they'd departed Cambridge after I met them on Friday evening. But there was something I didn't like about that.

Terry and Sam had told the police they'd given up and gone home, and that didn't jibe with their actions. They'd been camping out at The Eagle for a week and had told me they were in it for the long haul. It didn't add up.

I exercised caution as I drove past the house in Cambridge, expecting to see the jackals across the road, but there was not a journo in sight. They'd left off me, Michael was in Exeter, and they weren't bothering Rupert. Had they given up, just as Michael said they would?

It took a moment before I got out of the car. I breathed deeply, expelling all the worry, anger, and angst as I calmed myself. I wanted to present a positive front to Dad and Beryl, because they must be quite worried about me to make arrangements behind my back with Linus. I needed them to know that I was doing just fine — not true, but no matter — and that both the TIC and Rupert's schedule were under control. I may not be under control, but appearance, in this case, needed to be everything. *Sort yourself out, Julia. Put on a happy face.*

I slung my bag over my shoulder, took the cake box out of the boot and carried it as if I had been entrusted with the crown jewels. When I got to the door, I rang the bell with my nose. The door opened, and I almost dropped my cargo.

"Stephen!"

"You couldn't trust us to have something for your tea, could you?" He grinned at me, and my spirits lifted.

I slipped past him to set the box on the entry table and turned back to give him a massive hug before holding him at arm's length for a good look.

"You look wonderful," I said. But he didn't really.

Stephen's normal appearance wasn't terribly run-of-the-mill. Like Willow, he had found his own style. He wore his curly hair short and usually with a red tint, his spectacles sported turquoise frames, and he often chose boldly contrasting colors for his clothes. But today, his attire — although smart with coordinated tight trousers, jacket, and scarf — gave off a subdued, woodsy aura in russet and green. And his spectacles had tortoise-shell frames.

"Hmm," he said, catching my look. He ran his fingers through my hair and tilted my chin, probably noting the scratches.

"How are you?" I asked, before he seized the advantage.

He crossed his arms. "I'm fine. How are you?"

I crossed mine. "Fine."

"Jools—" he began.

"How is it that you're here on a Saturday?" I asked. Stephen owned a wildly popular hair salon in Hoxton, and he would normally be slammed on a weekend.

"I've decided to take a few days off," he replied, looking at the floor. "I've a fantastic manager, and she's well able to run the place."

"Time off — you?" Did he think I'd believe that one? Stephen had worked nonstop at making the salon a success, and he kept his hands on the day-to-day running with a vise grip. I squinted at him, daring him to look at me. "How's Clive?" I asked. It was an exploratory enquiry.

Clive and Stephen had been a couple for more than a year now. I thought they were a fine example of opposites attracting, what with Stephen's artistic talent and Clive being a mathematician. But at my question, Stephen continued to avoid my gaze, and that gave me my answer. "No, Stephen. What happened?"

"It didn't work out, that's all."

"This is awful — everyone is breaking up." I felt my emotions being pushed to the brink. "You and Clive, Tess and Chloe, Michael and—"

"Don't. Don't you dare say that," Stephen cut in, sticking an index finger in my face. "You and Michael are not broken up. Circumstances have pulled you apart briefly. That's all it is. And now, who are Tess and Chloe?"

I shrugged. "DI Callow and her girlfriend."

"DI Callow?" Stephen said, brightening up considerably. "Are you hot and heavy with the police now?"

I snorted with laughter. What a tonic Stephen was, and how thoughtful of Beryl to know he would cheer me up. Where was Beryl? Where was Dad?

"Are you here on your own?" I asked.

"Not quite," Stephen said, his eyes darting over my shoulder to the staircase. I whirled round to see that the gang of three was complete, for there stood Bianca.

CHAPTER 20

I had no words at the sight of my sister — her brownish hair swept back in an untidy, frizzy ponytail and wearing old denims and a sweater she must've left in a bureau upstairs all those years ago when she moved away. She was better even than chocolate cake. I threw my arms round her, and like a complete fool, I sobbed.

"It's okay, Jools," she said patting me on the back. "You just let it out, it's all right."

But it was over as soon as it had begun. I wiped my face and asked, "Why didn't you tell me you were coming for a visit? Where are the children? Where's Paul?"

Bianca spread her arms. "It's Mum's wild weekend away — I'm here on my own, just this once. Paul's minding the children, and his mother's helping out."

"This is such a lovely surprise."

"Good," Dad said, appearing from his study along with Beryl. "That's what we intended."

The comforting love of family surrounded me, but there was something else in the air I couldn't quite identify. "So, you all thought I needed cheering up?"

"We thought you needed an intervention," Stephen said.

"You what?"

"Come on," Bianca said, nodding toward the sitting room.

"Four against one — is that fair?" I asked, my initial joy quickly being replaced with the suspicion that I was going to be told off.

"My God," Stephen said, peeking into the bakery box. "Is that all for you, or are any of the rest of us allowed to have a taste?" He batted his innocent-looking eyes at me.

I sniffed. "I might share. Who's putting the kettle on?"

"Could we hold off on tea and cake for a few minutes?" Bee asked. "Let's sit down."

Fine. I marched into the sitting room as if walking the gangplank. Dad, Bianca, and Stephen took the sofa, Beryl one of the armchairs, and I the other. At least if I were going to be put on trial, I would be sitting comfortably instead of standing in the dock. I perched on the front edge of the cushion.

"Is this about double-booking myself yesterday morning? Because it was only a blip. It's all sorted now."

"It's about you punishing yourself," Bianca said.

"Punishing myself? What's that supposed to mean?"

"How do you feel about Nick's death, Jools?" Stephen asked.

I looked at him and then away. "What sort of a question is that? I feel horrible, of course. It's dreadful."

Bianca leaned forward. "But do you feel bad enough?"

"Do I what?"

"You think you should be drowning in some dramatic, full-on mourning — keening or some such thing — but you aren't," she said. "And so, you're blaming yourself for a lack of emotion."

My sister knew me too well. I looked down at my hands and mumbled, "I have plenty of emotion, just the wrong sort. His death is a terrible thing, and I should be sad — more sad than I am. But instead, I just want to scream."

"You've every right to feel angry," Beryl said. "You're remembering how it was when you were married, and we're remembering it, too. Everyone worried about you so. Your mum would go back and forth about how to help. Should she say something to you or shouldn't she?

"We saw what Nick did to you, Jools, when you two were married," Stephen said.

"Did to me? You mean, you think he abused me?" I shook my head. "No, Nick never hit me — he never did anything like that."

Rupert wiped the back of his hand across his mouth. "We know that. If I'd thought for one second he had laid a hand on you, you'd be visiting me in Her Majesty's prison now."

"But he didn't yell, either," I said, confused at having to defend Nick and, at the same time, wanting to blame him. "He didn't try to control me. There was no abuse. He never told me who my friends should be or where I should go. He never tried to tell me anything. He didn't care."

"That's true," Bianca said. "And you grew to be just like him — you lost your spirit. It was as if Nick had doused you with a fire hose. It's no wonder you're angry. With Nick dying, it's reminded you how it was then. But there's no need to pile the guilt on yourself."

"After Nick left for St. Kilda, how did you feel?" Stephen asked.

"Better," I said in a small voice. They waited. "All right, much better." I could remember it well. The weeks and months immediately after Nick departed, it was as if a clay mold round my entire being had cracked and broken off piece by piece. I was free. I had begun to spend more and more time at my parents' house over the following two years, until everyone thought I might just as well give up the flat and move back. Temporarily, we all said. Even so, it had been another two years before Nick and I had made the effort to get a divorce.

"The spark inside you that had gone out when you were with Nick, it came back," Dad said. "You reclaimed your life; you should be proud of that."

"You and Nick were chalk and cheese," Bianca said. "He was a loner, and you love life. You were a bad match. That's all there is to it."

"Yes," I said, the hot rush of fury streaking back, "a bad match. And that was down to me, wasn't it? What was I thinking marrying Nick Hawkins? What a stupid idea."

"We all make mistakes, Julia," Stephen said. "The thing is, you'd put it behind you until this happened. Now, Nick's death has dredged it up — all those dreary days and weeks and years."

"You've no reason to punish yourself because you aren't in bits over Nick dying," Bianca said.

Part of me knew they were right, but that didn't banish the guilt. Instead, it mushroomed, threatening to choke me. I breathed in and out quickly to keep the tears at bay, but they filled my eyes regardless. My body trembled as I fought to be free from that all-encompassing numbness that had reached out to me from the past and now, at his death, tried to reclaim me.

"He wasn't a terrible person," I managed to say. "But he did have a rather low affect."

"Low affect?" Bee repeated with an incredulous tone. "That's putting it mildly. His affect was so low I'm surprised people weren't constantly checking his pulse to make sure he was still alive." Her eyebrows shot up, and her eyes darted round the room. "Oh sorry, was that in bad taste?"

Here it came — the earthquake shook its way to the surface, and I pressed my lips together to keep it from escaping. But it was no use. I sputtered and popped and sounded like our kettle at the TIC until at last I broke out in screams of laughter. And they wouldn't quit. I snorted, gasped for air, and clutched my stomach, but I kept laughing. Dad and Beryl stared at me, their brows furrowed, but I saw Stephen grin, and Bianca, too.

As my laughter at last trailed off to the odd snort and rippling giggle, Dad let out an enormous sigh and took Beryl's hand. "Listen, Jools," he said, "there's something you need to know. Something I did before you and Nick split."

I wiped my eyes and blew my nose. "You gave him money to leave me."

Dad's jaw dropped. "Who told you that?" He threw Bianca an accusatory glare.

"Oh please," I said, "as if it wasn't clear to everyone but me that's what he'd wanted from the start."

"He came to me about this idea of moving to St. Kilda to track vagrant birds. Year-round." Dad shook his head. "We were so afraid you'd go, too, but then your mum said that perhaps this would help you see you had a choice."

"It isn't as if he said he was leaving me. He could never be that dramatic. 'Come if you want,' he said. There's a lovely invitation for you." I thought back to that afternoon. "I was stunned. It had really come out of the blue. I remember I rang you, and you did your best to act surprised." Dad's face went pink. "The next day, Mum stopped in. She tried to sound supportive, told me how lovely it is in the Outer Hebrides. She said, 'Just think of your days there. Day after day. Just you and Nick.' I'd been in a fog for twenty-four hours, but when she said that, I could see my life stretch out into years of nothingness. That decided it for me."

Bee grinned. "You stood up and shouted, 'He's out of his mind if he thinks I'm going to follow him to the ends of the earth so that he can catch sight of a handful of purple martins blown off course. Let him go to bloody St. Kilda, and good riddance to him.'" Laughing, Bee said, "Mum repeated that so many times we had it memorized by the end of the week."

I made a poor attempt at hiding a smile. "It was all well and good for Nick. I knew he would love that environment."

"But it wasn't for you," Beryl said. "And you realized that."

"The money Nick received wasn't a bribe," Dad insisted. "I donated to this institute he had formed. We had it arranged legally."

"Did you make Nick promise he'd stay away from me?" When Dad didn't answer, I added, "That's what I thought." I should've taken offense at my dad stepping in to help break up my marriage, but really, I couldn't be bothered. "But surely that money couldn't've lasted all these years? Do you think Nick wanted more money from you now?"

"He was never going to get any more money from me — that was part of the agreement. I don't know how he could've made it stretch this long."

"Terry and Sam contributed. Maybe Nick put them up to it at first — applying for the grant, but not including his name," I said, half to myself. "Except when they did apply, it was for money to move AIL to St. Margaret's at Cliffe in Kent. Nick would never have left St. Kilda, and when he found out what they'd done, he'd followed them down here and confronted them. They'd had to silence him. That could've been their motivation. But still, when did they have the opportunity?"

I felt four pairs of eyes on me and realized I probably should've kept those thoughts to myself.

"You've heard this from Inspector Callow?" Rupert asked.

It hardly mattered how I'd heard it. "She says they have an alibi," I said, "that they were both at work, not even in the area. Terry Fisk and Sam Redman. Do you know them, Dad? They were at uni with Nick." Dad had started his career at Cambridge before he gave up academia to teach his "citizen scientists" through appearances at spring and autumn festivals and on television.

Rupert frowned and thought. "Large fellow and the other one, dark, with glasses. Squints a lot. Yes, but I didn't know they were involved in AIL. Say, I thought Michael had put off the decision about the grant."

"SaraJane gave me the grant applications, because she thought I'd taken over everything from Michael, and so I read through them. That's how I know who they are."

"But how do you know so much about them?" Dad asked.

"It's amazing what people put into a grant application," I said, thinking we should change the subject before I got told off again. "Dad, SaraJane is a fantastic addition to the crew. You must find her invaluable. Hang on — don't you have an interview this afternoon with Radio Northumberland?"

"Julia," he began.

More evasive action needed. I reached over and clasped Stephen's and Bianca's hands, as they were the closest to me. "Thank you — all of you. I feel ever so much better. I can't say I'm finished being cross with myself for making the foolish decision to marry Nick in the first place, but I won't waste any more time worrying about it. Now, who's for tea and cake?"

CHAPTER 21

The company, the chocolate cake, Beryl's roast dinner, a couple of bottles of wine — these were the best restoratives. Everyone suggested I stay the night, and I was putty in their hands. After the meal, we gang of three washed up the dinner dishes, laughing and chatting as if we were twelve years old again, and ended up just as we always had, in Bianca's room with me on the floor, Bee at her dressing table, and Stephen sprawled across the bed on his back with his head hanging off the side.

"And so, that's it?" Bee asked him. "You broke it off for good with Clive?"

"I won't dwell on the past if Julia won't," Stephen said in a choked voice.

"Your face is scarlet, Stephen," I observed.

He sat up and coughed. "I can't believe I was able to do that for hours on end." He flopped back against the pillows. "Yes, that's that — the end of it. I'll never fall in love again."

"Wait!" Bee said. "That's one of Mum's old songs!"

We broke out in an enthusiastic rendition, but soon ran out of lyrics and collapsed in laughter.

"But I'm right," Stephen said with a sigh. "You know I am. It isn't easy to find someone that makes you look the way Bee does every time someone mentions Paul's name."

True. All the years of my sister's marriage, she would take on this little smile when the subject of her husband came up — as if they shared a secret.

"And you're the same these days." Stephen nodded at me.

"Don't," I said, with a rush of panic and passion. "I don't know. Don't say anything — you'll jinx it."

"Don't be afraid of it, Jools," Bee said. "And *you*" — she pointed a finger at Stephen — "you *will* find someone."

"Well, Ms. Broom and Ms. Lanchester," Stephen said as he got off the bed, whipped a towel off the back of Bianca's chair, and shook it out, "until my Mr. Right comes along, we'd better get to it." Stephen had decided Bianca needed a cut and said how handy it was that he always had his scissors with him. He turned her toward the mirror and tilted her head slightly, examining her shoulder-length hair that had a texture much like Dad's, tending toward bushy.

I replaced Stephen on the bed and spoke to the ceiling. "I can't believe I left Linus in charge of the TIC today — shows the state I was in that I'd let the earl work behind the counter."

"Especially since one of your loyal customers is a bird," Bianca said.

"Alfie," I said. "That is one smart rook. And Tennyson is adorable. She and Emmy would get along really well, Bee. I wish they could meet, because I think Tennyson could use a girlfriend. Not that Alfie isn't an exceptional companion. He's even helping me out a bit — do you know he could tell immediately that those journos were despicable people, and he harasses them every time they show up."

"They've backed off a bit, though, haven't they?"

"A bit," I said. "But one of them has kept it up." Yesterday, although I hadn't seen the jackals in the village, *Sightings* — one of the online rags — had slapped up a headline that read *Victim Had Been Pursued by Ex-Wife and Boyfriend in Murder Pact.* I couldn't quite laugh at that one yet. "Look, I've snapped a photo of them. You can see how horrible they are."

I pulled out my phone and found the photo I'd taken through the window of the TIC on Wednesday.

"They look like hacks, don't they?" Bianca asked, peering at the photo. "No respect for journalistic ethics, I'd say. Oh God, Stephen, you won't give me one of those, will you?"

Bee pointed to the auburn hair — the wedge half practically standing straight out. "Kitten woman," I said.

"Kitten woman?" Bee asked, laughing. "Where'd that come from?" I explained the muff on the hand-held recorder.

Stephen gave the photo a quick look and said, "That is what happens when people turn all DIY with their 'do."

"She cut it herself? How can you tell?"

"My dear, remember to whom you are speaking," Stephen said with a lofty air as he picked up comb and scissors. "She shouldn't have cropped the other half — too shabby. It's shave it or nothing." He glanced at the photo again. "That would be one wild head of hair if left alone. What she needs is a bit of product." He squinted, pausing with hands in midair. "Who's that one on the end?"

"The little weasel," I said, enlarging the photo, the better to see his wispy hair and pockets. "He made the mistake of stepping into my TIC, and I showed him out in short order."

"Stephen?" Bianca asked.

"Mmm," Stephen said, eyes still on the photo.

"Are you doing this or not? I'm about to lose my nerve."

* * *

Stephen worked magic on Bee's hair, giving her a couple of long layers and saying all she'd need to do would be to run her fingers through it. At least, that's all he'd had to do. He trimmed mine up. I didn't want him to do too much, or Rosy at The Hair Strand in the village would notice someone else had been at work on me. When he folded up the towel and headed downstairs to shake it outside, I stuck my head out the bedroom door.

"While you're down there, would you set a saucepan of milk on to heat, please? I could just do with a mug of cocoa."

"Your capacity for chocolate never ceases to amaze me," he replied over his shoulder. I took that as a "yes."

Bee and I sat on the bed with chins resting on our drawn-up knees.

"You're all right, aren't you?" she asked.

"I am," I said. "Mostly. I want to see Michael. I want to explain about Nick."

"Do you want to go and see him now?"

I shook my head. "He's in Exeter until tomorrow evening. That's good, though — it'll give me tomorrow to figure out how to explain it all."

We heard Stephen's voice downstairs. "'Night, Mum," and Beryl replied "Good night, my dear. So wonderful to see you."

Bianca glanced at the door and then at me. In a quiet voice, she said, "It's good, about Beryl and Dad."

I had long ago overcome my initial reservations about them. "Yeah, it is."

"She's lovely, really. And she's so good with the children."

"Yes." It was unlikely Beryl would become a grandmother through her son, so she had jumped in feetfirst to her role as stepgranny to Bianca's four children.

Bee sighed. "I still miss Mum. Every day."

I nodded. "So do I."

* * *

After a bit of a lie-in on Sunday morning and sitting in the study during Dad's interview with Radio Dorset, I gave everyone a kiss and drove back to Smeaton under dark and moody skies. It's one thing to solve the problems of the universe in the company of family and friends, but quite another when you set off alone to actually carry out the plan, and my spirits — initially lighter — had already started their downward journey. I'd dropped Bianca at the rail station in Cambridge on my way out of town.

"I'm sorry I can't stay longer," she had said, gathering her coat, scarf and bag.

"It's a dreadfully long journey for you — coming all the way from St. Ives on Friday and going back on Sunday."

Bee let a small smile escape. "First class," she whispered. "You've no idea what a difference that can make. And how much reading I can get done. It was such peace. Not that I want it all the time, but I don't mind it occasionally. And it was for a good cause." We hugged — arms bumping into windows and steering wheel.

"Thank you," I said, choked up again. As if their intervention had loosed some blockage in my emotional system, I'd found myself teary all weekend.

As Bee took hold of the door handle, she asked, "Did you tell Dad about your car?"

No, I hadn't, and I hadn't told Bee much. "Yobs," I said. "No need to worry him, and I've learned my lesson about where to park when I pull over for chips. Give my love to the children and Paul."

Bee disappeared into the rail station, and I got out of Cambridge amid light Sunday traffic. Midday opening at the TIC meant I'd time to stop at my Pipit Cottage for my usual duties — refill the feeders in the back garden, make myself a cup of tea, wash out a few bits of laundry and hang them outdoors. Still no rain, and perhaps I'd get them in later before it began. I had put away the remainder of the chocolate cake carefully. I had a plan for it, and it didn't involve my finishing it off before lunch. I took out my phone and stared at it. Should I check in with the police to let them know I would be back in the village? This was getting tiresome. I texted Tess and hoped that would suffice.

* * *

The threat of bad weather always puts a bit of a damper on visitors. At least if we didn't have crowds today, I could get a massive amount of work accomplished. Walking from my cottage to the TIC, I ran over my mental list of jobs for the afternoon — checking the details for the farmers market and the grand opening of the sweets shop, Sugar for My Honey, in a week's time. I would peruse the preliminary menus for

Smeaton's Summer Supper, checked the requisite health and safety requirements, marquee hire, and approval from the road-works division to close the high street.

I worked on automatic as I unlocked the door, turned on the lights, and flipped the sign to Open. I took one step toward the back to switch on the kettle and stopped dead.

There on the table, in pride of place, sat the Grecian urn.

All blood rushed from my head, and I had to brace myself against the wall to remain upright. What the hell was Nick doing still here?

I saw a note tucked just under the base of the urn and craned my neck, hoping to read it without getting any nearer, but no. I recognized Linus's even, regular, and quite small script, and I had to edge closer and closer before I could read his words.

> *"Dear Julia,*
>
> *As you can see, Ms. Hawkins did not stop by to collect her brother's remains. I wasn't quite sure what to do. It didn't seem appropriate to take them back to the Hall. If there is any problem, please let me know. I'm leaving the urn on the table, because I thought it better for you to see immediately that it had not been collected, instead of going about your business and coming upon it unawares.*
>
> *My very best,*
>
> *Linus*
>
> *P.S. What a delight Tennyson is, and Alfie's a gem. Do you know the girl's mother? Does she really work that many jobs? Is there something we can do to help?"*

I picked up the urn from the table and, holding it with both hands as if I'd won the gold cup at Ascot, and looked round the TIC, desperate for a hiding place. But my mind became muddled when I heard voices out on the pavement, laughter and talking. I threw open the door to the loo, and set Nick on the toilet one second before a crowd of hardy ramblers came in looking for a pub.

"That's the spirit," I said to them, a bit breathless. "What's a bit of rain to spoil a good walk?"

"No rain yet," one of them said cheerfully. "I don't think it'll start today."

I glanced out the window at skies that looked as if they would break open any second. "Well, and never mind if it does, right?" I gave them directions to both our village pubs, the Stoat and Hare and the Royal Oak, and offered a flier for the farmers market and a list of event dates for the estate, and they left discussing the summer supper.

That reminded me of lunch. With Nick out of sight — if not totally out of mind — I settled with a beef sandwich Beryl had sent along, abandoned TIC business, and looked ahead at Dad's weekly schedule. My second week at this. How much longer would I need to do it? I longed to relinquish this responsibility, to give it back to Michael, in whose hands I belonged. That is, in whose hands the job belonged.

I had refilled the kettle and I switched it on, when I noticed Gwen across the road. I went to the door and called out. "Fancy a cup of tea?"

She came over directly and we sat at the back table. Gwen picked through the remainders of several packets of biscuits I'd dumped into the tin.

"You should've heard her talk about him," she said. "'His Lordship' this and 'His Lordship' that." Gwen shook her head and smiled.

"Linus was equally impressed with Tennyson — and sounds as if he and Alfie hit it off, too." I played with half a digestive. "Say, Gwen, I should mention that the woman staying at the Stoat and Hare — the one who doesn't like to leave her room — she's my ex's sister."

Gwen reached for a shortbread finger. "Peg told me. She's a quiet sort, isn't she?"

"Mmm," I replied. "And her brother was the same way."

"She's nice about leaving while I do the room. She wanders up the lane to the church, for a bit of a break. I see her out the window chatting with a woman with dark hair, sort of. I thought it might be the vicar. She looked a bit unusual."

Next to Kathleen, wouldn't anyone? But, it couldn't be the vicar, Charles Eccles, or his wife, who was blond and a solicitor in Colchester, so gone most days. But Gwen was new to the village, so no surprise that she didn't know.

"You haven't seen Kathleen this morning, have you?" I had a fleeting thought of passing Nick off to Gwen, like a baton in a relay.

Gwen shook her head. "I don't go in on weekends."

"No, of course not." I'd ring Kathleen later. As a last resort, I'd march Nick up the high street and deliver him in person.

"You all right with . . . you know, everything?"

I nodded. "The police don't seem to be finding out much. Or at least, if they are, they aren't telling me about it. I know they questioned all of you at the pub about what you saw that afternoon."

"They didn't question me," Gwen said, "because they came round on Saturday afternoon, and that's not one of my days. But they spoke with Peg and Fred, and it sounds as if they had to interview everyone who attended the funeral reception. That must've been a load of work."

And all down to PC Moira Flynn. "Right. No joy there — the PC told me no one remembers seeing anything." I thought back to the crowd outside the pub that afternoon and envisioned the interior just as busy. Had everyone attending the funeral reception known one another, or could someone have slipped into the event unawares? Someone who could then dash over the road, find Nick, and kill him. What if instead of interviewing potential witnesses, police should've been looking at every single person as a suspect? A thrill ran through me like an electric current. Surely the police had thought of that, but I'd ask Tess to be sure.

"Thanks for the tea," Gwen said. "It's lovely to take a moment to sit and chat. But I'd best be off now — I've left

Tennyson working on a project with Alfie. It's that game with pairs of pictures that are covered up, and you try to match them by remembering where you'd seen the last one."

"I'd say he's a champ at that."

* * *

After Gwen left, I pulled up Dad's website. My one connection to Michael for almost a week. Pitiful.

I noticed that the children's feature in the corner, which had read, "Can you spot me?" and showed photos of well-concealed birds sitting on nests, had been replaced with the profile of a dark brown-gray goose with orange feet and bill. Next to it was a small cartoon figure of Rupert with a word balloon that read, "Does a bean goose eat beans on toast? Let's find out!"

My eyes filled with tears, and my throat constricted. "Does a bean goose eat beans on toast?" That was the very joke Michael and I had shared the day we spent at Minsmere. What a lovely morning that had been, just before we'd returned to our pub room to learn that Rupert and the Sudbury constabulary were searching for us.

Michael had left me a covert message in the guise of a joke about the bean goose. He was telling me it's all right, that this would be over and we'd be together again. My heart vibrated, as if it had been sent a confirmation text. I would go and see him. I had been back and forth about making an evening journey to Haverhill as a surprise when he returned from Exeter. I would do it.

I had a silly grin on my face when I heard the bell jingle, and it only grew when I saw who came in the door — Stephen.

"Here you are now," I said, getting up to meet him. "Could I interest you in signing up for a dig at the abbey — we've a sneaking suspicion the Druids were there ages before anyone else. Or how about this — the pensioners are putting on a tea dance at the church hall in June. Perhaps we could find you a dance partner."

Stephen didn't move from the door, and so I rabbited on in good spirits about Fotheringill estate events until I had reached him, where all words left me as I saw who stood in his shadow — a short man with wispy hair and a vest with a million Velcro pockets.

The little weasel.

CHAPTER 22

"*Ah!*" I screamed, taking hold of Stephen's arm and yanking him inside. "Get away from him, Stephen — don't speak to him. You get out of here this minute." I shook my fist at the intruder. "I'll ring the police. I know the DI, and she'll not stand for this. Come on, Stephen, come in here. I'll take care of this one. You can't trust him. He's one of them — one of those jackals."

"*Julia!*" Stephen clamped his hand on mine and spoke directly in my face. "Julia," he said when I'd stopped shouting and stood breathing heavily. "I'd like you meet a friend of mine, Gregory Cook."

"*A friend?*" My voice shot up an octave. "How can you even say that? He can't be a friend of yours. He's . . . he's . . ."

A weak smile crossed Gregory Cook's flushed face as he raised his eyebrows and asked, "The little weasel?"

I pulled my hand away from Stephen and crossed my arms tight enough to restrict my breathing. "I can't believe you brought him here. How could you do that after what I told you?" I saw the police foot patrol stroll by across the road and had half a mind to call them over, but Stephen stopped me.

"Let him explain, Julia. Give him a chance."

He got no chance, because the bell jingled and in came a family of five that scooted past the little weasel to get their entire number indoors. Apparently in denial about the impending weather, they were desperate for picnic supplies. I told them about Akash's shop, and then whipped past both Stephen and the little weasel to reach under the counter for a few children's activity packets put together by Willow. Behind me, the door jingled again, announcing the arrival of four birders — their telephoto lenses and rucksacks were a giveaway, and one of them held a grimy RSPB guidebook. Before I could get to them, the phone rang.

"Sorry, excuse me," I said to the family. "I won't be a moment." But when I turned, Stephen had picked up the phone and was saying, "Smeaton is the biggest secret Suffolk has — you will be smitten. You will be smitten with Smeaton." He raised his eyebrows to me and smiled. *Yes, all right — not half bad for a marketing slogan.*

I shifted my attention to the birders but found the little weasel deep in conversation with them. I broke them apart. Getting right down in his face and giving him an icy glare, I said, "Excuse me." He blushed and stepped back. I turned away from him and spoke to the visitors. "Thanks so very much for stopping in the center. I look forward to helping you. Can you excuse me for just a moment? Really, we're so happy to see you here. I'll just finish up with—"

"S'all right," one of them said, nodding to the little weasel. "He's just giving me a few tips on settings. Brilliant that you've got a photographer on staff here. Who would've thought?"

Another family with small children came in, and the noise level in the TIC tripled. "Oh, well, yes," I said and stepped away, straightening my cardigan and cutting my eyes at the little weasel. "In that case, carry on."

* * *

"First, let me say how very sorry I am to cause you any distress at all during this terrible time." Gregory kept his eyes on the floor as he spoke but glanced up at me once or twice.

We sat at the back table during a lull. Stephen had switched on the kettle during his last phone call and poured out a pot of tea, and when the TIC had emptied, the explanations had begun.

To begin, Stephen told me that he'd recognized an old friend in my photo of the jackals and had contacted Gregory to get the full story before bringing him to the TIC to tell his tale. Gregory had told him that he'd lost his position as lead photographer at a high-end fashion magazine when it had fallen on hard times and had made drastic cuts to its staff.

"They'll be left with little content and terrible art," Stephen said, "and I for one have already canceled my subscription for the salon. Let that be a lesson to them." Desperate for a job, Gregory had been taken on by *The People's News* as a stringer — a freelance photographer, but one with a tenuous association to the publication.

"I should never have become involved in such despicable activity," Gregory continued when I didn't speak. "It was wrong of me, and I completely understand if you would like me to leave immediately, but let me just say I'm grateful at least to have the opportunity to apologize."

"You were coerced," Stephen said. "And you were in need of work."

"That's no excuse for my behavior or for my association with those others. I'm happy to be free of them."

"But you're out of work again," Stephen pointed out.

"Yes, well, that seems insignificant when compared with what Ms. Lanchester and Mr. Sedgwick have been put through."

"Julia," I said at last, and reluctantly. "Call me Julia."

"It was a terrible mistake accepting their terms," Gregory said, shaking his head. "The first place they sent me was to you. 'Make your mark here,' they said, 'and you could get on full-time.' Why would I ever want to get on full-time with such a place?"

I could almost feel sorry for him, he looked so dejected, staring into his mug of tea. Almost, but not quite.

"Yet you continued to associate with the others. You continued to harass us. You used information illegally obtained from the police, and you splashed lurid headlines across the internet. These were pieces of evidence vital to the investigation that should've been kept quiet. The knife — how did you know about that?"

Gregory's head shook so violently I thought he might be having a seizure. "I don't know — I didn't have anything to do with that. There was this general assumed directive about where and when we would meet up, and somehow the others knew these things."

"You went along with them."

"The first couple of times because, as much as I hated it, I needed the work. If I didn't think about what I was doing, perhaps I could be . . ." Gregory rubbed the back of his neck. "By the time I caught up with them each day, they were already discussing things. 'The police say he's got the knife. The police say she knew all along.' It was dreadful."

I set my mug down hard on the table and covered my mouth, afraid I'd have to run into the loo. That those journos were discussing such things — throwing our lives and reputations around as if they were nothing. I trembled with rage. Stephen caught my free hand and held it tight.

"I'm so sorry," Gregory said again.

"Which one?" I whispered. "Did they all know, or was it one of them that spread the lies?"

"I remember at the beginning one of them, that big fellow, said something like 'We tell the truth about what we see,' but he said it as if he was repeating something he'd heard. I didn't like it. It wasn't ethical, and I suspected it was a load of lies. I wanted to know what you want to know — where were these leads coming from?" He shook his head slower now. "I couldn't spot the source. It was as if they all knew the same thing by the time I arrived. They'd all go off to the pub together, you see — up near Bury — and I didn't go. Weren't really my sort of crowd."

I refused to accept that he had no vital clues and pressed him. "Was it the twins?" I asked.

Gregory frowned. "Twins?"

"The two that dress alike," I explained. "Or was it kitten woman? Was she the one?" That smirk on her face had been imprinted on my brain.

Gregory cocked his head. "A kitten?"

"She's the one with the muffed recorder." I pointed vaguely out the door as if she still stood on the pavement in her brown duffel coat, waiting. But with my arm extended, I saw the crisscrossing thin lines of scabs from the brambles. No need to get into that story. I pulled my sleeve down and collar up.

"Olive, you mean." Gregory shuddered. "I just don't know for sure."

"You took pictures of us." I stated it as a fact, and he couldn't deny it.

His face turned a deep red. "One — at the police station that first day. But that was it, and I never turned it in. I couldn't stand it."

"You were with them the whole time with your cameras."

He nodded. "I took pictures of the village." I arched an unbelieving eyebrow at him. "Look," he said. "You look for yourself." He held out his camera and I began scanning the images on the screen. I scrolled quickly past several shots of the other journos — the big one, the twins, kitten woman, and after that, more pleasant photos appeared. I saw images of the turrets of Hoggin Hall against a blue sky, and a scene of the high street, empty. There, too, was a shot of the churchyard with the long grass growing like a high collar round the worn headstones and a silhouette of an enormous oak in the middle of a field with sheep bunched underneath its spreading branches.

I continued scrolling back quickly, but something flew by, and I stopped and said, "Wait, what was that?" I went forward a few shots and saw an image of Alfie perched across the road on the peak of the roof, one foot in the air as if he were in the middle of sentry duty. It made me smile. "That's quite good."

Gregory smiled, too — a pleased smile. "Birds. I photograph them just for a hobby. I like it."

"Gregory's posted his photos on the RSPB Flickr site, and they've used a couple of them on social media," Stephen said. "Show her the wren."

"No, Stephen, really, Julia doesn't need to see a load of . . ."

I handed his camera back. "Show me the wren."

Gregory obediently took the camera, ran his finger over the scroll button, and gave it back to me. I looked at the screen and laughed. Wrens are such tiny birds. This one, perched atop a wood railing, its short tail sticking straight up, had caught a fine feast — a dragonfly, its segmented body bursting from the bird's beak. There's a mouthful-and-a-half. A happy moment for a bird that must eat constantly to stay alive.

"This is lovely, really," I said.

"Look, Julia, is there something I can do to make up for this?" Gregory asked, with an undeniably obsequious air. "Do you want me to spy on those others for you? Try to find out who it is that's getting these details? Find out if there's a leak in the police team? I'll do it, I will. I'll follow them or I'll go to the pub with them and chat them up. Would that help?"

Pubs. I stared at the table, deep in thought as Stephen went to meet a visitor at the counter. Gregory was a photographer. Was there a way to use his talents? What did the investigation need a photo of — apart from the murderer, of course. A tiny plan blossomed in my mind. Terry Fisk and Sam Redman had told the police they'd returned to their respective homes, but I had my doubts. And, if they were still in Cambridge, I could just bet where they'd be. What would Inspector Callow say to photographic proof of that?

"Well," I said, smiling at Gregory for the first time, "as long as you're offering."

* * *

I gave Gregory the details — my own description of Terry and Sam — and where to find them.

"I know The Eagle," Gregory said.

"They'll probably be in the RAF bar."

Gregory nodded. "Lots of nooks and crannies there. I'll find a place so that I'm out of the way, but I can see the room. I'll use my phone so I don't look out of place, and I'll send you the photo as soon as I've got it."

I gave him my mobile number.

"Do you want to come along, Julia?" Gregory asked, ripping open one Velcro pocket after another until he found a handkerchief. "You could hide yourself away, but you'd be able to see for certain."

"No," Stephen said, giving me a wink, "she can't. Julia has plans this evening. Don't you?"

A nervous thrill ran through me. "Yeah. I have plans."

But it was not yet closing time — in fact, only time for tea, I realized when I heard a tapping at the door.

"Stephen, would you put the kettle on, please? We've visitors. You'll both stay?" I opened the door for Alfie who flew through to my mackintosh and dropped something in its pocket before settling on the back of an empty chair, cocking his head first at Stephen and then at Gregory.

Tennyson appeared next. "Hello, Julia. Oh — hello."

"Good afternoon," I said, putting my arm round the girl's shoulders. "I'd like you to meet two friends of mine."

Stephen kept his eyes on the rook and didn't move a muscle. "Jools," he said. Alfie shook out his feathers.

"Stephen and Gregory, I'd like you to meet Tennyson and Alfie. Gregory, I believe you and Alfie already know each other." I thought back to when I chased Gregory out of the TIC on Wednesday. The rook had been across the road, and he'd not said a word — that is, not made a noise — at the sight of this particular journo. "I apologize," I said to the bird. "You were right all along." I popped open the biscuit tin and let Alfie have first choice.

* * *

"What about you, Stephen — you'll come with me, won't you?" Gregory asked after the girl and bird had departed. "To the pub. That is . . . you know, if you don't need to hurry back to London." Gregory's face acquired a pink tint. "I could use an assistant."

"An assistant?" Stephen asked. His voice was casual, but I saw the gleam in his eye. "Well, I suppose. Perhaps I could watch the other door in case they come in that way. A stake-out." His voice finished in a whisper of excitement.

"Brilliant," Gregory said. "Now, before we're off, all right if I nip into the . . ." He looked round.

"Just behind you there," I said, and Gregory disappeared into the loo.

"So," I said to Stephen. "Gregory."

He held my gaze for a moment, eyebrows raised as if he didn't quite understand. But he knew me well enough to realize I wouldn't give up. He shrugged. "We've known each other for donkey's years. I ran into him about three years ago, and we had coffee. It was nice. But he was with someone. And by the time he wasn't, I was with Clive."

"And now you aren't with Clive," I said, turning my head as if to listen carefully. "And Gregory?"

"Unattached," Stephen said, a sly smile spreading over his face.

"Well, then—" I began, but Gregory emerged from the loo and brought the subject to a close.

"Sorry," he said, holding up the Grecian urn. "I wasn't sure what to do with this."

CHAPTER 23

I dawdled — so unlike me. After Stephen and Gregory left, I tidied up the TIC, took the rubbish out, and straightened the wall of leaflets and maps. I tried sitting in front of the computer to write the initial press release about Smeaton's Summer Supper, but I couldn't be still for the tremors of nervous anticipation that set my muscles twitching. At last, I set Nick on the table, locked up, and went back to my cottage where I changed clothes three times before settling on the first set of trousers and sweater I'd tried. I threw on a jacket and loaded myself along with my precious cargo — the last two slices of Nuala's chocolate cake — into Vesta's car and headed for Haverhill.

The road that led out of the village was deserted on a Sunday evening, although I could see a fair crowd at the Royal Oak on the other side of the green and at the Stoat and Hare at the bottom of Church Lane. I glanced at the first-floor windows above the pub and saw several rooms lighted. Was Kathleen hard at work on her history of the boiler gasket? Why hadn't she come to collect the Grecian urn? That was a question I thought I could answer — she couldn't stand the thought of Nick being in such an ostentatious container and didn't want to be reminded of it. I feared that I'd have Nick at the TIC until the appropriately plain ceramic urn arrived.

Michael's flat sat above an estate agent's office on a street of shops that were all closed up on this quiet Sunday evening. No sign of his car, which he always parked in front or round the corner, so I knew he hadn't arrived back from Exeter yet. I switched off the engine and settled in to wait, as the gloomy skies grew darker. I dismissed all other thoughts from my mind — Nick, AIL, Stephen and Gregory on a stakeout — and concentrated on this moment, and then the next one, and the one after that. I pulled my jacket closer about me and watched one car pass me and another pull over to park at the next corner. Michael? No, not his sea-foam-green Fiat. I yawned.

When he did pull up, I knew it in an instant. He stopped five or six doors down and didn't give Vesta's car a second glance. I watched as he got out, flung a holdall over his shoulder, and walked up the pavement to the building entrance, and then I waited, counting the steps he would take up the stairs to the door of his flat. I should give him time, let him settle in. I should let him at least put his holdall down and pour himself a drink. I got out of the car, dashed to the building entrance, and pressed the buzzer.

"Yes?" the intercom sputtered.

Out of breath more from nerves than exertion, I gasped, "Michael, it's Julia. I want to—" I got no further. The door buzzed and I heard the *click* as it unlocked. As if this offer was good for a limited time only, I threw open the door and sprinted up the stairs.

He met me at the top, taking hold of my hand, pulling me inside, and closing the door.

"What are you doing here?"

My face heated up. "No one followed me. They aren't around. I want to explain about . . . it's how I've been acting. I want you to understand why . . ." This wasn't going well. Where were the words I'd had only moments ago? I stuck my chin in the air, afraid I'd be sent packing. "I won't leave. You can't make me."

I'd expected him to argue, to tell me it was for my own good to stay away, tell me those journos would take advantage of any slip, tell me to give it time. But instead, he didn't tell me anything. Not with words, at least. In the dim light of the table lamp across the room, I could see his eyes were the blue of the sea on a clear day, and I felt a warm rush. The corner of his mouth tugged up into a smile as he leaned in.

He whispered, "I don't want you to leave."

And the barrier between us fell away. Had it been of my own invention? It had been only a week since we'd seen each other, but everything felt new again as his closeness sent shivers up my spine. He kissed me, lightly at first, grazing his lips over mine. I wrapped my arms round him and kissed him in earnest, and he put one hand behind my neck while the other hand got busy elsewhere. I braced myself up against the wall to keep from sinking to the floor. When I gave a little cry, we paused, and he leaned back for a moment. We were locked in one of those never-ending gazes — until I began unbuttoning his shirt as quickly as I could, and he walked backward to the sofa, pulling me along.

* * *

We just fit on his sofa, lying side by side. Under the heavy throw — my heat had dissipated and I'd noticed it was quite chilly in his flat — Michael's hand wandered up and down my thigh.

"I missed you," he said, giving me a quick kiss on the tip of my nose. "I missed this, and I missed all the rest."

I couldn't help but point out the obvious. "You shouldn't have left."

"You're right, I shouldn't've."

That had been an easy confession to extract. "Why did you? It was more than those journos."

"I did think I could keep them away from you, but they're persistent buggers. But also, I wasn't sure you needed me around. I thought you were reluctant to show how upset you were about Nick, and I thought it might be because of me. Because you didn't feel free to . . . grieve, I suppose."

My laugh was loud, but short, and Michael both grinned and frowned at me.

"That's irony for you," I said. "You wanted to give me space to grieve, and I had no grief in me." I gave a heavy sigh. "Nick's dying brought it all back — being married to him. It was not all that fantastic, you see, none of it. Not even from the beginning."

"You never say much about him."

"You never ask," I pointed out.

"Good God. Why would I do that?"

There's the difference between men and women. He never asked about Nick, and yet I'd asked enough about the two long-term girlfriends in Michael's past — Libby and the other one — that I could probably tell you how they took their tea.

"I got married for the wrong reasons," I said, but stopped. Hang on now, I wasn't the only one to blame here. "We both did. I was the daughter of a Cambridge ornithologist, and so to Nick, I was a path to achieve his heart's desire — to be alone, far from civilization, tracking vagrant birds. He got what he wanted."

Michael waited. I felt him stir, and at last he asked, "And you?"

"My reason was no better than his. It's because—" I squirmed — "all my friends were getting married and I was feeling left out. Isn't that the best reason in the world? For a while there, it seemed like I was going to a wedding every week and it just got to me. My friend Caroline's wedding was the tipping point. Nick and I were seeing each other, and when he proposed — not much of a proposal, as I recall — I thought, well, yes, why not join the crowd?" I shook my head at the memory. "Caroline was divorced a year later, and yet Nick and I drifted on for what seemed like forever."

"Did you never get along with him?"

"We didn't *not* get along. It was pretty much a flat-line marriage from the start. I grew angry with myself, but I couldn't admit to anyone how wrong I'd been. Too proud, too stubborn. And now I've been punishing myself, because instead of feeling sorrow at his death, I was angry all over again. And guilty, too. But no more."

We lay quiet for a moment as I did my best to banish the last of my guilt.

Michael's finger traced the scratches on my arms and neck. "Brambles," I said. "Silly, really. I'll explain later." It didn't seem quite the moment for tales of broken car windows and knives in doors.

"Did you get my text?" Michael asked.

"No, when?"

"About an hour before I got here."

"How did I miss it?" I asked, wanting to get up and find my phone, and yet not wanting to move. "Oh, wait. My phone's off. I sat in on Dad's radio interview this morning, and I forgot to turn it back on. Basil's good policy has rubbed off on me — silent phones."

Michael watched and waited, a small smile on his face.

"Yes, yes," I confessed. "Basil — you were right. Although, I think SaraJane's had a great deal to do with his shaping up."

Taking his victory well, he asked, "Are you hungry?"

Had he heard my tummy growl?

"I'm starving."

"Pizza?"

"The one with the Parma ham, please."

We pulled apart and dragged ourselves off the sofa. I gathered up clothes and Michael dug his phone out of his holdall and rang for a delivery. I gave his bare bottom a pat as I walked past on the way to the bathroom.

By the time I was out of the shower, Michael had dressed and opened a bottle of wine. I came out of the bedroom with mobile in hand, reading his text aloud. "I'll see u first thing in the morning. After all, it's your day off."

Michael gave an emphatic nod. "I was sick of being apart, too," he said. "On the drive back from Exeter, I decided I had a right to be a part of whatever you're going through." He paused, wine bottle in hand. "I do, don't I?"

Rarely did I see a soft spot in his usual hard shell of confidence. I slipped my arms round his waist from behind and rested my head on his back. "Of course you do."

The door buzzed, announcing the pizza's arrival, and we got to it, sitting at the kitchen table, which was so small our plates had to be set off center in order to fit on its surface. We didn't bother with conversation, only throwing each other a look now and then. Michael always said he enjoyed watching me eat pizza, because I did it as my American mum had done and used my hands. He said it showed the hedonistic side of me, and that suited him just fine.

I'd started in on my third piece, peeling off a long strip of prosciutto and dangling it over my open mouth. I'd taken the edge off my hunger, and now it was time to catch up.

"Peg didn't mean it to sound as if she was implicating you," I explained, beginning the story of our week apart. "She only told the police what she saw — that you'd turned into the drive. But the pub was heaving that afternoon, and she went straight back in, so she didn't see you leave. And anyway, Tess knows you weren't involved — she knows it's only those journos making things up."

"Tess, is it?" Michael asked. "How far you've come with the Sudbury constabulary."

"When she isn't being such a prig, she can be quite nice." I thought about the more personable side of Callow, and my spirits sagged. "She and Chloe broke up, and that's too bad. And Stephen and Clive aren't together any longer, either. That worried me — for us. It all looked so bleak."

Michael leaned over the table, cupped my face in his hands, and kissed me hard. He tasted of wine and cheese and garlic and cured meat, as did I. Mmm.

I proceeded to fill Michael in on everything I could think of. About Vesta and Willow leaving and how I visited the summerhouse and saw where Nick died, the brambles pushed away from the window like the curtain on a stage. I explained about Kathleen. I told him about Terry and Sam and the AIL, Gregory and Stephen being on a stakeout. That raised an eyebrow.

"Alfie knew all along that Gregory was the right sort," I explained.

"Alfie is a bird, isn't he?"

"He's a rook."

"Ah, well."

Michael refilled our wine glasses, and I thought we were in the right place for me to tell him the rest — about the knife in my cottage door and the broken window in my Fiat.

The storm clouds arrived and settled directly on his brow. "You should've moved out on the spot," he said, clattering our plates as he stacked them.

"I didn't need to — the police are all over the village. Linus has a string of people visiting to keep an eye on me. I've been perfectly safe."

"Going to visit those two alone?" Michael's eyes sparked like flint. "Without telling anyone?"

"In a pub in the middle of Cambridge. What could happen to me?"

Poor choice of words, as the back window of my car had been smashed on the way home that evening.

"And what good was *I* all this time?" His voice trembled with rage. "I thought it would be easier for you if I stayed away, but I left you in the middle of it."

"Are you saying I shouldn't have done any of that — gone to Cambridge, talked with Peg, looked at the summerhouse?"

He caught my hand and held it tightly. "I'm saying you shouldn't have done it without me." He exhaled, which seemed to blow away his anger and leaned back in his chair.

"Too right," I said. "Time to put an end to that."

He grinned and toyed with my fingers.

My phone dinged. I'd set it on the counter behind me, and when I leaned back to look, I could see I had a message from Gregory. I grabbed it, smearing tomato sauce across the screen.

"I'd say we found them," he wrote. The accompanying photo showed Terry Fisk and Sam Redman at a table, empty pint glasses in front of them. The photo had been taken from a slight angle, but that didn't mask their expressions — wide eyes and slack jaws. They looked gobsmacked. Caught!

I let out a whoop and turned the phone to Michael, who glanced at it and then held my hand still for another, closer examination.

"I know him," Michael said, frowning. "I know the one with the ponytail."

I paused in my celebration. "But how can you know him?"

"He came up to me in Cambridge on that Friday. We'd had to postpone the grants meeting, and I'd stopped in The Eagle for a sandwich. He looked surprised to see me, but then he kept watching, and next thing I knew he came up behind me in at the bar."

"Do you think he had followed you?" I asked, ignoring the next ding on my phone.

"Or he took advantage of the moment, because he recognized me from the foundation website. He spoke to me. He said he wanted to talk about his grant. I put a stop to it right there — I told him if he'd read the guidelines, he knew there should be no contact after the application goes in. I wouldn't let it look as if we're playing favorites."

"My God." I felt the heat rise in me, forcing me out of my chair like a rocket launch. "He wasn't supposed to be there that day. He told the police he'd been in Southampton. And even now he's lying, because he told Tess that he left Cambridge after the other night. I knew it wasn't true. The both of them had told me they would stick it out — to show how dedicated they are to getting the grant."

"Dedicated enough to kill for it," Michael said quietly. We both jumped when my phone rang.

"Gregory?" I answered. "This is amazing — well done, you. Stephen, too."

"Julia, did you see the second photo I sent? Did you see who it was they were looking at?"

"Did they spot you?"

"No, not me. Look for yourself."

"Hang on." I shifted the phone and switched to messages. Up popped a second text from Gregory, also with an accompanying snapshot. This one aimed at the doorway that led from another, larger room at the pub, and showed a woman with auburn hair — half-wedge, half-cropped — and a smirk on her face.

I sank back into my chair as all blood left my brain. Michael retrieved my phone just before it slid to the floor.

"Kitten woman," I whispered to him.

CHAPTER 24

"It's one of those journos — Olive Carboys," Michael said, looking at the photo. "What did you call her?"

"Her recorder that first day, I thought she was holding a kitten," I explained, but in a voice so weak Michael had to lean in to hear. "And she had scratches."

"She gave me a start, I can tell you that," Gregory said. "But she didn't see me. I was in that nook at the back. When I spotted her, I snapped the photo and ducked in here to the loo."

"Where's Stephen?"

"I left him out in the pub to keep an eye on the lot of them. Wait, I'll take a look." By now I'd turned the phone on speaker, and Michael and I hovered over it, holding our breath and listening as first one door, then another squeaked. "I think they're gone," Gregory whispered. "Yes," he said with confidence, "Stephen's giving me the nod."

The background noise increased to the usual pub level of clanking glasses and layers of conversation.

"She went over to them," we heard Stephen say. "They were talking, and I got up and moved closer to try to listen in."

"Stephen, you are not to do anything dangerous," I warned.

"It's a pub, Jools, what are they going to do in a crowd? It didn't matter, I couldn't hear a thing. She left, and after a minute, they did, too."

"Good work, the both of you," I said with pride.

"What's next?" Gregory said. "Should we try to follow them?"

"No," Michael said.

"Michael's right," I said. "We'll take care of this now."

"Mr. Sedgwick?" Gregory asked, his voice turning timid again. "Please let me apologize to you directly for any pain and suffering I've caused you this last week. It was never my intention to—"

"Julia's explained it all," Michael said. "Apology accepted. Don't think any more of it."

We both heard his sigh of relief.

"Next time we see you, the pints are on us, you two," I said. "Have a lovely evening."

* * *

"Proof. Tess can't deny this is direct proof of their guilt." I tapped my fork on the rim of my plate for emphasis.

Michael and I had decided to talk through what we'd learned before we contacted DI Callow. I had retrieved the chocolate cake from the boot of Vesta's car, and we settled on the sofa, each of us leaning against an end with our bare feet playing round in the middle.

"Kitten woman," I said — "Olive," Michael corrected — "has got something on Terry and Sam. It's obvious. She must have direct evidence that they killed Nick. She might be blackmailing them or something. The looks on their faces when she showed up at the pub! I'd say kitten woman better watch her step, because if they killed Nick over the grant, why wouldn't they kill her, too, to keep it quiet?"

"We don't know for certain how she got that information," Michael said in a speculative manner, "but if—" He stopped himself. "The best thing for us to do is to hand this all over to the police and let them run with it."

I sucked the fudge icing off my fork without answering. But I knew he was right. I had no desire to chase down that lot with a load of accusations. Far too dangerous. I picked up my phone.

"Now?" Michael asked. "You don't think it's a bit late."

I glanced at the time — just gone eleven.

"Remember the last time we said we'd wait to hand over evidence?" I asked.

He nodded to my phone. "Have at it."

I called before sending the photos. I wanted to know they would arrive fresh and would be seen immediately. DI Callow answered on the second ring.

"Julia, are you all right? Where are you?" Her tone was one of wide-awake impatience, as if I had broken my curfew and she stood tapping her toe at the front door.

"I'm fine — I'm in Haverhill with Michael."

"Yes, all right. What is it?"

"I'm sending you two photos taken this evening at The Eagle in Cambridge." Off the snapshots went. I waited, and Michael watched me wait. To the ensuing silence, I added, "They lied to you about leaving. And not only that — Terry lied to you about last Friday."

Michael's turn. He filled her in on his own sighting. "He never identified himself, and I didn't ask. When you questioned us about Nick, my first thought was that it had been him."

The blurred image of that Sunday afternoon when the two of us sat across the interrogation table at the Sudbury constabulary seemed eons ago, and yet, it had been exactly a week.

"So you see," I said, "Cambridge to Smeaton on that Friday afternoon, it's quite doable. An hour and he'd be there."

"Right, we'll get the pub's CCTV," Tess said. "Michael, you were looking into those journos. What have you found?"

"Well, the little weasel," he said — "Gregory" I corrected — "is harmless. He's the one that took those photos."

"And just how did that come about?" the DI asked. "That he was in the right pub and knew who to look for?"

I heard the suspicion in her voice, but I held my head high and owned up to it.

"As it happens," I said, "he's a friend of a friend, and when I realized that he might do a bit of—" I held up just in time. Probably not a good idea to use the word "surveillance" or point out to the DI that if *she* could have an informant — that fellow I'd met at The Den in Foxearth — then so could I. "You see, Terry and Sam would've recognized me or Michael. This seemed like a good plan. We needed proof to show you."

"How do you know you can trust the photographer? After all, he was one of those stalking you."

Because Alfie approved?

"Because my friend trusts him, that's why. Surely that means something."

"Michael, what about the others?"

"The big one's been sued for libel once before, so I'd say he's stepping carefully. But those two from *The People's News* — their site's been up, taken down, and gone up again. They seem able to dodge any complaints, and they're probably full of themselves. I'd say they've got nothing to lose and might try anything."

"And the woman?"

"Olive Carboys. I couldn't find her working anywhere before this. Her website, *Sightings*, is new. It's mostly filled with links that lead to royal gossip sites." Michael held up his phone so that I could see the screen and the headline splashed across it. *Murder Plot Widens — Did Ex-wife and Boyfriend Plan the Killing with Victim's Co-workers?*

In the span of a week, I had grown inured to these smear tactics, but not so inured that I didn't mutter "Cow" under my breath. Still, I kept to the issue at hand. "Will you pick them up now, Tess? Will you arrest Terry and Sam?"

"We will find them and question them, and we'll also question those who confirmed their alibis. But how was it the woman found those two?"

"I suppose," I said in a small voice, "she could've followed me."

We were all three silent. I thought about what that meant. If Olive the kitten woman had followed me to Cambridge when I went to meet Terry and Sam, she could've followed me away and to the roadside service, where the back window of my car had been smashed.

"But why would she do that?" I asked, as if we'd discussed the topic aloud.

"These hacks can get desperate enough to make their own news," Michael said.

"Are you staying there tonight, Julia?" Tess asked, and I knew she wasn't being a nosy parker.

"Yes. And tomorrow, I'm off to Minsmere for a location shoot, so I'll be well away from the village."

"Michael?"

"I'll be back at the cottage by tomorrow evening," he replied.

My heart was full. I leaned over for a swift kiss. What a lovely moment, apart from being on a three-way phone call with a detective inspector.

"I've some business to wrap up in Cambridge," Michael said, "but perhaps I should go with you to Minsmere?"

"No," I said, "there's no reason. I'll be far away listening for bitterns and waiting for the sand martins to return. I'll be back by late afternoon and I'll see you at the cottage."

Tess cleared her throat, and I blushed.

"And we will stay out of the case, Inspector Callow." Michael directed his voice to the phone, but his attention was all on me. I nodded briskly.

We ended the call, and Michael set his phone on the floor. As he did, a second, smaller, headline on *Sightings* caught my eye. *Where Will Victim's Remains Rest? "He wanted to return to his true love," says associate.*

Associate? Did Terry Fisk say that? Was kitten woman quoting him? Nick's true love was St. Kilda — would Terry take him back there? Would he like to drop by the TIC and collect the Grecian urn before winging his way to an extreme point off the coast of Britain to return Nick to the spot he longed to stay? I very much doubted it.

"What a load of rubbish." I kicked the phone with my toe and watched it slide away.

* * *

"Give my love to Miles," I said as I slung my bag over my shoulder and slipped on my shoes. That was a joke, of course, because Michael's older brother and I didn't quite get along. The first time we met, I had threatened him with bodily harm. Miles ran the family PR business and he had resented Michael's original departure from the fold and somehow blamed me. We'd yet to sort that out.

Michael, still in his pajama bottoms, held a mug of tea and leaned against the kitchen counter. "Look, Miles knew it was only temporary, this bit of work for him. There's no need for me to make a show of leaving. Why don't I just give him a ring and then I can go with you?"

"Would he believe you if you don't tell him face-to-face? Go on, make a clean break and then you'll be fresh and ready to take back all your responsibilities with Rupert. And you are welcome to them." I glanced out the window, saw the rain coming down in sheets, and thought about my trip to the coast.

"Good day for it," Michael said.

"Isn't it just? I'll have to make a dash for it." I gave Michael a kiss and lingered for a second one. "I'll stop at the TIC, but only for my mackintosh, and then it's straight to the coast." Nose to nose, I said, "I'll see you later."

I rang ahead to Basil. Good that he had everything in hand, and I wouldn't be needed until later, when Rupert arrived and I'd coordinate the filming of his segments. I took the turnoff to Smeaton and switched the wipers to "high." They swept the rain off in waves but helped not a bit. We'd have to stay indoors if it was like this at the coast. But that wouldn't matter, because there was a lovely spot in the Minsmere café with windows all round and bird feeders on the patio just outside. Rupert could talk, and over his shoulder viewers would see a host of greenfinches and goldfinches and all manner of finches feasting on sunflower seeds. Any brave souls who happened out to the reserve in the gale and took refuge in the café for a coffee would be rewarded with a ringside seat to watch Rupert film *A Bird in the Hand.*

When I sprinted from the car to the TIC and unlocked the door, I was met with the sight of the Grecian urn on the back table, and my second, although unconscious, reason for stopping in the village floated to the surface of my mind. Dutifully, Michael and I had left the evidence we'd gathered in the hands of the police, but it had been only after the phone conversation with Tess that I'd seen that second headline, the one about Nick's remains. What was kitten woman doing dredging up that business? Why had she ever even thought to mention his remains?

Unless she'd been chatting with someone about her circumstances — perhaps a family member in the village seeing to the business of death?

Each morning since Kathleen had arrived, she had vacated her room above the Stoat and Hare for Gwen to clean. She walked up Church Lane and, according to both Gwen and Kathleen, talked with the vicar. But it wasn't St. Swithun's male vicar. It was a woman — someone with dark hair "sort of," Gwen had said.

I left the urn where it sat, grabbed my mackintosh off the peg, but didn't take the time to put it on. I locked the door, ran the three steps to the car and threw my mack in the backseat as I dug for my phone. My call to Michael went straight to voicemail, and I had a vision of him standing across his brother's glass desk in the HMS, Ltd., offices with Miles's face a shocking shade of fuchsia. I left a brief message with little content, only to say I'd catch him up later.

I drove to the bottom of Church Lane and parked in front of the Stoat and Hare. Rainwater rushed through the street gutters on its way to overflowing the curb. I made a mad dash and leapt over the stream, arriving indoors with my bangs plastered to my forehead.

Not a soul in the pub — it was too early for even the earliest drinkers, and breakfast for hotel guests had long finished. A fresh pine scent mixed with the aroma of ale. Fred and Peg were behind the bar as he shifted bottles and restocked, while she stood with her hands on her hips. They each had a puzzled look.

"These things can't go walking off of their own accord, Peg." Fred scratched his chin with the back of his hand.

"I'm sure they'll turn up," Peg said. "Can't you make do in the meantime?"

I hadn't moved from the doorway but coughed to announce my presence.

"Good morning," I said. "Sorry to interrupt, but do you know if Kathleen is still upstairs?"

"Morning, Julia," Fred called over his shoulder as he lined up the bottles of whisky.

Peg came out from behind the bar. "Gwen's upstairs doing the rooms now, so Ms. Hawkins has left for a bit."

I needed Kathleen, but Gwen would be a good start. I could get a quick confirmation before marching into the church to confront that so-called journalist.

"Gwen," I said, "that's good. I just need a quick word with her." I bounded up the stairs.

The cleaning cart, parked in the corridor, signaled where I'd find Gwen — that and the loud, sucking motor of the vacuum as it was pulled across the carpet. I looked into the room. A suitcase in the corner and a couple of books on the table alongside a laptop were the only signs of occupancy, so Kathleen's room for certain. When Gwen took notice of me, I gave a little wave and she switched off the machine.

"Hiya," she said. "Your day off, isn't it?"

I felt a wee bit guilty seeing as how Gwen probably never had a day off, then I remembered that, at the moment, neither did I.

"Not quite. I'm on my way to Minsmere. We're filming for Rupert's program."

"You do all that as well as the estate work?" Gwen's eyes were wide. "And I thought I was busy."

"I used to be Dad's assistant, but now I'm only the TIC manager. It's just that I've filled in for a week or so, because of all that's happened." Best not to go into the details now. I pulled out my phone and brought up Gregory's photo of the person in question. "Gwen, you know the woman you've seen Kathleen talk with at the church? I know it's all the way at the top of the lane, but do you think — could this be the same woman?"

Gwen took my phone and held it at arm's length and then brought it closer, and enlarged the image.

"Yeah, she's the one. Isn't that odd?" She asked, almost to herself, eyes remaining on the photo. "From the distance, it's her haircut that makes me recognize her, but now, closer up, I sort of feel as if I've seen her before. But if she's the vicar, I suppose I have."

"She isn't the vicar," I said. "She's a bit of a nut job, and she's been hanging round the village recently. You might've seen her loitering on the pavement and that's why she looks familiar."

Gwen took another look and squinted. "Yeah, I suppose."

"If you see her, Gwen, don't talk to her. I'm hoping the police will see her off the estate."

"Is it that bad?"

"She's being such a bother they could do her for harassment. I'm sure the police'll take care of it." And if they didn't, I'd take care of her myself.

CHAPTER 25

I must rescue Kathleen, I thought, dashing down the hotel corridor and flying down the stairs. Little did she know she had been revealing intimate details of her brother's life not to the vicar of a church, but to a woman who lacked any moral compass and thought nothing of splashing lies about people all over the internet. Michael said it appeared her site had few followers, but that was entirely beside the point, as was the fact that Kathleen would be totally unaware of such salacious publicity. Small consolation.

As I headed toward the door of the pub, Peg called out, "Julia?"

"I'll be back, Peg," I replied over my shoulder. "Just nipping out for a moment."

I made ready to dive into the car for my mackintosh, but the tap had been turned off and not a raindrop fell, although the air remained heavy with moisture. So, I ran up the lane, dodging puddles and broken cobbles, through the lych-gate, into the churchyard, and up to the door. I paused for a moment in the covered porch, breathing hard, and ran my fingers through my damp hair.

The church, built of stone and flint, was cold and silent, the only light filtering through the huge, arched stained-glass windows. At first glance the vast space appeared empty, but then I spotted Kathleen sitting alone toward the front near the chapel, wearing her usual beige livery. She looked up at my entrance and watched as I walked up the center aisle, and sidestepped down her row, the wooden pew complaining loudly when I sat.

"Julia," she said, closing the book she had been reading. I caught sight of the title — *Ships and Their Mechanisms in the Eighteenth Century*.

"Hello, Kathleen, I'm sorry to disturb you."

"I wasn't praying, if that's what you think. It's only that this is a quiet place, and I retreat here."

"Of course. But you aren't always alone, are you? There's a woman you've met and spoken with?" I drew my phone out of my bag.

"Yes, the vicar," she replied looking over my shoulder as if to check for an imminent arrival. "Pleasant, but a bit talkative. She told me she sensed a loss in me and did I want to share it with her?"

Vile, despicable, slimy. "Is this her?" I held out my phone, my hand shaking, to show her Gregory's snapshot of kitten woman.

"Yes, it is. Not the usual look for a vicar, is it? But these days—"

"She's no vicar."

Kathleen's eyes shifted from the photo to my face and back. "But I thought she was carrying out her pastoral duties."

"Far from it. Has she been asking you personal questions about Nick?"

"Yes, and I didn't care to answer many of them."

I saw a stony look in Kathleen's eyes, and I dearly hoped she'd shown the same look to this Olive Carboys.

"She's been nosing around," I explained, "and she's caused a bit of a problem for us here in the village. I'll explain more later. Have you seen her today?"

"No. I've been alone until now."

"Would you let me know when you see her next? And don't feel obliged to speak to her at all. I don't think she should be bothering you, and I'm happy to report her."

"I wouldn't want to cause anyone trouble."

I'd like to cause kitten woman a great deal of trouble. "Oh, and also, Kathleen—"

She rushed to cut in, her cheeks pink. "I do apologize for not collecting the container with Nick's ashes. It was not fair of me to leave it like that, Julia, but I must confess to you that the sight of it goes against the very core of my being, and I didn't think I would be able to sleep if—"

"No, please, don't worry about it. You can leave it with me for as long as necessary." Perhaps I shouldn't have said that. Perhaps Kathleen would get on a plane today for Nova Scotia and leave me with the Grecian urn forever. "Well—" I stood and the pew groaned — "I'd best be off."

"Julia." Kathleen held up a hand and then dropped it to her lap, her eyes wandering round the church fixtures. "It's quite near, isn't it? The police told me the place where Nick was killed is on the grounds of the Hall, and I've seen the brick gate pillars across the road."

I nodded. "There's a small summerhouse off the drive. It's derelict at the moment, and rather overgrown. Do you want to see? Because if you do, I could take you over." *Please say no.* "The police are finished at the site, but I must tell you, Kathleen, that you're likely to see signs of . . ." The murder? Nick's blood? I couldn't bring myself to say those words to his sister.

"Yes, I understand. I can't quite decide if I should or shouldn't go. Thank you for your offer. Let me think about it."

* * *

I left her to her ships and their mechanisms and returned to the pub to find a couple of early drinkers at the bar and Peg writing up the lunch menu on the chalkboard.

"Sole with lemon sauce," I said. "Sounds lovely."

"Fred's none too happy about having to pull out his second-string cutlery for prep. You look as if you need a cup of tea," she said.

"God yes, I'm gasping." I hadn't forgotten about Minsmere, but it comforted me to think that Basil could handle it. I felt almost reluctant to leave the village. But I would do. I would be on my way after a quick cuppa.

Peg brought me a pot of tea and a massive fruit scone and butter. "Ooh, lovely," I said and got to work. When she hesitated at the table, and I said, "Sit, talk with me."

She sat. "No, it's only . . ." I could see the high color on her cheeks. "How are you?" she asked, in that sickroom voice people use.

"I'm fine, really." And for the first time in a week and a day, I meant it. But Peg must've noticed the state of me during the past week — everyone else had. "I'm better. Much better."

"That's a relief," she said. "It's only that you've been under such stress lately. But today I can see you look happy again."

Between the scone in my mouth and the tears in my eyes, I couldn't say much for a moment. Finally, I added, "Michael will be back this evening."

"Ah, that's lovely," Peg said.

"I tell you what. We'll come in for dinner."

"Brilliant. Everything's back to normal."

"Peg?" Fred called out the door of the kitchen.

"Right, love, just there." Off she went.

I polished off my scone and a second cup of tea before I rang Michael and Tess. Voicemail in both instances.

"She is harassing tenants and visitors to the estate," I said on the DI's message, "and I know that Lord Fotheringill will press charges as soon as he finds out." I sighed. "She's horrible, Tess. Can't you do something?"

On to Minsmere and the coast.

* * *

Despite the general circumstances, I felt a lightness — almost an ebullience — as I went on my way. I was free of the guilt that I had been dragging around with me for a week and almost free of the accompanying anger, too. I would spend midday on the coast and then return to my Pipit Cottage and Michael. We would have a celebration — a homecoming — and dine out on Fred's excellent food. Michael would pick out the wine. I wondered if the sole would be carried over to the dinner menu. Accompanied by local asparagus, of course. My tummy growled, and it wasn't even lunchtime.

And so I motored along in Vesta's car and allowed my clear mind to motor along with speculation, supposition, and imagination. Some might think that a dangerous mix, but to me it meant discovering lines of thought that would otherwise remain hidden. Perhaps I was holding too fast to this business about kitten woman's harassment. Shouldn't I be thinking of Nick's murderers instead? Terry and Sam's dark secret — that they would do anything to get what they wanted, to secure a grant that would set them up as respected ornithologists carrying out research in a not-so-remote place. But weren't the police taking care of them? It could already be finished. They may have confessed and been locked up. A tiny part of me wished I could've seen that.

Barely three-quarters of an hour into my journey, not far past Stowmarket, near a place called Forward Green, I met the rain again. Also, my bladder called out. Two cups of tea before a road trip — I should've known better. The rain had returned with a vengeance, and the water streaming down the windows didn't help my need for a loo. I pulled up at the Shepherd and Dog pub, forced to park along the road as vehicles and two tourist coaches sat chock-a-block in the car park. "Right, here's for it," I said to my mackintosh, which had lain idle in the backseat all morning. I held it over my head and made a run for it, hanging it with the rest of the rain gear on pegs just inside the pub.

Business accomplished, I bought a packet of crisps so the barman wouldn't look at me askance for using the facilities free of charge. I scanned both large rooms seeking an empty seat, but hordes of coach tourists sat hunkered over coffees waiting out the rain, so I stood while I finished my snack, and, brushing crisp crumbs from my fingers, I stepped out into the small, covered entry. The rain had not let up, so it was time I donned my mackintosh properly. I pulled my arms through and felt a drag in one pocket that caused me to list to the right. Alfie's treasures, which had been accumulating throughout these last few days.

When I stuck my hand in my pocket, I was met with a variety of shapes and textures — heavier bits at the bottom, with a wad of something soft. Unsure of what treasures the rook had left me, I scooped up and drew out the entire mass and found a folded beer mat from the Stoat and Hare, a large black button, two round stones, and something enormous, soft, and dark — the biggest spider I'd ever laid eyes on.

I squealed and flung it from my hand. It flopped to the ground, and the other objects scattered, landing in the gravel chippings of the car park. The spider lay still. My heart hammered in my chest as I stared at the thing, daring it to move.

It didn't, and not because it was dead, but because it wasn't a spider. When that realization hit me, laughter bubbled up and I glanced round, embarrassed at my initial reaction. I peered at the reddish-brown mass lying at the corner of the stone slab. It looked like spun wool with leaves and crumpled bits of paper tangled in it, almost like a nest.

Wool? Had Alfie picked up a stray skein of knitting wool from Three Bags Full? I bent over for a closer examination, the rain splashing in my face.

No, not wool. Not a spider. Hair.

CHAPTER 26

Rain overflowed the gutters of the pub roof and cascaded onto the chippings just beyond the *objet d'art* at my feet. For that's what it looked like, I decided — one of those mixed-media collages where everything from dolls' heads and machine bolts to broken coffee cups and muffin tins gets glued together. Alfie, the artist, had been rummaging in the bins out back of The Hair Strand in the village, had added other found objects, and had put his bits and bobs together in my mackintosh pocket.

The pub door pushed open, hitting me in the bum. "Sorry," said one of the tourists as they streamed out and trudged toward their coaches, several of them treading on the edges of Alfie's creation. Citizen scientist from birth, I knew what I must do. I reached down, swept up the collage — trying not to think that I had a handful of someone's hair — and stuffed it back into the pocket of my mack, adding the beer mat, button, black stones, and mossy twig that lay nearby. Tennyson would love this. She probably had a database listing all of Alfie's treasures, and I certainly couldn't deny her the chance to add these items to her species study.

I hurried to the car, throwing off my mack and tossing it in the passenger seat, as my phone rang.

"All finished at Minsmere?" Michael asked as one of the coaches pulled out of the car park and rolled past me.

"Finished? I'm not even there yet." A quick look at my watch told me I was well past my scheduled arrival. Although I'd begun with buckets of time, the morning had quite escaped me. "I suppose I'm a bit late, but with Basil, you know, it hardly matters. And you?"

"I'm in Cambridge, just had a talk with Miles."

"Poor Miles," I said, not really meaning it. "How did he take it?"

"Ah, he's all right. He's invited us to dinner at the weekend."

My punishment, I suppose. "Are you leaving for the village now?"

"I'm taking one more meeting for him, but it's here and it won't take long. You'd best be on your way."

"I told Peg we might have dinner at the Stoat and Hare this evening. A bit of a celebration — don't you think?"

"You'll wear your pink dress?"

He loved my flirty dress with the high hem and low back, but it had been seen far too often. I wondered if Dot had any other secrets hidden in the back of her dress shop.

"We'll just see about that," I said before we rang off. I hoped I had time for a bit of shopping later.

I heard rather than saw the other coach pull out as I remained parked on the side of the road with rain pouring down the windshield and obscuring my vision. I rang ahead to Basil, but as it turned out, he'd already started up with filming Rupert's segments. "He said you wouldn't mind." The sentence floated in the air, and I knew Basil worried that I'd shoot it down. But I was done with that.

"Fantastic. We'll watch the film when I arrive. And we'll talk about a new feature on smart birds. I've got the first one in mind already. Cheers, bye." I would give them all Alfie's particulars and provide visuals — the collage in my pocket with its long auburn hair as a unifying element.

Whacking that length of hair off all at once had been a drastic change for someone. I'd done the same thing when I moved to Smeaton — my blond locks that had reached halfway down my back replaced with a chin-length bob. The new me.

In my mind, I saw the scene from a year ago. Rosy at The Hair Strand carefully braiding my long tresses before cutting them off, so that she could send them away to the charity that makes wigs for children who lose their hair to cancer treatment. Mine had been plenty long for that. Certainly that mass of auburn hair, was, too. Why wasn't it braided and sent on its way to do good?

That is what happens when people turn all DIY with their 'do.

Stephen's voice in my head. He had said that when he looked at the photo of kitten woman, half-wedge, half-cropped. Reddish-brown hair. I glanced over to the passenger seat where lay my mack. I rang Rosy.

"It's about time you're coming in, isn't it?" she asked when I identified myself.

"Yes, I'm in desperate need of a trim" — I'd have to put her off as Stephen had just done that for me — "but right now, let me ask you a rather silly question. Have you cut any really long hair lately? As long as mine was?"

"No," she said, drawing out the word. "Why? Are you thinking of doing one of those fundraisers where all the villagers grow their hair out and there are prizes and we send off the hair to the charity?"

"Well, now, Rosy, you've caught me out, haven't you?" I said cheerily, as a string of enormous lorries roared past me. I raised my voice. "And I'll certainly need you in on the planning of that one. But can't talk now — I'll be in touch."

Confirmed — Rosy had not done this job. No, the hair had been cut by its owner, kitten woman. I felt certain of this. And to think I'd picked it up and stuffed it in my pocket. I rubbed the palms of my hands on my trousers, trying to wipe away any vestige of her. Why ever would she do that?

And then she had tossed it out. Why — and where? Alfie had recovered it and stuffed it in the pocket of my mackintosh. Why? Alfie was a collector, that's why.

The important thing to ask was could this be a way to be rid of her for good? Could she be charged with a crime for cutting her own hair and throwing it away? Sadly, I didn't think so.

But that didn't mean I wouldn't try. I rang Tess.

"Julia, where are you?"

Why must the police always know my whereabouts?

"On my way to Minsmere, remember?"

"Yes, right," she said. "Anyone with you?"

"No, the crew is already there. Dad, too. I'm running a bit late. Why?"

"I rang Terry Fisk just after we talked last night." The DI calling my prime suspect at midnight sent a shiver through me. "I said we'd further questions and I expected the two of them at the station at ten o'clock. They agreed to come in."

"And?"

"They've yet to appear. And they aren't answering calls. They haven't been seen at the pub in Cambridge. We contacted their old friend from uni where they were staying, and according to him, they left at seven this morning."

I checked the time — just now one o'clock. Their journey from Cambridge to Sudbury, which normally took an hour and a bit, had stretched into six.

"They've done a bunk?" I whispered.

"Apparently. You continue to Minsmere — best to stay clear of the village until this is settled. But ring me, would you, as soon as you arrive?" In the past, her clipped words, impersonal and full of police authority, would've set me off, but now they gave me comfort.

"You don't think they'd go to the village looking for me?"

"I'd say if they wanted to get away, they'd try to go as far as possible and fast, but still, it would be good to know you are out of the way. The thing is I don't know why they would bother—"

She broke off, and I heard Sergeant Glossop's voice in the background, saying something about a crash. A bit of reality settled on me — the police had to deal with it all, didn't they? Murder, smashed car windows, road-traffic accidents.

"Just there," she said away from the phone. "Julia, the thing is, the pub's sent us CCTV of Friday afternoon, the four-hour window of the murder. We see Terry Fisk approach Michael. It's a brief encounter, and the rest of the afternoon, he is sitting there alone, nursing a pint."

"No," I wailed, "that can't be. What if you have Nick's time of death wrong? How about that — it could've been later. Or earlier?"

I heard her sigh. "That question has been asked and answered. But it doesn't mean I won't ask it again. When a body has been left as long as this one and with the overnight temperatures, the more time passes, the wider the time frame of the murder grows."

"So, it's possible one of them did it. It isn't impossible." I grasped this straw of hope.

"I will go over the details again with the pathologist, but do not think you can take this and make more of it than it is. It remains unlikely."

"They had to have done it." I stamped my foot on the floor of the car. "If not Terry, then Sam. It could've been him."

"Redman maintains he was at work, and we've requested the CCTV feed from his company."

Sam Redman seemed the least likely murderer, but it was down to him.

"Tess, about that woman journo."

"Julia, unless it's an emergency, I'll have to ring you back."

"Yes, fine. Bye." I wouldn't let go of it, to be sure.

I shook my head to clear it and started the engine. I'd never arrive at Minsmere if I didn't get going, and so when my phone rang again, I had a thought not to answer until I saw Kathleen's name.

"Julia, I'm sorry to disturb you, but you did say to let you know if I saw that woman again. I had a most disturbing visit from her earlier."

That woman — she wouldn't let us be.

"Did you tell me her name?" Kathleen asked.

"Olive. What has she done? Kathleen, where are you? Did you see her at the church?"

She paused, as if sorting through my questions.

"No, I left the church following your warning. I came back here to the hotel, and Peg Phipps, the proprietor" — yes, yes, I knew who Peg was — "offered me a table in the dining room for my work. It was morning, and no one about. That Olive woman came looking for me. Apparently, she went up to my room first, and then she found me in here."

A cold shiver ran through me at the thought of Kathleen being tracked.

"What did she say to you?"

"She asked me where Nick's ashes were. She told me that it would help my grief if she could pray over them and so why didn't we get them now and do that?"

"That's dreadful, it's disgusting."

Not the praying part, but the entire subterfuge in order to invent more horrible headlines. Had the woman no conscience at all? How low would she stoop to scrape up lies and form them into her pseudo-journalism? What could she possibly gain from such an effort — a top job on the publication that spewed the most scandalous lies? Someone should remind her that *News of the World* was no more.

"Well, disconcerting, certainly," Kathleen said, and I could hear her regain control. "I told her I knew she was not the vicar and these were private matters, and I had someone locally taking care of the matter. I told her to leave. And so, Julia, I'm ringing to say that if she knows of our relationship, I may have dropped you in the middle of it, and I'm sorry."

I laughed but, mortified, tried to cover it with a cough. I blushed to hear that Kathleen thought we had a relationship, and I wondered if, after she left Smeaton, I should stay in touch. Was she still considered my sister-in-law?

"Are you in the dining room now?" I asked.

"Oh no, I've returned to my room. It was pleasant there to begin with, but people began arriving for lunch, you see." Monday — probably two tables occupied. Far too many people for Kathleen.

"Look, I will take care of this. You leave it with me." I should go this instant and confront this Olive, this kitten woman. I should not subject Kathleen to one more day of such harassment.

But I was meant to be at Minsmere.

Although, of course, Basil had things well in hand.

No, Tess said to stay away from the village.

But . . .

I felt dizzy, put my head back on the seat rest, and closed my eyes.

"There's one more thing, Julia." A pause. "The crematorium rang a few moments ago to say that the proper urn has arrived."

"Good, yes, that's fantastic," I said, at once embarrassed at my enthusiasm. "I mean, you must be relieved to know that will be sorted."

"I've told them I'd be by later today. May I stop round and collect Nick's ashes?"

There you are; it had been decided for me.

CHAPTER 27

Before I headed back to Smeaton, I sent two texts — one to Tess, accusing Olive of harassment, and one to Michael, with hugs and kisses, telling him Kathleen needed me and asking him to look in The Eagle before he departed Cambridge, just in case Terry or Sam were cowering in a dark corner.

I may not be able to prove those two killed Nick, but I could hand over Nick's ashes and rid the village once and for all of kitten woman, even if I had to frog-march her to the estate boundary and give her a swift kick in the bum to send her on her way. I tore down the A14 wishing Vesta's car had a wiper speed above high, and made it to the village in a half hour, coasting up to the Stoat and Hare before yanking on the hand brake. I had planned it all out on the drive. The police would need evidence of harassment, certainly — apart from what kitten woman had done to Michael and me, which probably came under the grimy umbrella of free speech. But she had misrepresented herself to Kathleen, and she had stalked her. Could we say that? Sightings — *ha*, I thought, seeing the wordplay in the name of her online rag — I would record sightings of her. She had visited Kathleen's room upstairs at the pub, and so I would begin with Peg and Gwen.

The rain had been reduced to sweeps of large drops followed by a pause followed by another sweep of drops — the clouds shaking out the last of their moisture. I grabbed my mack, but only threw it over my arm and hopped out of the car. I hadn't made it to the pub door before I heard such a clamor of cawing across the road that I stopped and looked back to see over the bridge that spanned the brook, a group of about a dozen rooks flying up and round, creating their own dark funnel cloud as they dived and soared. I squinted at another, larger, winged figure. Ah, a buzzard — a large predator, but the rooks were mobbing him, showing no fear in defending their nests and their territory, announcing to one and all that they would not stand for this invasion. I took a page from SaraJane's class book and envisioned all of us chasing kitten woman away in the same manner. I smiled.

As if in response to the mobbing, I heard a single cawing coming from behind the building. I followed the sound, walking around the back to the small yard between the pub and the outbuilding that housed the pub's rubbish and recycling bins.

Alfie perched on the very corner of the shed, flapping wildly and keeping up his complaints. Standing in the middle of the yard was Gwen.

"But I'm only taking out the veg trimmings for the compost," she said to the bird, hands in the air to show him a newspaper piled high with wilted lettuce leaves and potato peelings.

"Does he want them for himself?" I asked, and Gwen turned to me and laughed.

"If only — I've tried that one. It's something about this shed that's got him so agitated. It's been that way for a week or more."

Alfie turned his head, giving me his profile of gray beak and beady eye, before flying straight at me. Without thinking, I put my arms up in front of my face and felt the wind from his beating wings as he paused in midair and plucked at my sleeve with his beak.

"Here you go now, Alfie," Gwen called. "Door's open — it's all yours."

She stood holding the shed door wide. The rook twisted in midair, reversing direction, and flew straight into the darkness. Gwen and I stood quiet for a moment. The mobbing over the road had ceased, and I could hear the normal road traffic and, in the distance, the *yaffle* of a green woodpecker.

"Well, then," I said, "perhaps you could get him to sort the recycling for you while he's in there."

Gwen shook her head. "He's a quiet soul at home, you know. We've got a large corner of the sitting room for him. Thank God Derry didn't mind. We made it into a sort of loose wire cage, almost floor to ceiling and as big as a dinner table. Fitted it with his own tree branch and he roosts on that every night."

"Does he go in on his own?" I asked.

"Oh, yeah. He seems to like bedtime. He starts getting ready ages before we do — cleaning his feathers and such. He can do quite delicate work with his beak. We can hear that *clack-clack-clack* as he goes at it. While that's going on, we take turns reading stories aloud." Gwen gave me a nervous glance. "Tennyson and I do — Alfie doesn't read, of course."

"Not yet," I added.

"You've returned from your television program work, have you?" Gwen asked, checking her watch. "You were quick to the coast and back."

"Yes, well, I never quite made it. Something's come up and I wanted to ask you if you saw the woman you thought was the vicar go to Kathleen's room today?"

"I did," Gwen said, her eyes widening. "And it was odd in an unsettling way. She just appeared behind me in the room — gave me a fright, I can tell you. She asked where Kathleen was, as if I was supposed to keep track of the guests' whereabouts. I told her I didn't know, but perhaps she'd like to ask Fred about it. That sent her on her way."

"Good, you did the right thing. I've notified the police about her."

"But look now, there's something else. When you showed me that snapshot, and I could see her closer up, I thought she looked familiar. And now, I've remembered where it was the first time I saw her, but it doesn't make much sense. She's the one I turfed out of the kitchen that day of the funeral reception. Mind you, she looked a fair bit wilder that day. Her hair" — Gwen waved her hands round her head — "it was long and full, standing out in all directions. In the photo and what she looked like this morning, her hair's all cut off."

I had accepted that kitten woman aka Olive Carboys had whacked off her own hair but hadn't considered just where the event had occurred. But this had to work in our favor. "DIY hairdo," I said. "But why? She must be on the run. That's it. She'd been caught spreading lies elsewhere and authorities were in pursuit. She legged it and ended up here." This gave me such hope — hope that the police really would be able to do something.

Gwen's brow furrowed, and I realized I should offer an explanation, but before I could, she joined in my supposing. "And she wanted to give herself a new look for a fresh start?"

My hand flew up to my bob as I remembered starting over.

Gwen's hand touched her own multilayered, straight cut, dislodging a couple of tiny clips. She smiled with chagrin. "I tried that myself — cutting my own hair. I learned the hard way I'm no stylist."

I was about to recommend Rosy when Alfie flew out of the shed and perched on the edge of a stack of pallets near the back door of the pub. He had a beakful of something reddish-brown that looked like wool. He laid his prize down, ruffled and smoothed his feathers, and eyed us one at a time.

"My God," Gwen said. "Is that hair?"

"It's her hair," I replied. "The rest of it."

"What was it doing in there?" Gwen asked, nodding toward the shed.

"She was on the run and ended up here, and had to lay up somewhere to give herself the makeover. She must've been around all that afternoon — all weekend even."

The truth slapped me in the face — kitten woman was the anonymous tip. She had landed in Smeaton-under-Lyme by accident. Sleepy little village, she thought, just the place to lie low until whatever trouble she was in blew over. She'd boldly marched into the pub thinking no one would notice her in the crowd for the funeral reception. She'd given herself a botched makeover. Perhaps she'd slept rough and wandered the grounds of Hoggin Hall. The thought of her walking on Fotheringill land made me both nauseous and furious. She had come across Nick's body on Saturday afternoon and had phoned the police to tell them. What luck, she must've thought — just the tip she needed to start a new wave of destruction.

Ring Tess. Ring Michael.

"Is she dangerous, this woman?" Gwen asked.

"No, not dangerous. Just . . ." Evil? Delighting in others' despair? "Odd. Best to steer clear of her. Where will Tennyson go after school?"

"His Lordship has invited the two of us to the Hall for tea. She's chuffed, I can tell you. She printed off one of your leaflets and is studying up."

I put my hand on Gwen's arm and squeezed. "That's fantastic. I'm so glad you're doing this. Yes, good. You haven't met Thorne or Sheila Bugg yet, have you? You'll have such a lovely time."

Alfie had remained silent, turning his head to one, then the other of us, as if keeping up with the conversation and waiting for the moment he had something to contribute. It came when I took one step away to leave — he flapped twice and gave a complaining squawk, edging himself closer to the hair.

"Yes, all right," I said, scooping up the wad and stuffing it in the other pocket of my mack. "There now — satisfied?"

Apparently. He flew off.

* * *

As did I — off to the TIC to get ready for Kathleen to collect Nick's ashes. I left Vesta's car in front of the pub, needing to move my legs to make me think. I would sort through the latest influx of evidence and immediately turn it all over to the police. They would come to the same conclusion, surely. I began walking, but my pace quickened, and by the time I passed my cottage and the shops along the high street, I had stepped it up to a trot until, panting, I reached the TIC. I stepped in, keeping the lights off and the Closed sign up. I locked the door behind me. It was, after all, my day off. The rain may have stopped, but the air remained thick with moisture, warm and close. I hung up my mack and stripped off my sweater, leaving only a T-shirt layer until I had cooled down. I moved the Grecian urn from the back table to the front counter without a thought, as if it had become a part of the TIC décor. I would be happy to send Nick on his way with his sister.

Now to business. My call to Tess went to voicemail, as did the one to Sergeant Glossop. Third call's the charm — PC Moira Flynn answered.

I sat at our work table in the dim light and told her what I'd discovered about Olive Carboys — seen at the Stoat and Hare and most probably the source of the anonymous tip phoned into the police on that Saturday. "Can you tell DI Callow all this for me?" I asked. "I'm positive she's the one. Almost positive. Where is she, anyway — the inspector, that is? I would really like to speak with her."

"And she would like to speak with you, Ms. Lanchester. I believe DI Callow wants to explain to you the latest developments."

"Why? What's happened?" I took a hopeful stab. "Terry and Sam — has she found them?"

"Mr. Fisk and Mr. Redman, yes, the two persons of interest DI Callow had wanted to question. They have been located."

Have been located? That didn't sound good. "Are they . . . what?"

"They were in a car that failed to negotiate a turn on the road just outside of Foxearth. Speed may have been a factor."

Road-traffic accident. "They're dead?" I whispered.

"No, God no, I'm sorry — you mustn't think that. Bloody hell, I really need to get better at this," Moira muttered. "They are in hospital in Bury Saint Edmunds. I don't have any further details. Oh wait — unconscious."

They hadn't tried to escape — they had been on their way to the Sudbury police station. But why in such a hurry?

"Ms. Lanchester? Are you there?"

"Yes."

"The inspector said to hold tight and she'd ring you as soon as she possibly could. Hold tight, she said."

Yes, hold tight. I knew what that meant — don't go chasing after the suspects when they are in hospital.

"But I can tell you this," Moira said. "I've been trying to learn where Mr. Hawkins had stayed locally — his lodgings."

Nick staying somewhere local — that had not occurred to me, but of course he had to find lodgings. Had I thought he'd made a day trip all the way from St. Kilda to Smeaton and planned to head straight back after taking care of business?

"Well, I found it," Moira said, triumph in her voice. "He was in a B&B run by a Mrs. Banks over near West Wickham. Out in the country — not much round there."

Of course Nick would find the most isolated B&B possible.

"He booked for three nights," Moira continued, "but didn't return after the second one, according to Mrs. Banks. That would've been the Friday that he didn't return, of course. Left his kit — although she says there's not much of it. I'm just going over now to talk with her. But she did tell me this. Mr. Hawkins had a woman visitor while he was here."

* * *

The puzzle kept rearranging itself in my mind. One second, pieces fit together a particular way, and the next, they didn't. Who visited Nick? Had he contacted the online journalists himself, in hopes of exposing Terry and Sam's deceit, and kitten woman had paid him a visit? No, that made no sense. What would those online rags care about a foundation grant to track vagrant birds? They were much more interested in sex, lies, and murder.

I crawled under our tiny desk area to retrieve the grant applications that I'd stashed below. I would do as I was told and wait for Callow to ring. She would be pleased to learn I wasn't chasing after Olive Carboys the kitten woman. No, I'd leave that to the police. Meantime, I'd pore over the documents one more time in hopes of finding that one tiny piece of evidence that might be the key. On my hands and knees under the desk, rummaging round, I gave a thought to Terry and Sam lying in hospital and hoping they would be all right — and then wondered why I wished that.

The door of the TIC rattled, and the bell jingled a faint response. I started, bumping my head on the desk, but I stayed put, listening hard for another sound but hearing only my heart pounding.

Don't be an idiot, Julia, only tourists unable to read the Closed sign. Shove off, you ramblers, and let me sort this out. I remained under the desk awhile longer, well out of sight, just to be sure they'd moved along.

Finally, I climbed up off the floor. I would make myself a cup of tea, I thought, and ring Michael to tell him these latest developments. But first, I nipped into the loo.

I had only just turned on the tap to wash my hands, when a crash sent me almost through the roof. I heard glass tinkling to the floor and a heavy thud.

I turned to stone, too shocked to move as my mind rushed to imagine a reason for the noise. A car had crashed into the window of the TIC. A large rock had been thrown from a speeding lorry. Boys kicking a football. I had an urge to run out and, at the same time, block the door of the loo and hide. As these desires battled it out, I heard the sound of glass crunching underfoot, and a choked voice sobbed, "Look what she's done to you. Come on now. Come with me."

I didn't breathe. In the tiny slit between door and wall, I saw a figure moving past. I heard more crunching, then silence except for the pounding of my heart. I waited until I couldn't stand it any longer. I slid open the door an inch and peered out.

The front window remained intact, but broken glass lay strewn across the floor. The door had been the hit — I saw a brick on the floor against the far wall. A cold, damp gust of wind blew in the doorway while outside on this sleepy, gray Monday afternoon, the street was empty, everyone still at work or at school or in front of the telly. A single car passed without pause. I took one step into the room and surveyed the scene, my arms wrapped round my chest, hoping to stop the trembling. Apart from the door and the mess, it looked as if nothing had been touched, nothing stolen. The computer, printer, my mobile on the back table, my bag under the desk — everything accounted for.

No, wait. One thing gone — the Grecian urn.

CHAPTER 28

In a wild moment, I imagined that Kathleen had come to collect Nick's ashes and, finding the TIC locked, bashed in the door and made a run for it. I blamed the state of my nerves for the giggles this triggered, giggles I couldn't control until my phone rang, causing me to shout and jump back. But it was Michael ringing. I could see his name on the screen. I thought my mind played tricks on me, because as I reached for the phone, I could hear him shouting.

"*Julia? Julia!*"

He ran into the TIC holding his phone to his ear until he saw me, and I flew into his arms.

"Are you all right?" He stroked my hair. "What's all this? I was just ringing when I got close enough to see the door broken in." My phone continued to ring, and at last he ended the call, and the place was quiet enough for us to hear a loose piece of glass fall from the doorframe with a tiny, tinkling crash.

I opened my mouth. "I . . ." I stopped and tried to sort out where to begin. "I . . . I came back here because I was worried about Kathleen. She's being harassed, it's just awful. That kitten woman Olive Carboys let Kathleen believe she was the vicar. But Gwen has figured out that it was her

— kitten woman — she'd seen in the kitchen of the pub the Friday afternoon during the funeral reception. Alfie's been trying to tell me that with the hair, and I think she's somehow running away from trouble and washed up here in our village and found Nick's body. *She's* the anonymous caller to the police, I'm sure of it. But why? Just to get her headlines? I tried to ring Tess, but they're busy with Terry and Sam, who've been in a car crash and are in hospital. And now this."

Michael held fast, rubbing his hands on my arms. He frowned. Had I sounded that incoherent?

"You weren't at the cottage," he said, "so I thought you must be here. I could see something wrong with the door as I approached. Do you know who did it? What did they take?"

"I know who it did because I was here when it happened."

"You what?"

"In the loo — she didn't see me. I don't think she knew I was here."

"She?"

"Kitten woman," I practically shouted. "That's what I've been trying to tell you. She threw a brick through the door and came in."

"You saw her?"

"I saw a flash of reddish-brown hair" — I gave my mackintosh a sideways glance — "and I heard her say, 'Here you are.' She must've been talking to the urn." I shivered at the thought.

"Why in God's name would she break in here?"

"To steal Nick's ashes. To take him hostage. Can you imagine the next headlines?"

"Right," he said. "Police." But I heard his call go straight to Tess's voicemail. He hit "end" and shook his head.

"The foot patrol should be here soon," I said.

"Why would she do this?"

"Because she's mad," I said hotly. My fury burned just below the surface. "How dare she deceive a grieving family member and harass the rest of us. How is she allowed to get away with it — how could a sane person even want to do what she does? She's mental, that's what she is. She's barmy. Barking. She's off her nut. She's daft." I whirled round to pace and vent, but the TIC didn't afford pacing room. Instead, I came face-to-face with my mackintosh on its peg and saw, stuck to the outside of a pocket, a long, reddish-brown hair.

I was forever pulling a long, dark strand out of my food, Sam Redman had said. I whirled round to Michael.

"She's Daft Doris."

* * *

The sudden knowledge made me weak, and I grabbed at Michael as I sank into a chair. He didn't speak but pulled the other chair directly in front of me and sat, searching my face for the answer to the unasked question. Had I gone round the bend myself? It was no wonder, because I hadn't told him that part of my conversation at The Eagle with Terry and Sam. I forced my muscles to relax, and I inhaled and exhaled slowly. I must sound sane.

"Terry and Sam said Nick had a girlfriend on St. Kilda, someone who worked in the food services. They called her Daft Doris and said she was his 'shadow' and described her as wild-looking with a massive amount of reddish-brown hair. And Alfie found that hair" — I shook a finger at my mackintosh — "in the shed behind the pub. He put some of it in my pocket and brought out the rest when I stopped to see Gwen earlier."

Michael reached over, pulled a pocket open, and peered inside. "Alfie was trying to tell you that Olive had cut her hair and thrown it out at the pub?"

It did sound a bit batty.

"Rooks are smart," I said, looking at the table and remembering Alfie dropping the key to my cottage in my bag. "And they have a great memory for faces. They can identify objects and remember where they belong or where they saw it. Only the other day, Tennyson and I ran Alfie through an exercise."

"All right, she's no journo," Michael said. "She's Daft Doris. Alfie told you she cut her own hair."

"Actually, Stephen told me that."

"Well, good — there's someone I actually know. At least that part makes sense."

I needed Michael to catch up with my thoughts, which seemed to be sprinting ahead so fast even I was having trouble keeping pace.

"Daft Doris came down with Nick, I suppose. Or followed him. Nick might not have invited her along, but when she turned up, he probably just accepted it. And then he died. Did she see Terry or Sam do it? And she sorts of fell apart. But why all that subterfuge — pretending to be a journo? Why didn't she tell the police what happened? Maybe she truly is a bit . . . off. What do you think?"

"I think," he pulled out his phone once again, "we turn it all over to the police."

"Yes, please — let them take her away."

Michael rang the desk sergeant, gave him the pertinent details, and asked him to alert Callow and Glossop.

"Why don't you go back to the cottage and I'll wait here for the police?" Michael asked. "There's no need for you to stay. I'll explain, and when Callow's got her team to work, we'll follow you there."

"Yes." I nodded. "No." I shook my head but saw Michael's eyes spark. "Yes," I said, grabbing his arm. "Yes, back to the cottage, lock the door. It's just that first, I need to tell Kathleen what's happened. She's expecting to collect Nick's ashes — she could be on her way this very minute. I have to explain."

"Ring her."

I lifted my hand to my ear in a mock phone call. "Hello Kathleen, just ringing to say your brother's remains have been stolen by his girlfriend from St. Kilda who is, oh by the way, a nutter. Have a lovely afternoon. Cheers, bye." I took Michael's hands between mine and held them to my chest. "I can't do that to her. I need to tell her in person. She's just in her room at the pub. I'll walk up the high street in broad daylight and explain, and then I'll take myself straight to the cottage."

"I don't like it," Michael said. "I should go with you."

"You need to wait for the police. I won't be in any danger — Daft Doris has got what she wanted, hasn't she? Even if we don't know why."

A thought buzzed round in my head, but I couldn't hold still long enough to let it land. I leapt up and went for my mack but pulled my hand away.

"No, I'll leave that here. It's evidence and anyway, the rain has stopped, hasn't it?" I looked down at my bare arms. "It's warm enough I don't even need a sweater. Right, I'll be back to the cottage before you get there. I'll put the kettle on."

* * *

Michael stood out on the pavement and watched me go. I stopped and waved twice before the road curved and I lost sight of him. Past my cottage, past the shops, up the high street, and over the bridge that spanned the brook and where the road widened. In that magic way of spring, the clouds had broken up, turning from a heavy gray blanket to a few fluffy white pillows, and the fierce sunlight brought the world into sharp focus. I reached the door of the pub just as Peg stepped out with a rug to shake.

"Has summer suddenly arrived?" she asked, squinting in the light.

"Lovely, isn't it," I said, happy I'd shed my sweater before making the journey. "I've come to see Kathleen."

"Oh, she went out a bit ago."

"Out?"

"She left just after Gwen and Tennyson set off for the Hall."

For a moment, I couldn't imagine why Gwen and her daughter had gone to Hoggin Hall. "Yes, that's right," I said, as it came to me. "They were invited to tea with His Lordship."

"Gwen said Tennyson expected Alfie to go along, but he was nowhere in sight. That worried the girl a bit."

"I'd say he'll catch her up before long." Afternoon tea at the Hall. Sitting at the enormous table in the kitchen with tea, scones, Sheila's strawberry jam — it sounded like the most wonderful thing in the world at that moment.

Peg stood with one hand on the door. "I'd better return to my post. Fred's nipped off to Sudbury to replace cutlery that's gone missing, and so I'm on my own here."

"Gone missing? Have you had something stolen?"

"No, I don't think so," Peg said. "Things go walkabout occasionally. I once lost a stockpot for an entire year, because it had been packed away with the Christmas decorations. This time it's Fred's favorite filleting knife. And a pair of shears." Peg shook her head. "I told him they'd most likely turn up, but he does love the Cookshop, so off he went." Halfway in the door she stopped. "Cup of tea?"

"No, thanks, Peg. I need to talk with Kathleen. She didn't go up to the church, did she?"

"No, she's gone over the road. A stroll round the grounds, I suppose."

I looked across to the brick gate pillars that marked the drive. A stroll with a purpose — to see the place Nick had died. My heart sank at the thought of Kathleen making this journey alone, and I knew I couldn't let her do that.

"I believe I'll follow her on over — wouldn't want her to get lost," I said. But it was the last place I wanted to be — the summerhouse — and so I didn't move, and instead stood picking at one of the scabs on my arm.

Peg nodded to the thin crisscrossing tracks. "What have you done to yourself there?"

"I fell in the brambles," I said. "It was a silly thing." I stretched my arms out — the first time they'd seen the light of day in a fair while. My eyes traced the paths of the red lines as Michael's finger had traced them. How odd, I thought.

Give me a muffed recorder, shave half my head, and I'd look like kitten woman.

Peg returned to the pub, and I walked across the wide grass verge to the road. Traffic had picked up, and I stood at the edge waiting for my chance to dash across. As I waited, the thought that had been buzzing round in my mind alit at last.

I had fallen in the brambles outside the Little Chef on my way back from Cambridge after meeting Terry and Sam. But I was not the only one with scratches. Tess told me Nick had fallen in the brambles inside the summerhouse when he had been stabbed — he had had scratches. And Olive Carboys — Daft Doris — had scratches, too. From a kitten? That had been my first impression, but only because of the muffed recorder she held. Perhaps she had become tangled up in brambles, too.

The puzzle pieces snapped into place and I knew. I just knew. Gwen had caught Olive in the kitchen of the Stoat and Hare on the Friday afternoon during the busy funeral reception and sent her on her way. Olive may not have taken the soup spoons with her, but she'd taken a knife and shears. Fred's missing filleting knife — the murder weapon, the one left in my cottage door. Peg had been true to her word about avoiding those online rags, and she had not seen any reference to a knife and so had not made the connection among a missing knife, the wild woman in the kitchen, and Nick's death. And so, she had seen no reason to mention it to the police. Or to me. And the missing shears? They'd been used for Olive's DIY hairdo. Before or after she had tracked Nick down to the summerhouse where she had . . .

My hand flew to my mouth, and I retched as a cold fear washed over me. I scrambled for my phone just as traffic cleared enough for me to dash across the road. I ran straight for the drive. Kathleen might be wandering the grounds at this very moment, looking for the summerhouse. And where was Olive Carboys? She had been lurking in the shadows of the village. She'd been seen that morning and she had, only thirty minutes ago, broken in the door of the TIC and stolen Nick's ashes. I couldn't fathom why she would kill Nick, but if she had murdered once, why wouldn't she do it again? I paused and leaned up against one of the brick gate pillars. Anything might set Olive off again. Kathleen was in danger. I must find her. I pulled my phone from my bag.

"Are you at the cottage?" Michael's first words when he answered the call.

I'm sure he could tell I was not, what with all the road-traffic noises.

"Are the police there?" I asked.

"Not yet."

"Michael, she killed him. Olive Carboys. Daft Doris. She killed Nick."

"Julia? Where are you?"

"The scratches on my arms!" I shouted as a lorry rumbled by. I took off down the drive to escape the noise, searching in the trees on either side of the drive as I went. I saw no sign of life. "She has them, too, but the scratches aren't from kittens. Nick fell in the brambles when she stabbed him. Maybe she tried to grab him or fought with him or pushed him."

"You need to go to the cottage," Michael said in a demanding voice. "The police haven't arrived. I'll leave them to it and meet you there."

"Michael, I think Kathleen is in danger. She's gone off to find the summerhouse. She told me she wanted to see where Nick died. *Ah!*" Another piece of the puzzle snapped into place. "Terry and Sam! Remember how shocked they were to see her in the pub. It's because they knew she was Daft Doris, not because she was a journo blackmailing them."

"Don't go to the summerhouse."

"Kathleen," I begged him. "I can't leave her."

"You aren't there yet?"

"I'm on the drive."

"All right. Wait, Julia. Stop right where you are and I'll come to you."

Good thing he rang off before I replied. Of course if I could, I would do. I would stand stock still in the middle of the drive, but for the thought of Kathleen staring down at that wide, dark spot on the white stone floor. That was what drew me.

And the sound I heard.

I had reached the path that led to the summerhouse. The traffic noise behind me had faded, and now I could hear the cry of a single bird. Not a flashy "look at me" sort of *caw*, but a frantic, repeated *caw-caw-caw* interspersed with screeches and shrieks, an unending cacophony of distress.

"Alfie?" I called and listened. Quiet. "Alfie?" The clamor began again. I shot off into the brambles and down the path.

The heavy rain had made the earth soft and the coating of last year's beech leaves slippery. I dug my heels in for traction on the way down, but still my feet came out from under me twice and I ended up sliding down on my bum. As the trail began to climb to the knoll, my feet slipped and I had to take hold of an alder sapling to pull myself up. The rook's distress calls grew louder.

When the summerhouse came into view, I paused for a moment and scanned the wood. Nothing moved apart from the flutter of new leaves, setting the copse to dancing. I crept up the stone steps and peered inside.

The Grecian urn — Nick's remains — sat in pride of place on the table in the middle of the room, but askew, as the table itself leaned precariously. Scattered around the urn were bits of greenery — boxwood, I thought — and cowslips. Like a little altar. But my eyes were drawn away from the makeshift shrine by movement near the fireplace.

I heard a shuffling, a whimper, and I saw Alfie, caught in bird netting, hanging from a fireplace sconce.

CHAPTER 29

He lay upside down, his gray beak stuck through one of the holes, one leg thrust through another gap, while toes of the other grabbed at the thin black strands. His feathers stuck out in disarray. The fine black mesh lay like a shroud around him, and he hung motionless, watching me and muttering.

"My God." I dropped my bag and ran to him. "Alfie," I said, clasping my hands, too afraid to touch him lest I do damage. "Wait, stop," I told myself. "Be still, Alfie. Be patient." I studied his dilemma.

He hung about a foot below the mantel. "All right now, Alfie — let's try this," I said. I placed one hand under him for support, lifted the bundle and moved him onto the stone mantel. After a bit of scrambling, Alfie righted himself, both legs now thrust through holes but on solid stone. And still trapped.

"There now, that's a start." I kept a cheery note, hoping to calm the rook or myself, but my voice sounded artificial and tinny in my own ear. "You just hang on, I'll get you free. What a horrible thing to do to you. I hope you aren't hurt — your wings or anything. Do you think you're okay?" I rattled on barely knowing what I said. Alfie didn't move, as if steeling himself for whatever came next. But I'd nothing sharp in my bag to cut the netting, and so there was nothing else for it.

"Hold still, Alfie, I'm going to tear this apart and get you free, and then we'll both get out of here." I glanced over my shoulder and out the windows. I saw no one, but I knew Alfie hadn't put himself in the net. I should run for help, and yet I could not leave him.

I studied how the netting had been attached to the sconce — woven through with twine, wrapped round and round and tied in what looked like dozens of knots. I couldn't see where to begin and I chose one knot at random and picked at it, but to no avail. I shook my fists in frustration.

Alfie shifted. "No, no, now — sorry," I said, my heart in my throat and my voice tight. "We must stay calm."

The netting now flowed over his head like a great black veil and lay bunched up round his feet. I took up a loose piece, sticking my fingers in the holes, and gave a hard yank. The thin plastic line cut into my skin like wire, but I gritted my teeth and tried again. A couple of threads snapped, and I had a hole barely big enough for a wren.

Alfie needed more room than that to fly free. If he panicked and struggled, he could easily hook a toe, break a wing or pull out too many tail feathers as he fought. I really, really didn't want to harm Tennyson's only friend.

"You knew Olive was the one, didn't you, Alfie? Did you see what she did to Nick? Did she do this to you?" I babbled while I worked, talking through my clenched teeth lest I cry out. I saw beads of blood pop out on my fingers, following the line of netting.

At last I thought the hole large enough.

"Please don't move yet, Alfie. Not until I pull the net completely away, all right? You'll do that for me?" I positioned the hole over his head and slid the netting around his long gray beak and down his sleek black body. I even got it over his tail feathers. Almost free, but not quite. The rook lifted a foot, and I saw the problem — the thin net had become tangled tightly round one leg. I muttered an obscenity, and Alfie muttered, too.

"Now Alfie, this may take a minute. And you're going to need to let me mess with your leg. I'll be careful. But just you think of more pleasant things — think of teatime. Custard creams, ginger biscuits. And as soon as we're finished here—"

Before I could get my fingernails on the tangle, Alfie screeched and flapped, lifting off. I let go of the netting and it rose with him, like a trailing black cloud, but the net remained tied to the sconce, and he landed back on the mantel in a heap.

"Stupid bird. He wouldn't leave me alone."

I pivoted on the spot, but couldn't speak. Olive stood in the doorway. Her arms hung loosely at her side, but I could see the pair of shears she clutched in one hand — the kitchen variety, heavy and sharp that could cut through meat and crack bones with little trouble. She still wore her trademark duffel coat even though the day had turned sunny and warm. Crushed, dried leaves stuck to its hem, and a toggle button had gone missing. Her face had lost all color and her eyes seemed unfocused. Both she and her coat were stained and worn.

"I know who you are," I said, and I saw a faint smirk cross her lips. "Where's Kathleen?"

The smirk vanished. "She wanted to steal him from me. Did you think I would let her do that?"

Oh God, oh God, oh God. Kathleen's brother was dead, and all she had wanted to do was to take his remains back to her isolated sanctuary — a place that Nick would probably have loved. Instead, she'd been forced to endure days and days of civilization and deceit from a woman who had done the most horrible thing, and now . . . My eyes cut to a particularly large, dark stain on Olive's coat, and I swallowed hard.

We were two — Alfie and me — against one, but Olive armed with scissors and blocking our escape, had the advantage. I strained to hear sounds of Kathleen crying for help or the more hopeful noise of a car on the drive and Michael shouting for me, but I detected only the distant wheezy twittering of a greenfinch. If I could keep Olive distracted long enough, surely someone would come before she tried to take action. *Don't provoke her, Julia.*

"What have you done with Kathleen?" I demanded.

"I've got him back. She can't do anything now," she said, brandishing the shears at me. I flinched as I imagined drops of Kathleen's blood shaken off the blade and flying through the air toward me. Olive thrust her chin in the air.

I pointed at her weapon. "You keep those things away from me."

"She wouldn't let me see him." Olive's voice was full of incredulity. "I had to do something. Nick is mine, not hers. And he's not yours, either." Olive shook the shears at me as she advanced. I took a step back and ran into the mantel. I heard a rustle of feathers behind me and a *clack-clack*. Alfie's beak.

She stopped at the table and gazed down on her funeral arrangement.

Out of the corner of my eye, I could see the window where police had cut the brambles away and where they had done their best to clean up a pool of blood. "You killed him."

"We belonged together, but he didn't understand." She ran a finger over the urn. "He wanted *you* back," she said in a pitiful voice.

"He what?" I snapped at her. "Are you out of your—"

She raised the shears, her face hardening.

"You're a fool," I said. "All those other people thought that's what he was doing here, but they'd never met Nick, and so they didn't know better. But you — you knew him, and yet you believed that?"

"He said he had to see you."

"Because he wanted money for his birds."

"He left me on the island to come and find you," she insisted with a sob. "But I came after him and tried to tell him we were meant to be together."

"*You're not listening to me!*"

Her eyes widened and focused. For a moment, I thought I could reason with her. I took a breath to get hold of myself. "Nick's coming here had nothing to do with us getting back together."

"He printed out a picture of you and Michael."

"Because he wanted to know what Michael looked like. Nick wanted to talk with Michael."

Olive's gaze became unfocused again. "He looked at the picture and said, 'She's cut her hair.' I knew then what I had to do. The day he came here, I followed him to this place. He was walking out in the wood. Birds, of course. And so, I went across the road and borrowed these" — she waved the shears in the air — "and I used them. 'There,'" I said to him. "'I've cut my hair, too, just as she did.' But he said that was no matter to him. He told me to leave, go back to St. Kilda. He had something to sort out." She frowned at the urn.

"But you'd taken more than scissors from the pub kitchen. You'd taken a knife, too."

"Filleting knife." Olive nodded. "Quite a good one, actually. I should know. I can't tell you how many fish I've gutted working in the canteen on that island."

"And the knife was a bit of persuasion?" I shouldn't've been so sarcastic, but she took no notice.

"He needed to know I was sincere. That he could never leave me. Why didn't he understand that?"

So much for reasoning.

From deep in my bag near the door, my phone rang. It was a glorious sound.

"That's Michael," I said. "He's coming for me. He'll be here any minute. You'd better go. You could escape if you leave now." I liked the idea of the police in pursuit of Daft Doris as she ran across the estate with a Grecian urn in her arms — far better than facing her here in the summerhouse.

"That's Michael," she repeated, taunting me in a sing-song voice. "I have Nick's phone, you see, and Michael just received my text saying I've got you and I'm taking you to that little cottage of yours. I told him I'd do to you what I did to Nick. My Nick." Her face wadded up, her chin trembled, and my patience wore thin.

"A little late for tears, isn't it?"

"*You*" — she pointed the scissors at me — "you and that perfect boyfriend of yours had everything, and I had nothing. You needed to suffer."

"So that was why you hounded us, you thought we had to suffer? The entire reason for splashing lies over the internet? You and your filthy cohorts."

"How easy it is to find a group of like-minded individuals," she said, and giggled. "Except for that little one — he was useless."

She had murdered Nick to keep him from leaving her and then turned round as quick as you please and did her best to make Michael and me miserable. For one second, I marveled at how easy it was these days, to throw up a website and toss out a load of lies. I longed for days I barely remembered when such immediate destruction could've taken ages.

"What about Terry and Sam? Did they know you were here?"

Olive frowned, and shook her head, the shears mimicking the movement. "Bad boys, they were. Terry saw me that night he followed you from the pub. You're remarkably easy to follow, I might say. Never paid any attention to the same car behind you every time you left your precious village. After Terry saw me, I had to have a talk with them. I told them they'd better be on their way. Imagine my surprise when they decided to be brave and head in the direction of the constabulary in Sudbury. Such a bad idea. We had a little chase on the road. They scare awfully easily. And then they crashed their car. Are they dead?" she asked, her eyebrows raised in hope.

"Look," I said, holding my hands up in surrender, "you've got what you wanted. Nick." I nodded to the urn. "He's yours forever. Off you go now, back to St. Kilda. Wasn't that your plan — to spend eternity together, just you and Nick's ashes?"

Caw-caw-caw — Alfie started up again at top volume in my ear. But a booming voice drowned out even the rook's clamor.

"*You're not taking him anywhere!*"

Olive whirled round and staggered back.

Kathleen stood in the doorway, her arms spread and hands braced against the doorjamb, so that her thin cardigan hung down like wings. Her hair, loosed from its tidy bun, flew in all directions round her head like a halo. An avenging angel in beige. She ran the back of her hand across her forehead, leaving behind a muddy streak, before launching herself at Olive and tackling her at the waist. They toppled to the floor, knocking into the table, which gave up its last breath, and collapsed. The Grecian urn fell to the floor with a *clank*.

Before I could move, Alfie gave a single screech and, somehow free of his constraints, took off over my head straight at Olive. Olive screamed, "Nick! Nick!" and thrashed while Kathleen struggled to keep hold of her. My eyes were on the shears as Olive waved her arms about, my stomach in a knot of fear that she would run the rook through or stab Kathleen. I reached out, but had to bob and weave to keep the weapon out of my face. When the scissors waved too close to Kathleen, I saw a crimson streak bloom on her sleeve. Olive saw it, too, and taking advantage, kicked free of Kathleen's restraints.

She came at me, jabbing the air, pointing to the urn and shouting something incomprehensible. I jumped back, but my foot got caught on a long stem of brambles growing through one of the broken windows, and I fell back onto my bum. Olive jumped on top of me, and I gasped for breath and beat at her face. Above us, Alfie dived at her again and again — a one-rook mobbing — before shooting straight out the door, leaving behind a single black feather that floated to the floor.

Olive scrambled off me. I scooted away and my hand touched cold metal. The urn. Perhaps I could toss it out the window and she'd run after it like a dog. I reached for it, but when Olive saw my hands touch the handles, she screeched louder that the rook and made for me again.

"Julia!" Kathleen shouted.

With both hands, I flung the urn toward Kathleen, and she caught it in midair. When Olive whirled round and started for her, I leapt up off the floor. Kathleen pitched the urn back to me and then I to her again. Olive whirled one way and then another. In a wild, silly moment, I wondered if Kathleen and I could keep up the rugby game until Olive was too dizzy to continue.

But Kathleen's next toss went wide and it landed off to my right with a clank and skittered across the stone. Olive flung her arm out and I couldn't get out of the way fast enough. I saw a glint of metal, and I felt a hot streak on my forehead.

Blood. I saw blood everywhere, just as I had imagined it had been with Nick. Olive disappeared from my sight and I fell, waving my arms in empty air, unable to catch hold of anything. It felt as if I floated in slow motion until, with a *clank*, my head hit. Just before the red curtain fell over my eyes, I thought I saw Michael fly through the door in a blur of black feathers, and I heard Olive scream.

CHAPTER 30

I lay straddling that border between asleep and awake, where I'd just as soon drift off again as open my eyes. As I contemplated my options, I felt the flutter of wings on my cheek. No, not wings — lips. Soft kisses on my eyelids, my cheeks, my lips followed by sweet, whispered words that I strained to hear.

". . . sorry, so sorry . . . my fault . . . never again . . . I know . . . love you . . ."

"Is she awake yet?" I heard Stephen ask.

I felt Michael get up off the bed.

I cracked my eyes open a slit and saw, on a bedside table, a mountain of grapes — red and green bunches piled so high they looked like an avalanche hazard, or a monoculture still life. *I'm in hospital*, I thought. It's what we do when we visit someone in hospital — we bring grapes. Bury Saint Edmunds, I supposed. We'd no hospital in the village.

"No, not awake yet." I heard Michael speak in quiet tones. I shifted my gaze and saw he stood at the door with Stephen. "But the doctor said it's all right, that she needed the rest. She lost a lot of blood."

"Why don't you go home and change clothes?" Stephen asked. "You look like you just walked out of a slasher film."

"No, not until I talk to her."

"There's no need to punish yourself," Stephen said.

"I abandoned her," Michael replied sharply. "I should never have left. I'd no good reason. Afraid of what she felt about Nick? Where was the courage in that? And what good did it do? If I'd been around, it wouldn't have come to this. I won't go until I see her awake."

"Awake," I said and blinked, but my raspy voice seemed to belie my declaration. I cleared my throat. "I'm awake."

Michael appeared at my side. His eyes were rimmed red as if he'd taken a felt-tip marker to them. Swollen, too. His shirt, stuffed into his trousers, had no buttons, and the front of it looked as if he'd tried to mop up a large spill of . . .

"Hiya," he said, staring deep into my eyes and taking my hand. "How do you feel?"

"Good, yeah. I guess. I'm all right." I thought about the question. "Am I?"

He nodded. "Your forehead."

My forehead felt stiff, and I couldn't quite lift my eyebrows.

"A cut," Michael said. "And you hit your head when you fell, but you landed on the urn. It was just cheap metal, so it gave. Lucky" — he took a couple of quick breaths as if he didn't like the word — "lucky it wasn't the stone floor."

A jumble of images tumbled through my mind. It would take a while to put them in any proper order, but I could recall the highlights well enough.

"Is that my blood?" I said, pointing an index finger at him while noting the tubes coming out the back of my hand.

"I didn't have anything else to press on the wound."

I caught one image as it went sailing past. "I remember you coming in. You and Alfie."

"She tried to put me off by texting me you were at the cottage," Michael said. "She used Nick's phone, but I didn't realize that. It delayed me, I should've been there quicker. When I finally got to the drive to the Hall, Alfie came hurtling out of the trees and nearly knocked me flat. At least, I figured that's who it was. He kept squawking and flying just behind me until I'd got to the summerhouse."

"What about Kathleen?"

"She'd wrestled the shears out of Olive's hand and had her pinned to the ground," Michael said, "so I went straight to you. But you'd lost consciousness, and I couldn't wake you. There was blood, and I thought you'd stopped breathing," he said, his voice breaking at the end.

"Had I stopped breathing?"

"No, but I . . ."

"Well, that's all right then," I said, and patted his hand, which used up what little energy I had mustered. "I'm fine. I'm awake." We were alive and seemed to be reasonably well, and I, for one, felt cozy and comfy and a bit sleepy. "Is Stephen still here?"

"I am, darling," he said. He moved closer to the bed, and I saw he wore red denims and a tight purple jacket and glasses with turquoise frames.

"Stephen, you're in color again," I said.

He straightened the jacket. "In celebration of you solving Nick's murder."

I doubted that was the main reason.

"Where's Gregory?" I asked.

Stephen glanced over his shoulder and out into the corridor. "Gone to the hospital canteen for a cup of tea." He frowned. "With Mum and Rupert."

"Oh my, are you that far along already?"

He blushed and shrugged his shoulders.

"And are these all from you two?" I asked, nodding at the Mount Everest of grapes.

"God, no," Stephen said. "You've had everyone in that village of yours popping in. I doubt if there's a single grape left within a twenty-five-mile radius."

"Would you like one?" I asked.

Stephen laughed. "No, thank you. I think I'll go chase down Gregory and see if he needs rescuing. You're a brave woman, Jools. I'll see you later." He gave me a kiss on the cheek and was gone.

Michael sat down on the edge of my bed.

"Is it still Monday?" I asked.

"No, Tuesday morning."

"Have you been here all night?" From the state of him, I believed I could answer that question. Then I saw the chair in the corner with a blanket in a heap and my suspicion was confirmed. "Is that where you slept? That's not much of a bed."

"Mostly I watched you. You woke up once during the night and smiled at me. I slept a bit after that."

"Tuesday morning," I murmured. "I have a great deal of work to do."

Michael shook his head. "Don't even try that one on. Linus has closed the TIC until repairs to the door are carried out."

"You thought I wanted to go into work? The thought hadn't even crossed my mind," I said. "I don't need to. I can work from the cottage. I only need to check a few details for the farmers market tomorrow."

"You will do nothing. I've found all your files, and I've got it in hand."

"Have you?" I smiled. "Well, that's all right then." Didn't that work out well? This would be the perfect way to show the world Michael had returned. "You just be sure to keep your eye on those asparagus farmers — they're a dodgy lot."

"They try anything and I'll sic Alfie on them."

"Alfie. Is he all right?"

"He is."

"Tennyson?"

"They were all having a grand tea at the Hall and knew nothing until Callow knocked on the front door."

"Kathleen wasn't hurt?"

"A cut on her arm, not as bad as yours. Mind you, I wouldn't want to get on her bad side," Michael said. "She kept a firm hold on Olive and didn't let go until the police arrived."

"She looked a bit mad herself when she appeared in that doorway."

"She'd been walking the grounds looking for the summerhouse, she said, but slipped and fell in that drainage ditch."

I sighed with relief. But that hollow look had not quite left Michael's face. I stroked the back of his hand with my finger.

"A few minutes ago," I said, "before I opened my eyes, you were talking to me." I watched his face, which remained inscrutable. "I heard what you said. I heard those words."

His eyes were like midnight. "Good."

I said those same words to him, and the corner of his mouth tugged up into a smile.

"Now," I said. "Give us a kiss."

He obliged, and I responded with a yawn. My eyelids felt as if they had lead weights attached.

"I think I'll take a bit of a kip," I said. "I'm all right now, you know that. You go on home, and I'll see you later."

* * *

When I awoke again, the world was in focus, and the sun spilled out from the window and over the foot of my bed. I felt those stirrings of a well person, wanting to get up and get on with things. A young man in scrubs stood next to the bedside table with its mountain of fruit.

"Hello," I said. "Care for a grape?"

"Ah, there she is now," he said, giving me a grin.

"Are you the doctor?" I asked.

"No, love, I'm the charge nurse." He took my pulse and looked into my eyes and scribbled something on his clipboard. "How are you feeling?"

"Fine, thanks. I've a bit of a headache. And could I clean my teeth? Feels rather fuzzy in there."

"Clean teeth are a good start. Shall I bring everything to you, or would you like to get out of bed?"

I looked at my hand and saw I was free of tubes.

"I'd love to get up."

For all my good intentions, I wobbled at first and he had to place a firm hand on my elbow and guide me to the loo, but once inside, I was spoilt for choice of grab bars to keep me upright. I used the toilet, cleaned my teeth, and splashed water on my face. I felt like a new woman. In the mirror, I examined my forehead and saw a long thin red line stretched almost the whole way across it, and it seemed to be held together with clear glue. My bangs were slicked back out of the way, but at least they hadn't shaved any hair off — God knows what Stephen would've made of that.

The charge nurse waited just outside the loo door and guided me back to bed, sat me upright, and fluffed my pillows. "I could just do with a cup of tea," I said, mostly to myself.

"Perhaps your friend here will go off to the canteen and fetch you a cuppa," he replied and nodded to the door. It was Tess. Or was it DI Callow? The black business suit gave me no clue.

"I will indeed," Tess said. "Would you like anything else?"

Oh, good, it was Tess. "Hello," I said. "Well, since you asked, I wouldn't mind a bite of something."

"You've a meal coming before too long," the charge nurse said.

I felt sure the meal would not be one of Fred's burgers and a massive pile of chips, which I was rather in the mood for. "Just a biscuit? I'm starving."

"Well, we can't let you starve, now can we?" he asked. "I'd suggest the lemon drizzle — it's not half bad."

"Yes, please, tea and cake. Just what I need."

Alone with nothing to read and no one to talk with while I waited for Tess to return, I ate a couple of grapes and wondered where my phone had got to. I wondered if Michael was at the cottage, in bed asleep. I wondered if Stephen had returned to London and if Gregory had gone with him. I wondered if Beryl and Rupert had gone back to Cambridge or if they were staying over at Hoggin Hall — Linus had offered before. I wondered . . . Good thing Tess didn't take too long, because my mind felt like an overinflated balloon about to pop.

"Thanks," I said, taking my cup and lemon drizzle from her. She perched on the edge of the chair with her own tea and cake.

"How are you feeling?"

I swallowed and pointed to my super-glued forehead. I'd also located the bump on the back of my head, and it was quite sore. "No concussion, the nurse said, so I'll be fine. It's all over, that's what's important. It is, isn't it? They've taken Olive off?"

"They have, but here's something. Her real name actually is Doris. Doris Oliver."

"So Daft Doris suited her. But she's not that swift at thinking up an alias, is she?"

"She's tried several different names the last few years," Tess said. "She's been cautioned in Blackpool and Leeds for fraud and threats with a deadly weapon, but slipped out of police reach and disappeared each time. Perhaps she thought she'd be safe on St. Kilda."

"Terry and Sam?"

"They're all right. She ran them off the road when they were driving to Sudbury. The woman who runs the B&B where Nick stayed identified her. She had stolen an old Vauxhall Corsa from a farm — just goes to show it's never a good idea to leave the key in a car, even when you live in the country."

"And she slept rough?"

"In the car. She'd parked it on the northeast boundary of the estate. She told us where." Tess put her cup on the windowsill and sat up straight. "Your decision to go after Ms. Hawkins" — *Right, here it comes, my dressing down* — "it was a brave act."

I exhaled with relief.

"But foolish. You should've waited. Michael had called us, and we were on our way. As was he."

"She had caught Alfie in a net," I said. "There's no telling what she would've done. Without Alfie distracting her, Olive — Doris — might've caught Kathleen before Kathleen caught her."

"Yes, all right. I'm glad you weren't hurt worse."

"She took the knife from the Stoat and Hare, you know that?" Tess nodded. "Her scratches — I finally realized she got them from the brambles, and I remember you said Nick had scratches from the brambles." I stretched out my arm and saw how my own had started to fade. "And you know about how she cut her own hair off?"

"Michael turned over the evidence found in the pocket of your mackintosh, I hear."

"Alfie again," I said.

"Yes, a remarkable bird. Look, I wanted to tell you that PC Flynn came across Mr. Hawkins's laptop at the B&B and found a document titled 'The Case for St. Kilda.' In it, he lays out the problem of Fisk and Redman wanting to move the institute to Kent, and why it should stay on the island. He had two draft emails — one to you and one to Michael. In them, he requested clarification of the grant process and how he wanted to put his case to you in person. In the one addressed to you, he wrote that he hoped you could put your past differences aside and you would intercede for him on this important issue." Tess lifted her eyebrows. "You were right about why he came to find you. It was about the birds."

"I did try to tell you all. But then, I had convinced myself that Terry and Sam were murderers, so it's not as if I was completely right." My victory was tinged with sadness. I took a deep, deep breath and blew away the last cobwebs of anger and guilt. "Poor Nick. He did so love to be in the middle of nowhere with his birds."

I heard the rattle of a trolley in the corridor, and a young woman popped her head in the door. "Hello, good evening. I've a lovely dinner for you, shall I bring it in?"

Tess stood to leave. "I wanted to tell you — it seems I've a massive amount of holiday time built up, and so I've decided to take a chunk of it."

I could well believe the massive amount of holiday time — DI Callow lived to work — but found it curious she would want to tell me about her plans.

"That's lovely. Where are you off to?"

"Cornwall. A good jaunt on the motorbike." Her face turned an uncharacteristic pink.

"I thought you wanted to sell the motorbike." And then I twigged it. "Are you going alone?" I asked with all innocence.

She smiled. "No, as it happens, I'm not."

I love happy endings.

CHAPTER 31

On Friday afternoon, Kathleen and I stood out on the pavement in front of the TIC waiting for her cab. She couldn't leave the country fast enough and had booked a flight as soon as the police had allowed with the caveat that she might be recalled to testify. I could see the fear on Kathleen's face when she heard that possibility, but Tess had reassured her that it was extremely unlikely to happen, because Olive — that is, Doris — had confessed to killing Nick. Only the question of her sanity remained.

When Kathleen had arrived at the TIC, she had declined tea, only wanting to show me that Nick's remains were now in a brown ceramic container with no decoration whatsoever. She also wanted to say goodbye before she returned to her island home.

"Your village is lovely," she said. "And your market on Wednesday looked quite well attended."

Kathleen hadn't ventured forth from her hotel room to the farmers market but had been able to observe it all from her window. I had been allowed to attend, but no one would let me do any actual work, and so I had parked myself at one of the WI tables with tea and cake until it was time for lunch, when I'd had a grilled sausage. A successful day all round.

"If you are ever back here for any reason, Kathleen, I hope you'll visit."

"Thank you," she replied. "And if you ever travel to Nova Scotia, please let me know."

Having each extended invitations that had absolutely no chance of being fulfilled, we stood for a moment, wordless. At last, I pulled a card out of my pocket.

"Here's my email address," I said.

"Lovely," Kathleen said, with a relieved smile. "And here's mine."

I waved as her cab sped off toward the Sudbury rail station, and when it was out of sight, I propped open our shiny new TIC door to allow the fresh breeze to blow in. I remained where I was, eyes closed, breathing deeply of spring and letting a gust of wind lift my bangs, which I'd carefully combed over the cut on my forehead. I waited for the sun to make a brief appearance between the billowing white clouds.

I waited for Michael, too. Then, I spotted him up the high street and watched as he walked toward me. He wore a dark suit and white shirt, his jacket unbuttoned and his tie loosened and a black leather work bag slung across his shoulder. He looked gorgeous.

He greeted me with a kiss and wrapped his arms round me. I knew he was hiding his face, not wanting me to see. I leaned back until I could see his eyes burning like blue flames.

"Well?" I asked.

He'd met that morning with the decision makers at BBC Two about a one-hour program. He had mentioned the idea in a casual way to someone only two days ago and had been asked immediately for details. The two of us had dashed off a brief proposal. He had described the topic in glowing general terms, and I had sprinkled in enough practical details to make it look like a firm plan.

He held me in suspense for a moment, but I saw the corner of his mouth twitch. "They liked it," he said, and smiled.

"Yes!" I kissed him again. "Congratulations, Mr. Executive Producer."

"My name won't be the only one on the credits — we'll be listed together."

"This is fantastic," I said. "Dad will be so pleased."

Michael looked over his shoulder, up the high street. "Here he is now," he said, "the star of the new television program, *Every Trick in the Rook*."

Alfie soared over our heads, banked right and straight through the open door of the TIC.

From indoors came a hiss, pop, and wheeze.

"What's that?" Michael asked.

"Alfie," I said. "He switched the kettle on."

THE END

AUTHOR'S NOTE

The inspiration for Alfie came from Esther Woolfson's book *Corvus*, the true story of living for more than twenty-five years with a rook (named Chicken) that her daughter brought home as a fledgling. It is a lovely tale of getting close to a different species and our perceptions of intelligence and companionship. In writing my piece of fiction and creating Alfie, maybe I stretched a rook's abilities — and then again, maybe I didn't.

For ideas, inspiration, guidance, and encouragement, many thanks go to Colleen Mohyde of the Doe Coover Agency, editor Kate Miciak, and my fellow writers and critique group (Kara Pomeroy, Joan Shott, and Louise Creighton). And grateful thanks to you, the reader, who enjoys a mystery grounded in our natural world.

ADDITIONAL NOTE

Many thanks to Joffe Books, publishing director Kate Lyall Grant, and to my agent Christina Hogrebe (Jane Rotrosen Agency) for re-publishing my Birds of a Feather series!

THE JOFFE BOOKS STORY

We began in 2014 when Jasper agreed to publish his mum's much-rejected romance novel and it became a bestseller.

Since then we've grown into the largest independent publisher in the UK. We're extremely proud to publish some of the very best writers in the world, including Joy Ellis, Faith Martin, Caro Ramsay, Helen Forrester, Simon Brett and Robert Goddard. Everyone at Joffe Books loves reading and we never forget that it all begins with the magic of an author telling a story.

We are proud to publish talented first-time authors, as well as established writers whose books we love introducing to a new generation of readers.

We won Trade Publisher of the Year at the Independent Publishing Awards in 2023. We have been shortlisted for Independent Publisher of the Year at the British Book Awards for the last four years, and were shortlisted for the Diversity and Inclusivity Award at the 2022 Independent Publishing Awards. In 2023 we were shortlisted for Publisher of the Year at the RNA Industry Awards.

We built this company with your help, and we love to hear from you, so please email us about absolutely anything bookish at feedback@joffebooks.com

If you want to receive free books every Friday and hear about all our new releases, join our mailing list: www.joffebooks.com/contact

And when you tell your friends about us, just remember: it's pronounced Joffe as in coffee or toffee!

ALSO BY MARTY WINGATE

BIRDS OF A FEATHER SERIES

Book 1: THE RHYME OF THE MAGPIE
Book 2: EMPTY NEST
Book 3: EVERY TRICK IN THE ROOK

THE POTTING SHED MYSTERIES

Book 1: THE GARDEN PLOT
Book 2: THE RED BOOK OF PRIMROSE HOUSE
Book 3: BETWEEN A ROCK AND A HARD PLACE
Book 4: THE SKELETON GARDEN
Book 5: THE BLUEBONNET BETRAYAL
Book 6: BEST-LAID PLANTS
Book 7: MIDSUMMER MAYHEM
Book 7.5: CHRISTMAS AT GREENOAK
Book 8: BITTERSWEET HERBS

Made in the USA
Columbia, SC
21 April 2024

34684643R00169